THE DANTE GAME

Jane Langton is the author of eight other Homer Kelly mysteries, including *Natural Enemy*, *Emily Dickinson is Dead*, and *God in Concord*. She lives in Lincoln, Massachusetts.

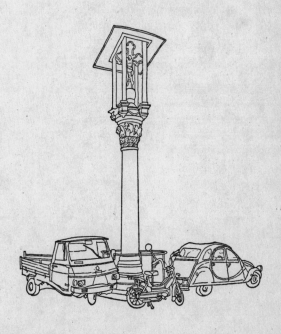

THE
DANTE
GAME

JANE LANGTON

Illustrations by the author
Blackboard sketches by Giovanni Zibo

PENGUIN BOOKS

PENGUIN BOOKS
Published by the Penguin Group
Viking Penguin, a division of Penguin Books USA Inc.,
375 Hudson Street, New York, New York 10014, U.S.A.
Penguin Books Ltd, 27 Wrights Lane, London W8 5TZ, England
Penguin Books Australia Ltd, Ringwood, Victoria, Australia
Penguin Books Canada Ltd, 10 Alcorn Avenue, Suite 300,
Toronto, Ontario, Canada M4V 3B2
Penguin Books (N.Z.) Ltd, 182–190 Wairau Road,
Auckland 10, New Zealand

Penguin Books Ltd, Registered Offices:
Harmondsworth, Middlesex, England

First published in the United States of America
by Viking Penguin, a division of Penguin Books USA Inc., 1991
Published in Penguin Books 1992

3 5 7 9 10 8 6 4 2

PUBLISHER'S NOTE
This is a work of fiction. Names, characters, places, and incidents either are
the product of the author's imagination or are used fictitiously, and any
resemblance to actual persons, living or dead, events, or locales is entirely
coincidental.

Drawings by the author

Grateful acknowledgment is made for permission to reprint extracts
from The Divine Comedy by Dante, translated by Dorothy L. Sayers,
published by Penguin Books Ltd.

THE LIBRARY OF CONGRESS HAS CATALOGUED THE HARDCOVER AS FOLLOWS:
Langton, Jane.
The Dante game/by Jane Langton.
p. cm.
ISBN 0-670-83439-4 (hc.)
ISBN 0 14 01.3887 0 (pbk.)
I. Title.
PS3562.A515D28 1991
813'.54—dc20 90-50427

Printed in the United States of America
Set in Linotron Aldus
Designed by Ann Gold

FOR ILSE PLUME

THE DANTE GAME

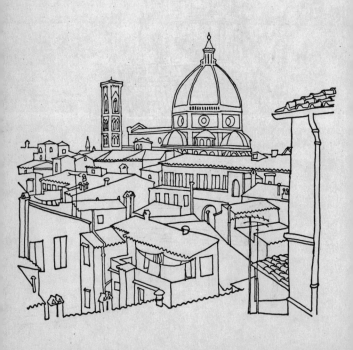

CHAPTER 1

∎∎∎∎∎∎∎∎∎∎∎∎

As the geometer his mind applies
  To square the circle . . .
           Paradiso XXXIII, 133, 134.

I t was a matter of simple geometry.
     On the tourist map of Florence the cathedral was a
large pink blob like a polyhedron. A puzzled traveller
could put a finger on the blob, look up at the red-tiled rooftops and find the dome rising above everything else, a great
rounded octagonal shape like a segmented melon.

This year it was the point of intersection for an extraordinary convergence.

Along one line marched the Vatican Curia with all the
pomp and splendor of a pontifical procession—His Holiness
in white, accompanied by a crimson swirl of cardinals, sweeping across the pages of the calendar from one Easter celebration to the next. Behind them ran the Archbishop of
Florence, trying to catch up.

Along another path trotted Leonardo Bindo, bowing and
smiling, dapper and plump, with Matteo Luzzi strolling in
his wake, encumbered by baggage—zippered cases of Rugers,
Sigs, Winchesters, and a queer-looking assault rifle with a
telescopic combat sight.

And there were other meandering paths. Sooner or later
they too would conform themselves to the same course, and
meet the following Easter at the Cathedral of Florence.

One was Julia Smith's. For Julia the cathedral was only
a bright projected image on a screen in a college classroom
in New York City. She watched as a warm breeze from the

1

open window made the screen billow, while the instructor discussed the Problem of the Dome. *I could go there*, thought Julia. *I could see it for myself. I could go to Italy in June.*

This sort of decisiveness was unusual for Julia Smith. Normally Julia let things rise to the surface slowly. Dynamic action was not her best suit. Whatever other strong points she possessed were overshadowed by her beauty. If there was more to her than a perfect surface, it took a while to find it. From the very beginning when every good fairy had hovered over her cradle, Julia had attracted admiring attention. She had been a strapping baby. Her DNA molecules were packed with sparkling chromosomes, a gene of perfection governing all the rest.

Now she had grown into the promise of that perfection. There was a liquid depth to her eye, a glow to the round curve of her cheek, a delicacy of nose and mouth, a luxuriance of curling yellow hair, an exuberance of breast and hip.

It had been a burden to her, as she grew up into it. By the time she was thirteen Julia had become wary of her own blossoming. She was pestered everywhere. She couldn't go out for dinner with her parents without attracting the attention of some old lecher at another table. She would feel his ogling gaze and dread the moment when he would come across the floor and say to her father, "Your daughter is a very pretty girl."

Here in this college classroom she was older than the other kids sprawled around her in the heavy chairs—old enough to have lived through a number of vicissitudes, including the deaths of her parents, a short unhappy marriage and several turbulent affairs. She had been scalded, she had scalded in return. Finally, emerging from a crude episode with the police, she had abandoned all that and gone back to school.

By this time Julia had learned to protect herself. With her friends she carried on a comfortable kind of easy kidding. On the street she wore heavy trousers, thick canvas shoes and oversized men's shirts trailing below the hip. She was handy with a screwdriver and a soldering iron. She could repair a tape deck or a bicycle, replace a spark plug, change a tire. She was cautious. She knew how easily she could cut a swath. She had learned to sit back and wait, to see what happened, to hold in check her own impulsive affection.

This spring there had been too many clumsy encroachments. Julia felt dragged down, as though a couple of folding chairs had entangled themselves in her clothing and were bumping awkwardly behind her.

Now, staring up at the cut-away diagram of Brunelleschi's dome, she thought, *I could get away. I could go to Florence and see all that.*

As for the building itself, rising out of Tuscany like a man-made hill of marble, it had been nearly seven centuries since the poet Dante Alighieri had witnessed the laying of the foundation. For six hundred and ninety-nine years the Cathedral of Florence had sailed ponderously around the sun, swinging in orbit with other massive mountains—the Matterhorn, Mont Blanc, Pike's Peak—its southern side exposed to the light, its northern flank perpetually in shadow.

CHAPTER 2

■ ■ ■ ■ ■ ■ ■ ■ ■ ■ ■ ■ ■

Come, we have far to go; let us advance.
                              Inferno IV, 22.

The crack of the mallet that started all these balls rolling in the direction of the Cathedral of Florence was an announcement by the pope on Easter Sunday morning. From the balcony of the Apostolic Palace, addressing the crowd gathered below him on Saint Peter's Square, he launched a new crusade, an *Anno Sacro Anti-droga*, a Holy Year Against Drugs.

The announcement was followed at once by a television drive, an international campaign on Vatican Radio, and an official poster, an image of His Holiness embracing a repentant young addict.

Copies of the poster were carried by truck, local train, country bus, donkey and camel to every parish church, along cart tracks in the Sonora Desert, along the coast of Kenya to Mombasa, up the Orinoco to high settlements in the Andes. Wherever young people gathered—in the bars of Miami, in the labyrinthine alleys of Calcutta, in the video-game arcades of Barcelona—the strong piping voice of the Holy Father was transmitted by satellite, repeating in all the languages at his command, "Rejoice with me, for I have found my sheep which was lost."

It wasn't the announcement itself that was so astonishing, or the public relations campaign or the posters. It was the result. The crusade was working.

The cardinals were flabbergasted, and so were the citizens

of Rome and indeed the entire population of Italy. Praise for the papal crusade poured in from New York, from Paris, from Tokyo. Mothers and fathers of every faith blessed the name of the Roman pontiff.

The frenzy of repentance began in Naples, where a saintly young man appeared out of nowhere, leading a ragtag band of boys and girls to Rome. They had sworn off, they said, they had given up amphetamines and heroin and cocaine and crack, and here they were in Saint Peter's Square, two thousand strong, seeking the blessing of the holy father. Legions of schoolchildren signed a pledge of purity. *Never, never, never,* they swore, would an illegal substance enter their bodies—*mai, mai, mai!* A powerful elected official in Turin made a public confession, "for the sake of the Christ child and the children of Italy." Drug offenders in prison gathered to pray. A strange wave of adolescent weeping spread around the world.

"His Holiness is a wonder-worker," said the Italian Minister for Public Health. "Here it is, still only the month of April, and already we see a sharp decline in the rate of new addiction."

"How astonishing!" marveled the Vatican prelate in charge of the crusade. "In our wildest dreams we never imagined such a miracle."

CHAPTER 3

∎∎∎∎∎∎∎∎∎∎∎

know thee, filthy as thou art . . .
                    Inferno VIII, 39.

In some quarters there was less satisfaction with the extraordinary success of the crusade.

Among the most disgruntled in the city of Florence was Leonardo Bindo. Signor Bindo was the manager of the Banca degli Innocenti in Piazza Santissima Annunziata. The bank was named for the ancient foundling hospital across the way, and the square for its local church.

On the rainy morning in mid-April when yet another pilgrimage arrived in Saint Peter's Square—this time it was a trainload of young penitents from Paris—Bindo sat at his desk in Florence looking gloomily at the Roman daily paper *Il Messaggero*. The front page showed a sea of heads, all turned in the direction of the faraway tiny figure of the Holy Father.

Bindo tossed the paper across the desk to Matteo Luzzi. "This morning I had to cancel a shipment. It was very expensive, but there was no use throwing good money after bad. God knows I've always supported His Holiness, but this is outrageous." Angrily he quoted Dante, *"Rapacious wolves in shepherds' garb behold in every pasture!"*

Matteo's choirboy face beamed with recognition. *"Rapacious wolves*—you mean the pope who threw Dante out of Florence and then turned up as a villain in *The Divine Comedy, vero?"*

Bindo laughed. "I'm reminded of the way your head-

Ospedale degli Innocenti

master threw you out of that seminary. I'm glad your education wasn't altogether wasted." He looked with appreciation at Matteo's rosy cheeks and congratulated himself on finding someone so presentable. How lucky to have discovered a boy so proficient in a single useful calling and yet so winning at the same time!

Of course Matteo lacked Bindo's broad vision and large-scale grasp of things, but what could you expect of the son of a whore? Well, no, that was unfair. Matteo's mother was not a common prostitute. Bindo himself had known her in her professional capacity, and he was aware that her clientele was strictly upmarket. And young Matteo had profited from his mother's rich associations by picking up a few social graces, including a scrappy understanding of the English language.

Bindo rose and stared out at the rain beating down on the stony square. A nun in full habit hurried past the window, her long skirts lifting and plunging in the wind. "I think," he said portentously, "I have found someone to do what is required in this matter." He turned and looked accusingly at Matteo. "Since you refuse to handle it yourself."

Matteo lifted his hands in horror. "I told you. I'm not a believer, but even so, it would be tempting fate."

Bindo sighed, and sat down at his desk. "It's ironic. Roberto Mori is a priest, and yet *he* is willing."

Matteo looked surprised. "He's a priest?"

"A priest who has lost his calling, but still a priest. You understand"—Bindo looked piercingly at Matteo—"he has no knowledge of our concerns. He doesn't know me. And of course you must cherish his ignorance like the virginity of a young girl. He's never to know our private reasons for this action. The man's an idealist, a fool. His own motives are"—Bindo rolled his eyes at the ceiling—"idiotic, ridiculous, insane! But for our purposes they are precious, they are magnificent works of art. In the long run they will protect us. Fortunately he's here in Florence and available."

"Here in Florence?" Matteo raised his eyebrows. "What good will that do? Surely the action must be in Rome?"

Bindo smiled. "Ah, but I'm working on that matter with the assistance of my friend the archbishop."

"The archbishop? You don't mean the Archbishop of Florence? But he's a very holy man. Surely he would not—"

"The holiness of the archbishop is our good fortune." And then Bindo recited his favorite maxim, "All things can be made to serve." He looked up as his secretary popped in to say that Signor Zibo was waiting in the outer office. "*Un momento*," he told her. Bending forward as she left the room, he gave Matteo his instructions.

Matteo listened, and murmured his questions, and listened some more, and nodded.

"Here's the letter," said Bindo. "And wait. Give him this too." He stuffed a wad of bills into a manila envelope.

"But it must be a million lire," said Matteo.

Bindo looked at him severely. "I will require a receipt for the exact amount, and his signature. Is that understood?"

"Oh, *si*." Matteo stood up sullenly.

"Stop, don't use the street door. Go out the other way."

Impatiently Bindo watched Matteo leave the office. Then he hurried to the door separating him from the main chamber of the bank where the tellers were doing business. Throwing it open, he welcomed his next visitor.

"*Buon giorno*, Professor Zibo. You've come to sign the lease. What a great day it must be for you! Now your new school can begin. I'm happy to see the property of the city of Florence put to such a good use."

Settling his guest in a chair, Bindo jerked open a drawer and produced the lease, a contract between the Comune di Firenze and Giovanni Zibo, and smoothed it on the table with the pink palm of his hand. "The American School of Florentine Studies, it sounds very splendid. They'll be doctoral candidates, your students? Teachers, professors?"

Zee suppressed an urge to whip out his sketchbook and

get down on paper Signor Bindo's wonderful roundness, his spherical head, his goggling eyes. His pencil twitched in his pocket, eager to inscribe circles for those chubby cheeks, that cozy chin. "No, no, most of the students will be young undergraduates, taking their third college year abroad."

Zee scribbled his name on the lease, and Bindo looked solemn. "You understand, Professor Zibo, the city is not responsible for any unsatisfactory condition of the Villa L'Ombrellino. The comune rents it to you at this low figure because the renovations for the new trade center are incomplete. When the city is ready to continue, your school must vacate the premises. Is that understood?"

"I trust the roof won't fly off in the next breeze?"

The banker frowned. "Professor Zibo, I thought you understood the terms as we outlined them the other day?"

"No, no, I was only joking."

Outside the bank and all over the city of Florence it was raining harder than ever. Falling drops struck the yellow water of the Arno in a million steely shafts, and battered the red-tiled rooftops on both sides of the river. The Lungarno arcade was empty. No one was making pastel portraits of tourists or rendering the Ponte Vecchio in watercolor. A queue of shivering Norwegians waited to enter the Uffizi. Above the low skyline of the city the dome of the cathedral rose wet and red to the platform of the lantern, where a few tourists huddled in slickers and hooded jackets, worn out by their long climb up the four hundred and sixty-three steps of the narrow curving stairs.

Zee came out of the bank and paused in the doorway to pull out his sketchbook and note down the pleasing spherical forms of Signor Bindo.

Mist collected on his drawing, blown from the fountains in the center of the square. Zee mopped it off with his sleeve, and thought of the third circle of the Inferno, where it rained all the time, *one ceaseless, heavy, cold, accursed quench.* Like Leonardo Bindo and Matteo Luzzi, Zee could quote

Dante. For him it was not merely part of the mental equipment of an educated Italian, it was the great occupation of a lifetime, one of the two driving forces that got him up in the morning and urged him through the day and sent him to bed at night.

The other was a collection of wretched memories.

Now with the signing of the lease for the new school, an unknown and unsuspected third force was about to enter his life. Dante would have called it one of the teeth by which the love of higher things grips the soul, a ratchet revolving the heart toward God.

In Dante's case the ratchet had been a woman of Florence, Beatrice Portinari. For Zee it would be an American woman, a student in his new school. But whether she would become for him one of those earthly objects by which the soul is hooked, or merely a random piece of carnal folly, only time would tell. At this moment Giovanni Zibo was unaware that she existed.

Putting away his sketchbook, he bowed his head and hurried out into the rain.

And ran smack into another pedestrian. There was a jarring shock, and Zee staggered back. *"Mi scusi."*

A tall man in a Milwaukee Brewers cap was holding his head and muttering, "Jesus."

"Are you all right?" said Zee in English. "I am so sorry. Can I help you?"

Rain beat down on both of them. The man looked bewildered. He fumbled with the camera around his neck. "Oh, God, I don't know. I'm looking for the Doomo."

"Duomo," corrected Zee politely, and he pointed to the dome of the cathedral rising conspicuously above the housetops on the southwest side of the square.

"Oh, is that it? Oh, hell, I already been there. Jesus, look at the rain. I thought this place was supposed to be so, you know, beautiful." The tourist waved a cold blue hand at the rain-soaked facade of the foundling hospital, where the nine arches of Brunelleschi's arcade rested serenely upon their ten perfect columns. "Back in Milwaukee this would be a park, with, you know, trees. What's so great about this?" Turning his back on the sporting sea creatures in the fountains, he stared at the melancholy carriages waiting for passengers, the sodden horses drooping their heads. "It don't look beautiful to me."

Zee listened to the whining voice and wondered why the man had ever left home. Taking pity on him, he explained how to get to the Palazzo Davanzati, where surely the poor fool would enjoy the display of fourteenth-century domestic life. Then, with a nod, Zee mopped at his streaming hair and hurried away to catch a bus to the place where he had parked his car.

He didn't look back to see the man from Milwaukee turn away from the great tourist spectacles of the city of Florence and enter the Banca degli Innocenti for a chat with the manager, Leonardo Bindo, that fascinating geometrical study in circles inscribed upon circles.

Signor Bindo was not happy to see the man from Milwaukee, whose name—Earl—he could not pronounce. He spoke to him angrily in English. "I've told you never to come here."

"Oh, Jesus, the phone. I can't work the goddamned phone. Those goddamned tokens, Jesus."

Bindo listened to Earl's peevish complaints, feeling for him nothing but contempt. When the product in which he was dealing worked its way to the bottom, all the way down into the hands of this piece of filth, he lost interest in it altogether. He felt more respect for the men who handled it on its long journey from the high mountains of the Hindu Kush. Sometimes Bindo compared himself with his colleagues in Milan and Naples and Turin, busy professional men who had no interest in the substance except as a profitable commodity like pharmaceuticals or cement. To his own wide-ranging imagination there was something romantic

about its travels along the dangerous road to eventual con-
sumption on the street—the long passage that carried it from
some poppy field on a mountain hillside in Pakistan to a set
of rusty oil drums on the Northwest Frontier, then through
the Khyber Pass on donkeys, and at last, by a fantastic series
of further adventures, to a conversion laboratory in Milan
to become heroin by a hideously corrosive chemical process.

That was excitement, that was daring. Bindo envisioned
the cleverness of the turbaned tribesmen, the resourcefulness
of the brave couriers, the exhilaration of living precariously
every day on the verge of discovery and death. But as for
the pushers on the street, *beh*, who gave a damn about them?
They were dirt under Bindo's feet. More contemptible still
were the ultimate consumers, the sick offal of the city squares
and back alleys, the dregs of the human race. If they perished
from their obsession with the substance he bought and sold,
it was no concern of his. Another crop of customers would
rise up at once to take their place.

Or rather, they would have risen up, if His Holiness had
not announced his new crusade, his *Anno Sacro Anti-droga*.

CHAPTER 4

■ ■ ■ ■ ■ ■ ■ ■ ■ ■ ■

Say I submit and go—suppose I fall
  Into some folly? . . .

                                                  Inferno II, 34, 35.

"My umbrella," said the Archbishop of Florence, getting down on his knees to look behind the heap of rubbers in the bottom of his wardrobe. "I seem to have mislaid it."

"Excellency, I have it right here." The priest who was the archbishop's secretary helped him to his feet, accompanied him to the door of the archiepiscopal palace, popped open the umbrella and put it in his hand. Then he reached forward and buttoned the archbishop's coat. "It's very wet, Excellency."

The palace of the archbishop was near the cathedral. Holding his umbrella slanted against the rain, he hurried across the square, past the Baptistery and along the great cliff of the north side of the church, to enter the vast space of Santa Maria del Fiore through the door called the Porta della Mandorla. In the sacristy he permitted another assisting priest to robe him, although he would much rather have done it himself. Being waited on was a continual penance, but he accepted these services humbly and tried to be thankful.

The daily morning ritual of ten o'clock mass was not strictly required of the archbishop, but he was a man of great simplicity and strong faith, and he felt it his duty to celebrate the Eucharist every day with the common folk of his famous parish. This sort of devotion had won him a reputation for

15

saintliness, a regard that pained him, since he felt himself unworthy.

Worshippers were few this morning because of the rain. In the enormous hollow spaces under the dome the archbishop's voice was almost lost, but to those receiving the body and precious blood at the entrance to the sanctuary his words seemed, as always, meant for their ears alone. Today it was mostly elderly women lifting their faces to the cup, except for the young officer of the police who often appeared at ten o'clock.

After the service the archbishop pulled off chasuble, stole and alb with his own hands and hurried back through the rain, trying to work up the courage to make a long-distance phone call to a certain cardinal in the Vatican.

When he burst into his study, his secretary was already putting the call through. The archbishop barely had time to catch his breath before the phone was put into his hand. "He's on the line, Excellency."

Pulling himself together, the archbishop spoke up heartily, "Your Eminence? Good morning! I hope I'm not calling at an inconvenient time?"

"Of course not," said the Prefect for the Pontifical Household. "When I'm told to expect a call from Your Excellency, I'm eager to receive it any moment of the day."

"Well, then, I'll get down to business right away. Were you aware, Your Eminence, that the city of Florence will celebrate next year the seven-hundredth anniversary of the consecration of our cathedral?"

"No, I didn't know that. Congratulations! But I suppose it means a lot of fuss on your part, all sorts of celebrations and special services?"

"Well, of course, Your Eminence. We've already set up a committee. Actually, we've set up a number of committees. But the most important task has been assigned to me." The archbishop cleared his throat. "Your Eminence, I have been delegated to ask if His Holiness would honor the occasion with his presence. You can imagine how much it would mean to us all."

"Ah, I see!" The cardinal prefect laughed. "Of course you would think of the Holy Father at such a time. And I feel sure he will be delighted to attend, if it can be fitted into his calendar. It's a good thing you called today. We're just making up a broad outline of his schedule for next year. What day were you thinking of?"

"Ah, there now, that's the difficulty. It's Easter Sunday morning. Of course I understand how busy—"

"Easter Sunday! But that's impossible. You must know that."

"Your Eminence, it would be only for an hour. He could simply pop in and pop out. We've made all sorts of—"

"Pop in and pop out! His Holiness? What are you thinking of? On Easter Sunday? You know perfectly well what his schedule is like. One enormous event follows another—on Holy Thursday the washing of feet in the basilica, on Good Friday the celebration of the Passion, followed by the torchlight procession and the Via Crucis in the Colosseum, on Holy Saturday a ceremonial conclusion to the Holy Year Against Drugs, on Easter Sunday—"

"But, Your Eminence, if he flew up by helicopter! We will cordon off a landing place beside the cathedral. He would merely mount a platform on the cathedral steps, give his blessing, send into flight the little mechanical dove to set off the fireworks—the old ceremony of the Explosion of the Cart, Your Eminence—and then get back in his helicopter and return to Rome in plenty of time for his appearance at noon on worldwide television."

"I assure you, it is utterly impossible. Now, my friend, do you have other business? I'm afraid I have a busy morning."

"But, please, Your Eminence, let me describe our project in detail."

"Forgive me, Your Excellency, I must go."

"I will call again another time."

The archbishop leaned back and shut his eyes with fatigue. He had failed. It was too bad—Signor Bindo would be disappointed. It had been Bindo's idea in the first place to invite the Holy Father. He must be informed at once.

But to the archbishop's surprise Leonardo Bindo merely laughed. "He said no? That means nothing. You mustn't give up, Your Excellency. You must try again."

"But you don't know how difficult it is to change anyone's mind at the Vatican. You must remember, my dear Signor Bindo, *Roma locuta est, causa finita est.* When Rome speaks, the matter is finished."

"Your Excellency, I assure you, the cardinal only needs time to get used to the idea. You must call him again in a day or two."

Reluctantly the archbishop agreed, although his heart wasn't in it.

It was time for lunch. The Archbishop of Florence was ascetic by long habit, and his secretary had to wheedle him into eating a bowl of soup at his desk. For Leonardo Bindo it was a different matter. Lunch was the central ornament of the day. Bindo always dined properly at a restaurant around the corner on Via de' Servi.

But first he would stop in at Santissima Annunziata. The church was a famous shrine, frequented by the rich wives of several of the bank's major depositors, and it did no harm to display his piety.

The clouds were parting as Bindo walked out into the square. Sunshine sparkled on the wet ribs of the cathedral dome and glittered in the splashes thrown up by the whining wheels of motorbikes as they tore through the puddles on the pavement.

To his mild disappointment he was alone in the church except for one ragged old woman kneeling before the famous old painting of the Annunciation, which had been finished by an angel, according to legend.

As he finished his perfunctory prayers and got to his feet, the old woman got up too, and touched his arm. "I'll tell you a secret, Signore. That is the real one."

"The real one, Signora?"

"The real mother of God. The others, they are not real. Only this one."

"Ah, I see." Bindo smiled at the old woman. "*Grazie tante*, Signora. I did not know it."

CHAPTER 5

▪ ▪ ▪ ▪ ▪ ▪ ▪ ▪ ▪ ▪ ▪ ▪ ▪

Florence, rejoice, because thy soaring fame
  Beats its broad wings across both land and sea,
  And all the deep of Hell rings with thy name!
                                              Inferno XXVI, 1–3.

They stood together on the north side of the Villa
L'Ombrellino, Giovanni Zibo and Lucretia Van Ott,
the two founding professors of the American School
of Florentine Studies, looking down across the river at the
city of Florence.

There it lay with its fabled domes and towers, filmed
over with a pearly haze as the rain withdrew over Monte
Morello. They could not see the life on the streets—the
stream of motorbikes flying along Via Cavour, the coffee
drinkers in the corner bars, the old man riding a bicycle
along Via Ghibellina with a ladder on his shoulder, the American pusher in a Milwaukee Brewers cap shambling into
Piazza Santo Spirito to peddle his wares. Nor could they hear
the roar of the traffic, the lumbering wheeze of city buses,
the whistles of policemen in white helmets, the murmurs of
lovers embracing on street corners, the clatter of metal shutters rolling down over shop windows, the hoarse cheerful
greetings of shopkeepers entering restaurants and cafes. Here
there was only a sprinkling of church bells from across the
river, the distant horns of cars far below at Porta Romana,
and the spatter and plop of raindrops falling from the olive
trees below the parapet.

"Well," said Lucretia grudgingly, "the view is certainly
very fine."

Zee glanced at her anxiously. Now that he had signed the lease, it was important that she be satisfied. Lucretia was to be his colleague in the new school, just as she had been for the last five years at the University of Florence, and her contribution would be crucial. Lucretia was Dutch. She spoke five languages. She was an authority on the art of the Italian Renaissance. Taller than Zee, she was a handsome woman with light hair cut short like Hans Brinker's. She was always in a hurry, her long skirt whipping in the breeze of her forward stride. Beneath her jaw a little curve of skin betrayed the fact that she was no longer altogether young.

Now they turned their backs on the view and looked at the villa.

"But it's falling down," exclaimed Lucretia in dismay.

Zee's heart sank. It was true. The place was even more dilapidated than he remembered. Had the stucco on the loggia been crumbling like that last week?

Signor Bindo had given him a key. Entering on the north side between a pair of busts wrapped in plastic, they toured the villa slowly, examining it inside and out, choosing places for classrooms, a library, a dormitory, private spaces for the staff.

The Florentine comune had achieved a number of necessary repairs before running out of money for the renovation of its new trade center, but much remained to be done. In the dormitory wing the plumbing was new, but everywhere else it was practically prehistoric. The plaster on the walls was cracked, and grey mildew crept over the faded frescoes lining the central hall. In the garden the playful bronze umbrella that had given L'Ombrellino its name had been reconstructed, but all the stairways needed repair, and some of the tiles on the three great terraces were missing. The tower was shabby. Wisps of grass grew between the toes of the stone maidens adorning the parapet overlooking the city.

But the maidens were goddesses, after all, and the villa itself was of a grand design. Once it had belonged to the mistress of Edward VII, Mrs. Keppel. Under her dominion it had been gussied up with crystal chandeliers and vases of tuberoses and porcelain pagodas from the Brighton Pavilion. Now the place seemed an empty shell.

Nothing, however, could be more distinguished than its seventeenth-century history. For fourteen years the villa had been the home of Galileo. It was here that he had written the work for which he was condemned by the Holy Office of the Inquisition. *You, Galileo, have made yourself vehemently suspect of heresy*—the awful condemnation conferred luster on the villa, in spite of the bushy tangles sprawling where there had once been orderly gardens, in spite of the shattered greenhouses, in spite of the uninhabitable tower and the antiquated kitchen.

Now, examining the kitchen, Lucretia stopped frowning and began to laugh. Zee's spirits rose. Once again they wan-

dered through the spacious rooms, and this time Zee invented
comic names for them, marble-cold though they were—the
Drawing Room of the Queen Mother, the Rumpus Room of
the Crown Prince, the Pavilion of the Concubines, the Antechamber of the Grand Vizier, the Dining Salon of the
Grand Duke, the Pleasure Dome of Kubla Khan.

Leaving the house, they explored the grounds. Pulling
out his sketchbook, Zee scribbled swift portraits of the goddesses on the parapet. Most of them were tugging ineffec-
tively at cascading draperies that failed to conceal their
youthful breasts and long magnificent thighs.

"Look, there's another one," said Lucretia, forcing a path
through a jungle of overgrown hedges to the last of the
marble women. Like the others it was no particular goddess,
only a miscellaneous nymph, a potluck dryad. Lucretia
grinned at Zee. "It's really very grand, the whole thing. But,
good God, there's so much to do."

"Books," said Zee. "Books first."

"Furniture," said Lucretia. "Beds, chairs. No, first we've
got to line up the staff. A cook! How do we find a cook?"

Anxiously they thrashed their way out of the hedges. The trustees of the new school were far away across the Atlantic in Massachusetts, but Zee could feel their eyes on his back as his little Saab plunged down the steep declivity of Via di Bellosguardo.

"September," the president of the trustees had said. "We'll provide the students and the rest of the faculty if you people will prepare the physical plant and be ready to begin in September."

CHAPTER 6

Those men do violence to God. . .
                    Inferno XI, 46.

The day that had begun with rain was now bright and hot. Reluctantly Matteo Luzzi pulled a dark wool suit out of the back of his closet. As he tucked in the black dickey and fastened the Roman collar, he was already sweltering.

When he emerged on the street he at once became Father Matteo. Old women murmured, "God bless you, Father," young girls smiled at the cherubic curly-headed priest. In spite of himself Matteo felt noble and holy. Benignly he smiled back as if he would be glad to stop for a chat, but, alas, he was on an errand of mercy.

From infancy Matteo had been destined for the priesthood. His mother's girlfriends, in spite of their calling, had clasped their hands at the angelic child and gushed, "The boy will be a priest." It had been the dearest wish of his mother, as she carted him here and there in the company of one wealthy patron after another. Somehow she failed to see little Matteo scissoring off the wings of butterflies to watch the frantic zigzag crawling of the mutilated insect bodies. From butterflies he went on to cats, and at the seminary there had been an unfortunate episode involving the death by gunshot of another student.

It was an accident, everyone agreed, and no charges were brought against Matteo, but he was quietly expelled just the same.

Mercato Centrale

"Guns and cars," complained the rector to Matteo's mother. "The boy thinks of nothing else, when his head should be filled with visions of Christ on the cross."

Leaving the school was no loss to Matteo. He had been a feeble student anyway, dreaming during class, drawing sports cars in his notebook, with long streaks of speed streaming from Jaguars and Alfa Romeos. Often in the morning he played hookey, going after birds with a shotgun he kept in an abandoned garage behind the cafeteria.

Thereafter firearms and fast cars became Matteo's life. The one led directly to the other. Providing a service with the first earned him the second. Unfortunately he had smashed his last car, a sporty Nissan Pulsar, but walked away from the collision unscathed. His mother said it was the intervention of the Blessed Virgin—although the Virgin had not protected the driver of the other car, a pretty young schoolteacher from Lucca.

At the moment Matteo had no wheels to play with. He was saving his money for a Maserati. Signor Bindo kept him short, but he hinted that this business with the insane idealist would result in a lump sum sooner or later.

The idealist had an apartment in the neighborhood of the *Mercato Centrale*. Matteo, perspiring in his priestly collar and dark suit, made his way among the stalls. Here everything was movement and color and loud music, with sunshine glittering on the hoods of cars and the windshields of parked motorbikes, reflecting brightly from the racks of sunglasses, sparkling in the miniature fountain above a bowl of fresh coconut. American tourists bought wallets and T-shirts, housewives lugged plastic bags of groceries by their stretched handles, swaggering kids in leather jackets fingered the gold neck-chains, boys bounced a soccer ball against the rough stone facade of the church of San Lorenzo. Where was the idealist's apartment?

Then Matteo's eye was caught by a flashy Maserati parked at one side of the street. *Gesùmmaria*, it was just

what he liked best. Himself, of course, he would choose the
red rather than the black.

Roberto Mori waited for Matteo, looking down at the
market from above, his eye roving among the shoppers,
searching for a priest. Through the open window floated all
the lively smells of the market, the reek of hanging carcasses,
the fragrance of ripe fruit trucked up from the south.

Roberto had spent the morning at his new job in the
Department of City Museums. As a former professor of
Christian archeology he had hoped to work with the artifacts
dug up from the foundation of the ancient church under the
cathedral Instead he was a mere bureaucrat, assigning keys
to janitors and cleaning women, granting or denying permission for school visits and special tours.

It was a disappointment. But Roberto's sense of himself
was no longer bound up with his calling. It had once meant
much to him to be a distinguished professor at the Gregorian
University in Rome, but he had long since stopped regretting
his lost ambition. Now all his passionate attention was di-
rected elsewhere.

His visitor was late. The market was closing. With a
noise like the roll of a drum one of the carts rumbled away
over the stony street. Now the other merchants followed
suit, dropping gold chains into velvet boxes, stowing away
the plastic statuettes of Michelangelo's *David*, tossing purses
into paper bags, collapsing the awnings, folding everything
down into the carts.

Where was Father Matteo?

Then Roberto saw him, a young priest on the sidewalk
beside a parked sports car. He was walking around it, slapping
the hood, stroking the sleek surface, peering in at the dashboard. It seemed an odd thing for a priest to do. Roberto
watched him turn away from the car and look up and down
the street. Ah, now he was coming.

Walking out into the hall, Roberto watched his visitor
climb the stairs. *"Buon giorno*, Father," he said amiably, as

Father Matteo paused to stare. It happened all the time. People seemed to need a moment to get used to him. It was a nuisance, but Roberto was accustomed to it.

In the apartment they settled down on two uncomfortable wooden chairs. Matteo held the letter and the envelope full of money on his lap and gazed admiringly at his host. Signor Bindo would be interested to hear that the man looked like a film star. Then, remembering what he had come for, he handed over Bindo's letter.

"It's from one of the cardinals in the Vatican. He wishes you to know that he regrets your official silencing by the Congregation for the Doctrine of the Faith."

"One of the cardinals?" said Roberto. "Which cardinal?"

Matteo shook his head. "He can't give his name. He's one of many who feel the same way. He wants you to know that he shares your views."

"My views?" Roberto's strong handsome face took on an expression of amused doubt. "And what are my views supposed to be?"

Matteo recited his memorized list. "More democratic procedures in the church, an end to the doctrine of papal infallibility, a more liberal practice of releasing priests from their vows, a role for women in the hierarchy, an end to priestly celibacy, the possibility of divorce—"

"Next, Father Matteo, you will be talking about abortion," said Roberto gently, smiling at the eager young priest.

Matteo looked surprised. Clearly it had been the next shocking word on his tongue.

"*Mi scusi,*" said Roberto, opening the letter from the cardinal, reading it swiftly. At once his doubts fell away. The three closely written sheets had been penned on the stationery of the Council for Public Affairs of the Church, one of the august departments within the Vatican Secretariat of State. Roberto had visited the office, high on the top floor of the Apostolic Palace. He could picture the prelate writing the letter at his desk, looking up now and then to glance at

Bernini's colonnade, craning his neck to see the play of light and shade on the facade of the Basilica of Saint Peter. The letter was signed only *Your friend*, with a polite final command, *Please destroy*. Roberto was deeply moved.

Smiling, he folded the letter and held it in his hand. For the first time he felt supported by a brother in the church—comforted, endorsed, sanctioned at last. It was so much more than he had expected; he longed to express his joy.

But the vacuous young priest was not the right audience. Father Matteo was looking around inquisitively at the spare furnishings of the small apartment. He asked a nosy question. "How do you support yourself now, Father?"

Roberto explained his job in the Department of City Museums. And he cautioned Father Matteo not to address him publicly as a priest.

"Of course not." Matteo leaned forward, excited to be sharing confidences with a man so distinguished. "*Anch' io.* I too must become someone else. The soutane,"—he ran his finger around the edge of the stiff collar—"it's much too conspicuous. People will remember a priest." Then he handed the envelope full of lire to Father Roberto. "The cardinal also wished me to give you this. It will take care of extra expenses for a little while. You must count it and sign a receipt."

Roberto took the envelope. "The cardinal wishes it?"

"Yes, yes, the cardinal."

CHAPTER 7

▪▪▪▪▪▪▪▪▪▪▪▪▪

For all their eyelids with an iron wire
  Are stitched and sealed . . .
                    Purgatorio XIII, 70, 71.

The Archbishop of Florence tried again a few days later, urged on by the vigorous encouragement of Leonardo Bindo. Bravely he dialed the Vatican switchboard himself, and asked to speak to the cardinal who was Prefect for the Pontifical Household.

The prefect was wary. Was His Excellency going to raise the same impossible request for the pope's presence in Florence on Easter morning the following year?

He was. "I just want to be sure, Your Eminence," said the archbishop hurriedly, "that you understand how eager we are to pay for everything, and how thorough our security arrangements will be. Here in this city we have access to hundreds of men in uniform to protect the safety of His Holiness—the polizia, the carabinieri, the soldati—"

"How can I make it clear to you that such a visit is unthinkable? Your Excellency, I brought the matter up at our weekly *congresso*, and they all laughed merrily at such a suggestion. I assure you—"

"But, Your Eminence, have you spoken to the holy father himself?"

There was a pause. "No, but I don't need to. He can't possibly do such a thing."

Leaning forward at his desk, the archbishop knocked over a hideous marble paperweight in the shape of an obelisk, the gift of his niece. It fell with a crash, but he paid no attention,

31

and spoke passionately into the telephone. "I beg you, Your Eminence, for this one thing, only this, that you will ask His Holiness."

There was another pause, and then the prefect sighed. "Well, perhaps. But not today. Not tomorrow. I can't promise when I will have an opportunity."

"Thank you, Your Eminence. Let it be at your convenience. I'm deeply grateful."

The polite tug of war went on for weeks. The archbishop was a courteous person, but his program committee in the person of Leonardo Bindo continued to nag him to pester the Vatican.

The archbishop had to keep forcing himself to call the prefect and appeal to him once again.

At first his badgering phone calls bore no fruit. The responses were always the same. "I'm sorry, Your Excellency, I've had no time to speak to His Holiness. We've been far too busy planning his trip to the Orient"—"Oh, Your Excellency, not again! I can't possibly speak to him now. There's a general audience this afternoon. Seven hundred African priests and thirty bishops!"—"Oh, Archbishop, not today. I've just returned from poolside at Castel Gandolfo. The Holy Father is taking a complete rest. I couldn't possibly disturb him."

After this last rebuff the archbishop spoke up in mild complaint, "But my committee is pressuring me, Your Eminence. I've got to tell them something."

"Then tell them no," responded the prefect angrily. "I simply cannot hurry the Holy Father."

"Oh, no, no, no, it's all right," stuttered the archbishop. 'I will await his decision with patience. Let it be entirely at your convenience."

When the prefect called at last to announce the pope's decision, the archbishop felt no hope. He was stunned to learn that the holy father had been enthusiastic about the project. He would pop in and pop out on Easter Sunday morning as the archbishop suggested, arriving by helicopter at an early hour, returning to Rome in time for the all-important eleven o'clock mass in the Basilica of Saint Peter.

The archbishop began to splutter his gratitude, but the prefect interrupted to warn him that the holy father would come *if and only if* the security arrangements were worked out in advance, *if and only if* thirty members of the Vatican Vigilanza and the Swiss Guard were present at the ceremony, having been quartered in Florence the day before.

"Oh, but of course," cried the archbishop. "Certainly! Money no object. I will write to His Holiness at once to express our gratitude. Our prayers have been answered."

At once he called Signor Bindo, to tell him the good news.

Signor Bindo was overjoyed.

CHAPTER 8

For better waters heading with the wind
  My ship of genius now shakes out her sail. . . .

                              Purgatorio I, 1, 2.

It was left to the trustees back in Boston to advertise for
students. Before long a sign went up on bulletin boards
all over the university—

STUDY ABROAD

The American School of Florentine Studies,
Villa L'Ombrellino, Florence,
will open its doors this fall to eleven
resident students. Applicants must be above
sophomore rank. Postgraduates, alumni
and alumnae may also apply.

Applications are available in the office of
the Department of Comparative Literature.

The notice looked splendid and inviting, but the staff was
still incomplete. The two Florentine professors had yet to be
balanced by two recruits from the United States.

For instruction in Italian history the obvious choice was
Augustus Himmelfahrt, a specialist at the University of Chicago, who had written a thick book on the subject.

Himmelfahrt was delighted. At once he made an excited
transatlantic call to inquire about accommodations. Would
his room at the villa have a private bath?

"Of course," said Zee, instantly identifying him as a

shit. Zee had spent twelve years of his life teaching at American and Italian institutions of higher learning, and he knew the varieties of academic imbecility very well. Pulling out his pen, he began doodling a portrait of Himmelfahrt on the pad beside the phone, a cartoon face with a tiny nose and a colossal chin. He didn't tell Himmelfahrt that the only private bath in the villa was an old one with a vast tub holding fifty gallons, heated by a gadget with a rusty ten-gallon tank.

There remained only a single post to fill, that of instructor of contemporary Italian literature. One possible American candidate after another refused the offer. Either they were pregnant or in the throes of a divorce or already under contract for next year.

"What about Kelly?" suggested the chairman of the Department of Comparative Literature. "You know that guy at Harvard who used to be a detective? He's mostly American Lit, but he's always going on about Alberto Moravia or Italo Calvino. Try Homer Kelly."

"Oh, I know Kelly," said the president of the trustees. "Isn't he something of a wild man? Well, not exactly wild, just sort of exaggerated, if you know what I mean?"

"Exaggerated? Well, perhaps." There was a ruminative pause, and then the department chairman concluded stuffily, "But sound, I would say. The man is altogether sound."

It was true that Homer Kelly was an exaggerated person, somewhere at one end of the curve of human possibility. Taller than most people, Homer was given to various forms of hyperbole. For one thing he was noisy and gregarious, indulging in spasms of euphoria that alternated with fits of gloom. For another he had a habit of tripping over his own large feet, and he didn't know how to repair a light fixture. Thirdly he was nosy and inquisitive and apt to spring to conclusions by leaps of intuition rather than logical reasoning. Lastly Homer Kelly was rapacious of experience, wallowing in the present moment, greeting the morning with savage appetite.

When the call came, Homer was on his knees in his front yard in Concord, groping at oak leaves under a bush. When he heard the phone ring inside the house, he sat up suddenly, and a twig lashed his eye. Whimpering, he ran up the steps, snatched at the phone and barked, "Ouch, ouch, hello?"

Thus he wasn't in the most receptive mood to accept a teaching post in a foreign land. "I'll think it over," he said, mopping his streaming eye.

"Good God, Mary," he said to his wife when she came back from shopping, "I can't read all those Italian novels over the summer."

But Mary was thrilled. "How wonderful. I'll come too. I'll go to Rome and find out about all those American artists abroad, friends of the Brownings and so on. I'll write another book."

"But, listen, my dear—"

"Nonsense, Homer. Look, I'll help. We'll read those people together. And we'll study Italian. And while we're about it, let's read *The Divine Comedy*. It's one of the supreme works of art in the western world, and it's been out since the fourteenth century, so it's high time."

Meanwhile on the other side of the ocean in the Villa L'Ombrellino, Giovanni Zibo went on with his preparations. He bought a secondhand van and spent a hot afternoon in the middle of May painting the school's name on its two front doors. Lucretia ordered twenty mattresses from the Casa del Materasso on Piazzale al Prato. She drove off to a shop on Via Franceso Ferrucci for a set of cheap mirrors of wavy glass. The wardrobes, bedsteads, desks and chairs came from a warehouse in Pisa.

"Soap," she cried, staring at Zee. "Toilet paper. What else have I forgotten? Wastebaskets!" And she rushed off again to consult the yellow pages. She hired a cook, Alberto Fraticelli, and a chambermaid, Alberto's wife, Isabella. She found a gardener, Franco Spoleto. She advertised for a sec-

retary to occupy the school office on the second floor of the villa, a handsome chamber with a ceiling of blue clouds.

Books in English for the American students were a problem. They were so expensive.

"Perhaps the American faculty members could bring them from the United States," suggested Lucretia.

"Well, we can try," said Zee, and he called Professor Kelly.

Homer was agreeable. "Which edition of *The Divine Comedy* do you want, Professor Zibo?" he said, speaking to the Italian professor for the first time.

"Call me Zee. I thought the Sayers edition, Professor Kelly."

"My name is Homer. Oh, good, that's the one we're using." Homer showed off. Deepening his voice to a roar, he intoned the first lines of Dante's *Inferno* in the Sayers translation—

> "Midway this way of life we're bound upon,
>   I woke to find myself in a dark wood,
>   Where the right road was wholly lost and gone.

That's the translation you want?"

"Oh, yes, that's the one. It's not perfect, and sometimes she strains too hard after rhymes, but the notes are excellent, don't you agree?"

And then Zee hung up, and went on groping through the tangled branches of his own dark wood. By now it was the way life presented itself to him, a dusky vista of narrow glimmering passages between the trunks of sullen trees.

During this second week in June, Julia Smith arrived in Florence. She found a room at once in a third-class pensione near the railroad station and settled down to see the sights. First the cathedral, then the Uffizi, then Michelangelo's *David*, then the Palazzo Vecchio.

At the end of the third day Julia climbed the stairs to

her room in tears, disappointed by the stony city choked
with tourists, worn out with the stares and catcalls, suffering
from loneliness.

Perhaps she should never have come. Perhaps she was
wasting the remains of her small inheritance.

Julia had been eager to experience at first hand a city
crowded with works of art, but somehow it wasn't what she
had expected. She had longed to be surrounded by greatness,
she had hungered for the flesh of genius, but so far she was
still starving.

What good did it do to look at something, and then move

on to look at something else? It was too passive. She wanted
to live in the famous buildings, she wanted to move into one
of the monks' cells decorated by Fra Angelico at San Marco,
she wanted to pluck the bronze pears from Ghiberti's Doors
of Paradise. She wanted to *do* something with the city of
Florence. It was no good just gawking.

Then one day in the Bargello she came upon a flock of
American kids standing in a semicircle before Donatello's
Saint George. They were listening to a lecture. They were
going to school in Florence.

Enviously Julia stood on the sidelines. When the lecture
was over, she asked the instructor about the school.

"I'm sorry, but our list is filled for next fall. But there's
a new American school over across the river in Bellosguardo.
You might try there."

He gave her the address, then watched her go, cursing
his limited enrollment. How that stunning woman would
have ornamented his class of stupid girls!

"Oh, Mr. Braithwaite," tittered Melanie Bulger, "Cyn-
thia and I think you look just like Saint George."

There was a chorus of giggles. Julia disappeared down
the stairs.

CHAPTER 9

▪▪▪▪▪▪▪▪▪▪▪▪

O Tuscan, walking thus with words discreet
  Alive through the city of fire. . . .
                              Inferno X, 22, 23.

Once again the bell in the Campanile was ringing for ten o'clock mass. The bell had a deep vigorous note, one that thrilled the archbishop and shook the delicate membranes of his spirit, even after all these years.

Taking his place at the altar, the old man noticed that attendance was larger than usual this morning. Some of the communicants were tourists, coming forward self-consciously, humbly trying to follow local practice. The archbishop ignored their strange sporty clothing, their bare legs. One American girl with yellow hair was wearing too many clothes on this warm day—men's shirts and pants, how odd! The archbishop refrained from making judgments. He was grateful, as always, that these people were here at all.

Once again he was glad to see the young officer of the polizia among them. As the boy put up his homely face to receive the host, the archbishop smiled at him, enjoying his modesty, his avoidance of any unctuous show of piety.

The service was a momentary relief from the increasing pressure on the archbishop. Preparations for the celebration of the seven hundredth anniversary of the cathedral had mushroomed. Committees were springing up around him like weeds, proliferating and exfoliating in all directions. He had never heard of Parkinson's Law, but the growth of his committees was a perfect example of its inexorable sway.

There were promotional committees to oversee publicity

in the newspapers and on television, artistic committees to design banners to hang over the city streets, construction committees to set up bleachers for important people in front of the Duomo, tactful committees to choose the important people, sacred committees to increase the splendor of the Easter service, floral committees, traffic committees, tradesmen's committees, Vatican liaison committees, papal protocol committees, clean-up committees, and of course the all-important committees concerned with the safety of the Holy Father.

Over the entire writhing mass one faithful overseer exercised control, the manager of the Banca degli Innocenti, Leonardo Bindo. The archbishop had come to rely on his calm authority and swift decisiveness, and now he leaned on him more and more. Signor Bindo was his rod and staff.

This morning the subject under discussion was the *Scoppio del Carro*, the Explosion of the Cart.

"But surely we don't need a committee for that," said the archbishop. "It's always been well managed. After all, for how many centuries has it been part of the Easter celebration at the cathedral?"

"Nevertheless I think it should be placed under the oversight of a special artistic director. I suspect the cart could do with a repainting, and perhaps a regilding of the Pazzi dolphins. Surely it suffers damage every year from the explosion."

"Ah, yes, I see. Of course." In the end the archbishop always agreed with Signor Bindo.

"And the oxen to pull the cart through the streets, they must be the finest in Tuscany, the whitest, the biggest. I suggest we send someone to Arezzo to choose among the very best. Perfection above all."

It was their watchword. "Of course," sighed the archbishop. "Perfection above all."

Leonardo Bindo kept all these matters in hand. He had a way of ordering things in his head, masterfully controlling every detail. Like an artist he dabbed a little here and a little there, preserving at every moment the balance of the picture as a whole.

Some of the picture, of course, was private, indecipherable to anyone but himself. His correspondence with Roberto Mori was a matter of this kind.

Composing the letters for a fictional prelate in the Vatican called for all his enterprise and cleverness. He enjoyed the intellectual challenge of warping his mind in a direction completely at odds with his own conservative belief. At the Biblioteca Nazionale he spent an entire day ferreting out articles by dissident churchmen, by Hans Küng of Austria, by Leonardo Boff of Brazil, by a certain rebellious priest in California, by truculent nuns in Chicago. His notes were full of distasteful phrases to be sprinkled into his letters like cherries in a cake—"the language of modern man," "the courage to be Christian," "the apostolic succession of every member of the church," "the internationalization of the Roman Curia," "the participation of the laity," "the need for spontaneity in worship." What nonsense! Idiotic phrases rattled out of his typewriter, day after day.

But Bindo threw the whole force of his gifted imagination into his lying letters. They were more than clever, they were magical. They were alive with brilliant touches, sincere with high purpose, homely with personality—"Ah, I have spilled coffee on this letter! Forgive me, Father!"

Matteo Luzzi took them to Roberto Mori one at a time.

Matteo's second appointment was for the lunch hour, but once again he was late. This time it was the fault of a stunning American girl among the tourists waiting to see the Michelangelo sculptures at San Lorenzo. Matteo hung around for half an hour, flirting with her in English, extracting only monosyllables in reply. The girl had covered half her face with sunglasses, she had hidden most of her golden hair under a man's hat, and disguised her delicious curves with a couple of long shirts. But Matteo was a connoisseur of classy girls. He could see the goddess underneath.

Not until the door opened and the waiting tourists were admitted did he release her and turn languidly away, remembering his mission to Roberto Mori.

Father Roberto was delighted to see him. At once he reached for the letter in Matteo's hand. "From the cardinal?" he said eagerly.

"*Si, si*, of course it is from the cardinal."

Matteo watched as Father Roberto tore open the envelope and read Bindo's clever concoction of insane mellifluous phrases.

"Can you wait while I compose a reply?" Roberto's face was flushed with pleasure.

"Of course."

Roberto sat down at a narrow table and drove his pen swiftly over a sheet of paper. His letter was different from Bindo's. It poured out of him without calculation—earnest, reverent, charged with his ardent willingness to serve. As he handed it to Matteo, his face was transfigured.

Matteo took the letter and promised to send it by the proper channels at once. Then he lingered. He had begun to fall under the spell of the passionate and handsome priest, who had been silenced by the Vatican just as he, Matteo, had been expelled from the seminary. There was something compelling about him, a kind of authority very different from that of Signor Bindo.

"I have to get a job," he complained to Roberto. "And a new place to live."

He did not explain that it was Leonardo Bindo who was insisting that he be usefully occupied, that he should not hang around all day doing nothing.

Nor did he go into the grubby details of his landlady's outrage. The usual thing had happened. Matteo had begun by charming her, but after a few months she was no longer charmed, she was infuriated, and now he had frightened the poor woman out of her wits. This morning when she had complained about his delinquent rent, he had sprayed her sofa with birdshot. She had thrown him out.

"The cardinal wants you to get a job?" said Roberto innocently.

"The cardinal? Oh, *si, si,* the cardinal." Matteo lied easily. "He wishes to conceal my involvement. I'm to be occupied with ordinary things."

"But I think I can solve your problem. There's a school here, a new school. They're looking for a secretary. See, here's the ad in *La Nazione.* And you could live there too, I think."

It was the new American school at Villa L'Ombrellino. Matteo rode out to Bellosguardo on the bus and climbed the hill. He was interviewed by Lucretia Van Ott, who hired him at once.

Returning to Bindo's office, Matteo bragged of his success. "And I'll be living there," he said proudly. "It's a big villa, a new American school on the other side of the river."

"Not the Villa L'Ombrellino?" Bindo was mildly astonished. "But I have recently prepared their lease. Professor Zibo signed it. It's a lovely place, *vero?*"

Matteo made a face. "*Beh,* it is old." More to his taste would have been a brand-new structure of glass and steel like a hotel in Milan, with color-coordinated furnishings and everything push-button—the television, the air conditioning, the stereo, the shower.

After Matteo left him, Roberto unfolded the cardinal's letter and read it eagerly once again, tasting the sweetness of the words of praise. But he shook his head at the caution scribbled at the bottom of the page, "Destroy."

Soon, perhaps, but not yet. For the moment he couldn't bear to lose it. Carefully Roberto put the letter back in its envelope and hid it with the first in the table drawer.

CHAPTER 10

▪▪▪▪▪▪▪▪▪▪▪▪▪▪

Beatrice gazed on heav'n and I on her. . . .
                              Paradiso II, 22.

There was no great rush of applications from would-be
students to the American School of Florentine Studies.
"The announcement came out too late," said the president of the trustees. "Everything was too rushed. Next year
it will be different."

Nine of the accepted students were juniors at the university, two were older women alumnae. At the last minute,
during the final week of preparations in August, two of the
younger applicants dropped out, leaving holes in the
enrollment.

The first was filled when an American girl wandered up
the driveway of the villa one day and spoke to Franco Spoleto,
the gardener, who was working with a bucket of patching
plaster, repairing cracks in the wall.

"The office?" she said, and then she tried it clumsily in
Italian. *"Il uffizio?"*

Franco looked at her openmouthed, then pointed at the
villa. *"Là,"* he said. "Wait, I take you." Putting down his
trowel, he hurried gallantly ahead of her, sweeping open the
door, staring avidly as she entered ahead of him.

Lucretia and Zee looked up as Julia paused in the doorway
of the office and inspected the ceiling of blue clouds. "I'd
like to come to your school this fall. Am I too late to apply?"

"Well, it just so happens," said Lucretia, "that we've

had a cancellation. I don't suppose you have a transcript with you?"

"No, I'm sorry." But when Julia described her background as a graduate student in art history at N.Y.U., they accepted her at once.

"What do you think?" said Lucretia to Zee, after she went away.

Zee was speechless. He gestured feebly and tried to go back to his class notes, then gave up and began drawing in the margin a portrait of the girl from New York City.

The second replacement was a graduate of the University of Padua. He phoned one day from Florence, having heard about the school, he said, from a friend.

Lucretia was delighted. "He speaks both English and Italian," she told Zee. "His father's from Pittsburgh, his mother from Bergamo, which explains his name, Tommaso O'Toole."

"Why would a kid with his background want to come here?"

"Heaven knows, but let's be grateful that he does. Now the roster is full again."

"And you found us a secretary, Matteo what's-his-name. How did he happen to turn up?"

"Luzzi, Matteo Luzzi. He answered our ad. He's a seminarian who changed his mind about being a priest."

"Well, he looks like an angel," said Zee. "It's too bad he can't spell."

CHAPTER 11

██████████████████

. . . my spirit now is burning
So to go on, and see this venture through.
                    Inferno II,136–137.

On the thirty-first of August, Homer and Mary Kelly had worked their way through Dante's entire *Divine Comedy*, all the way through *Hell* and *Purgatory* to the topmost realms of *Paradise*.

Hoarsely Mary read the last line of the last canto—

The love that moves the sun and the other stars—

and then they packed their bags and books and flew to Milan and spent the night in a hotel, and took the train to Florence and climbed wearily into a taxi. While they gawked out the window, turning their heads left and right, pointing and exclaiming, the taxi found its way across the Arno, raced out to the Porta Romana, zoomed up the winding streets to the Piazza di Bellosguardo and turned into the driveway of the Villa L'Ombrellino.

Homer and Mary jounced in the backseat and stared. The surface of the road was a morass of careening tire tracks. There were marble nymphs and goddesses at every turn. Shrubbery sprang up waist-high around Cupid and Psyche. As the taxi rounded a curve, the villa reared up on their left, an expanse of sunlit buildings partly covered with scaffolding. At one side rose a pockmarked tower.

They pulled up behind another taxi. A portly man in a

rumpled seersucker suit was getting out. "Himmelfahrt," said Homer, "the Italian history man from the University of Chicago."

Professor Himmelfahrt was in a state of shock. His first glance at the Villa L'Ombrellino had filled him with dismay. "Good lord," he mumbled, jerking at his luggage, his breast churning. The taxi driver jabbered at him. Fifteen thousand lire? Good God. Himmelfahrt pawed through his handful of thousand-lire notes, angrily convinced he was being cheated. And where was the welcoming committee? Where were the formal gardens? Nobody had warned him about the run-down condition of the buildings. Dumping his heavy bags on the driveway, Himmelfahrt slicked strands of hair over his bald head, and turned in surprise as Homer and Mary Kelly came up behind him and introduced themselves.

"We've got your history of Italy," said Homer genially, and Himmelfahrt cheered up at once, not knowing that Homer had merely opened the book and slammed it shut again, because the damned thing was totally impenetrable.

Ah, here was the welcoming committee. Himmelfahrt

beamed at Lucretia Van Ott and Professor Zibo. There were
greetings and handshakes. A student took Mary's heaviest
bag. The boxes of books were lugged out of the trunk.

"*Avanti!*" said Lucretia, beaming and waving them up
the stairs, while Zee made polite remarks, congratulating
himself at the same time on his prophetic portrait of Himmelfahrt. The big chin was there, and the tiny nose. But
look at the man's tiny lipless mouth, *minuscola!* He should
have guessed.

The student carrying Mary Kelly's bag was Ned Saltmarsh, a plump boy with pink cheeks, striped shorts and
orange socks. "Lordy," he said, heaving and puffing, "it's
heavy."

"Let me help," said Mary.

"No, no, I've got it," gasped Ned, dragging the bag across
the cracked tiles, lacerating its canvas bottom. Mary followed, feeling a momentary dismay. Here on the terrace of
this Florentine villa under the gaze of these half-draped marble goddesses, Ned's orange socks were an affront to the soft
Italian sky and the ancient cypress trees and the hillside from
which Galileo had looked at the heavens. Was this kid a
typical example of the student body? For Homer's sake, Mary
hoped he wasn't.

The room assigned to the Kellys was on the third level
of the dormitory wing, an elegant chamber with painted
panelling. It was several doors removed from a modern bath
which was to be shared with Professors Zibo and Van Ott.

Mary looked out the window at the blue haze to the
south beyond the statuary around the driveway, and reminded herself that only thirty-six hours ago she had been
scraping at the filth behind a radiator in Concord, in a last-
minute attempt to make the house fit for a tenant. She was
exhausted. "I'll just close my eyes for a minute," she said,
dropping on the bed.

Far away across the central mass of the villa in the opposite wing, Himmelfahrt gulped with consternation at the dilapidation of his magnificent private bath.

Homer went downstairs and found Zee, who hurried him to the door. "The view. We'll get it over with before lunch."

They came out on the north side of the house, passing through a loggia with busts of Galileo and the poet Ugo Foscolo. Zee led Homer across the lawn to a low wall, where another bevy of sculptured nymphs turned contemptuously away from whatever lay below. "Prepare yourself," said Zee.

The sky was opening, the distance widening. "Good God," said Homer.

In coming to Florence he had assumed he would be let down. A place so ballyhooed couldn't possibly be everything people said. But here it was, a vision fanciful but real—Brunelleschi's great dome, church steeples and towers familiar to Dante and Michelangelo and Machiavelli—spread out on a platter.

"I'm speechless," he said. "It's like a fairy city. I'm sorry. That's a silly thing to say."

"It's all right," said Zee. "This view is famous for inspiring remarkable people to say commonplace things. Don't apologize." He began pointing out landmarks, identifying bell towers and domes.

Homer listened, and watched the pointing finger. Zee's speech was almost without accent. He spoke with small pauses, dredging up surprising words from some thesaurus in his mind. He had taught in the United States, Homer knew that. How old was he? And why did he look so familiar? His face was gaunt, but his eyes were clear and curious, and his mouth was enclosed in small parenthetical wrinkles. He gave the impression of a man of sprightly good humor put to the rack, or a starved ascetic like Saint Jerome.

They went back to the house and headed for the dining room. In the entrance hall on the south side of the villa Homer was attracted by the buzzing noise of a small gasoline engine below the terrace on the driveway. Glancing out the window he saw a pretty girl zooming up the hill on a little motorbike, dodging expertly around the deepest ruts. Her shoes on the pedals had spike heels, her jeans were skin tight, her hair was an explosion of bleached curls.

"Good God, what's that?" said Homer in a state of rapture.

"Oh, that's Isabella Fraticelli. She's the chambermaid. She's married to Alberto Fraticelli, the cook."

"No, no," said Homer, "I mean what's that thing she's riding? I saw them on the street. That little zephyr, that floating wisp of thistledown?" Desire tugged at his vitals. "How much do they cost?"

"The motorbike? It's the smallest kind, a Honda 50, I think." Zee looked up with amusement at Homer's enormous frame. "You'd never fit. You're much too tall. Maybe you could use a Vespa, one of the bigger ones."

"But would it have the same buoyancy? Would it fly through the air barely touching the ground, like Isabella's?"

Zee laughed, and greeted Mary as she came down the stairs. Then he hurried ahead of them into the dining room, and Homer took his wife's arm. "But I know who he is now. Don't you recognize him? Now that I see him, I remember his name."

Mary frowned. "Well, perhaps. I think I've seen a picture of him somewhere."

"Of course. It was all over the Boston papers about ten years ago. He was convicted of murdering his wife. He spent five years in Walpole State Prison."

CHAPTER 12

. . . .

Down must we go, to that dark world and blind. . . .
                                        Inferno IV, 13.

The dining room was a large chamber with a columned entry, a marble fireplace and tall windows overlooking yet another terrace.

To Homer the grandeur of the villa was a little hollow. He had looked it up in a book. To his disappointment the place spoke less of Galileo than of Mrs. Keppel, with her tasteful Edwardian pretensions. There were no surprises, no awkward dead ends, no peculiar crannies. It was a movie set for the beautiful people of the first half of the twentieth century—for Osbert Sitwell and Christian Dior, for Cecil Beaton and the high society of Florence.

The room was noisy. Homer wished the beautiful people had left behind a few rugs and curtains to soften the impact of youthful voices ricocheting off marble floors and plaster walls. Whenever the kitchen door flapped open, the banging of pots and pans and the high-pitched conversation in the kitchen added to the pandemonium. Isabella Fraticelli, the girl who had arrived on the little moped, came hurrying in with a serving dish. She was still wearing her skinny black jeans and teetering heels. Isabella was assisted by a young man whose magnificent physique was displayed in a tight-fitting black T-shirt.

"Is that her husband, the cook?" Homer muttered to Zee.

"No, no, that's Franco, the gardener. He lends a hand everywhere." Homer refrained from remarking that Franco was lending a hand to Isabella's hip every time he brushed past her in the doorway. In fact they always seemed to arrive in the narrow passage simultaneously, pausing to bump together, giggling. Of the cook himself there was no trace, except for the violent clashing of crockery and an occasional angry shout.

Lucretia clapped her hands loudly and then in the silence introduced Homer and Mary to the room at large. Himmelfahrt came hurrying in, and had to be introduced too.

Quickly Lucretia pronounced the names of all the young students, who smiled politely and began dishing up bowls of minestrone and tearing off chunks of bread and helping themselves to platefuls of salad.

Homer couldn't remember which of the kids was which. Three or four of the girls were Debbies. Another was Sukey. The plump young boy in the striped shorts was Ned. A pair of taller boys with fair hair were Kevin and Winthrop. A good-looking dark-haired boy was Tommaso O'Toole. She introduced Homer and Mary to Matteo Luzzi, the school secretary, a beautiful young Italian with a mop of brown curls.

Then Lucretia took Homer and Mary across the room to meet a couple of older women sitting by themselves, Dorothy Orme and Joan Jakes.

Homer and Mary nodded and smiled, then filled their plates and settled down at a small table with Professor Zee. There was an extra chair, but when Himmelfahrt began lowering himself into it, Zee warned him away. "I'm sorry. I'm saving it for someone else."

Himmelfahrt was not to be denied a seat at what he perceived to be the head table. Pulling up another chair, he sat down beside Mary Kelly, and began a long history of his family. It turned out that the Himmelfahrts had been margraves of Brandenburg, related by marriage to the dukes of Schleswig.

Mary made appreciative noises, and let her attention wander to the students. She couldn't help comparing the American kids with the young Italians—with Matteo the secretary, Franco the gardener, and Isabella the chambermaid-waitress. How green the Americans looked! So young and callow and bursting with health, so plump of cheek, so juicily packed with fresh fruit from California and orange juice from Florida and vegetables from Georgia. Were they as wholesome as they looked, or had they brought along supplies of controlled substances in their baggage? If so, the effect was invisible. Their eye sockets were not hollow, their complexions were bright. Their clothing was cheerful too, loose and sporty in mismatched hues, unlike the cruel blacks of the Italians. A couple of the boys had odd haircuts, but the hair of the girls fell over their shoulders in long shining floods.

By contrast Isabella and Franco and Matteo were poised and majestic. Young as they were, they seemed a dozen years older than the Americans. They were monarchs who by some quirk of fate had been enslaved by a crowd of giant children.

The din grew louder. "*Silenzio!*" cried Lucretia, clapping her hands again. The clashing in the kitchen stopped. The American kids paused in mid-shout. Laughing, Lucretia pulled up another chair and sat down beside Homer, then leaped up and ran to the serving table for a basket of fruit. Zee turned to look at the door, but the person for whom he had been waiting didn't come. Somewhere a clock chimed, and there was a general upheaval. Everyone got up. Chairs scraped across the marble floor, plates were piled on the center table.

The cook appeared in the kitchen door, watching the exodus, smoking a cigarette. Alberto Fraticelli was a pale melancholy-looking man with a bald head, obviously a good deal older than his wife.

"It's the first class of the school year," said Lucretia to Mary. "Why don't you go?"

"Zee's Dante class, you mean? He's very good?"

But Lucretia merely said, "Just go."

CHAPTER 13

▪ ▪ ▪ ▪ ▪ ▪ ▪ ▪ ▪ ▪ ▪ ▪ ▪ ▪ ▪ ▪

Canst thou be Virgil? thou that fount of splendour
Whence poured so wide a stream of lordly speech?
                                    Inferno I: 79, 80.

The classroom was another spacious chamber, as big as a ballroom. Zee had nicknamed it the Drawing Room of the Queen Mother. At one side it was dignified by a pair of orange columns streaked like marble, but the portable blackboard and the folding chairs gave it the homely air of a rec room in a church basement. All that was missing was the Ping-Pong table.

Homer and Mary sat down at the back and watched as the three Debbies came in and sat down together, followed by the two older women and three of the boys. Matteo the secretary was there, slouching in a chair in the front row. Ned Saltmarsh ostentatiously put his books on the seat beside him, turned to glower at the three Debbies and announced, "This is for Julia."

"So?" said one of the Debbies, and the three of them laughed. "Where's Sukey?" said another Debbie. "Maybe I'd better go and see," said the third Debbie.

But then Sukey ran in and stood angrily in front of Matteo. "It's happened again," she said furiously. "Something's missing from my room. First it was my boyfriend's picture, and now it's my bathing suit. It's that maid. I mean, like I saw her poking around like she was supposed to be dusting or something, but she was snooping, I swear. You've got to search her room. Honestly, I didn't come here to be ripped off."

Matteo yawned and promised to investigate. "Like a detective, yes?"

Sukey plumped herself down and jerked out her notebook, as Zee came into the room and arranged his papers on the plastic table beside the blackboard.

Picking up a piece of chalk, he glanced around at the rows of students. Homer suspected he was searching for the person who hadn't appeared in the dining room. Apparently that mysterious person was missing once again. Zee smiled wanly at Homer and Mary, and then began drawing a picture on the blackboard, a brisk sketch of a tiny vessel tossed by giant waves.

Turning to the class, he cleared his throat and spoke up in Italian.

The students stared back at him blankly, their pencils poised over the fresh new pages of their notebooks. Did he expect them to read Dante in Italian?

But at once he put it into English—

No sea for cockleboats is this great main
  Through which my prow carves out adventurous ways,
  Nor may the steersman stint of toil and pain.

"The *Paradiso*," he explained. "Canto twenty-three. In other words, we're embarked on a difficult quest. Welcome aboard."

Everyone laughed, partly in relief, partly in sudden commitment. Zee was warning that much would be required of them, and at once it was just what they wanted. For a moment they all imagined this was why they had flown across the Atlantic. It was for this that they had stuffed their shapeless zippered bags and backpacks with summer clothing and winter parkas, with tiny radios and cassette players, with condoms and contraceptives and blow-dryers with the wrong sort of plugs and traveler's checks provided by parents who

were thankful to see the last of them for a while. Here was a teacher worth a journey of three thousand miles.

They listened and scribbled as he dashed off another little Dante pushing blindly through a forest in his long gown and hooded cap. Then he recited the first lines of the *Inferno*, canto I. It was the stanza Homer had shouted at him across the ocean, back in May—

> *Midway this way of life we're bound upon,*
> *I woke to find myself in a dark wood,*
> *Where the right road was wholly lost and gone.*

He explained that the Roman poet Virgil, representing human reason, would lead Dante out of the wood on a conducted tour of Hell and Purgatory. "But not Paradise," warned Zee. "Only Beatrice, personifying Revelation, can take him there."

And then, like Dante in the dark wood, Zee lost his way. He dropped the chalk, picked it up and dropped it again.

Someone had come in silently. Swiftly she sat down in a chair in one of the empty rows.

All heads turned. One of the older women smiled at her, the boys became gawky and self-conscious, the three Debbies grew solemn with envy, and Ned Saltmarsh promptly moved back to sit down beside the new arrival with a conspicuous taking of possession.

It was Julia Smith. Head down, she opened her notebook and plucked out a pen. Ned pushed close, whispering, displaying a scab on his arm, looking for sympathy.

Clearing his throat, Zee tried to gather the scattered threads of everyone's attention (his own as well) by swiping at the blackboard once again and scrawling on it the gate of Hell, with its ominous warning, LAY DOWN ALL HOPE, YOU THAT GO IN BY ME.

Then he spoke of the miserable race of the damned, whose blessings on earth had done them no good—*Those who have lost the good of intellect.*

His chalk screaked. Some of the kids took notes, *lost the good of intellect*, some let their attention drift away. *Charon ferries the damned across the river Acheron.* Kevin Banks put his foot under the rung of Ned's chair and lifted it ever so slightly. Ned turned and glowered. A wasp wandered aimlessly around the classroom, trying to find its way back to the smashed figs on the terrace. Sukey reared back from it in fright, and screamed as it settled in her bangs. She clawed at the wasp, it stung her, and the class came to a tumultuous halt.

Dorothy Orme took charge. Dorothy had been a registered nurse, and now she escorted the sobbing Sukey to the kitchen for a poultice of baking soda.

Zee, white-faced, put down his chalk and turned away as Julia Smith gathered up her books and went out with the others, Ned Saltmarsh bobbing at her elbow.

Homer took Mary by the arm and led her outside for a

DANTE IN THE DARK WOOD

look at the city below the wall. "Who is that girl?" he said. "The one who came in late?"

"I don't know, but she certainly is stunning." Then Mary caught her first sight of the celebrated view. "Oh, Homer, how fabulous, how amazing. Oh, wow."

CHAPTER 14

■ ■ ■ ■ ■ ■ ■ ■ ■ ■ ■ ■ ■ ■

Voluptuous Cleopatra, who love slew.
                              Inferno V, 63.

The chambermaid Isabella Fraticelli was restless. Isabella was a clever flirtatious girl, eager for excitement.
Once upon a time it had been exciting to be married to Alberto, an older man of whom her parents disapproved. But now Alberto was fat and bald, and it was no longer any fun to be his wife. It was intoxicating instead to play games with the gardener, Franco Spoleto, who was handsome as a Greek god. Franco was obviously thrilled too. Who could tell where his fascination with her might end? Images from films flooded Isabella's mind, naked celebrities on satin sheets, swooning with ecstasy in each other's arms.

And now Matteo was here, with his blue eyes and charming curls. Matteo had studied in seminary, he had wanted to be a priest. To Isabella there was a forbidden sexual attractiveness about men who had taken sacred vows. And in Matteo's case there was the added wonder that he was not really a priest. He had the appeal of forbidden fruit, and yet he was available, he was free to make love if he wished.

Matteo's room was on the third floor of the east wing, down the corridor from the one Isabella shared with Alberto. Did Matteo take a nap after lunch?

Isabella helped Alberto wash the lunch dishes, and then she took off her apron and fluffed her hair.

"Where are you going?" said Alberto, looking at her suspiciously.

"For a walk," said Isabella sulkily. "Is there anything wrong with that?"

"For a walk? You're not going for a walk. Here, look at all these onions. Cut them up!"

"Onions, *uffa!*" Isabella turned and pranced out of the kitchen. As the door swung shut behind her, an onion hit it with a thump.

Chopping onions, cleaning toilets! Isabella fumed as she ran lightly up the stairs. The whole job was beneath her!

But at least she had the free use of a key. As a chambermaid she could enter every closed door, inspect every privacy. Now Isabella took out her key and approached Matteo's room, meaning to creep into his bed and run her fingers through his hair.

But when she opened Matteo's door, she had a shock. He was not in the bed. He was standing at the window, oiling a gun. Around him lay an arsenal of firearms.

Angrily he shouted at her to get out. In confusion Isabella backed away. Matteo slammed the door in her face.

Porca miseria! Isabella's feelings were deeply hurt. Offended, she went looking for Franco Spoleto. Franco would not shout at her. Franco would be sweet to her. And how thrilling, to tell him Matteo Luzzi's secret!

Matteo saw them together. Looking down from his high window over the landscape, across the hills and valleys south of Florence, the tower of Villa Montauto, the convent of La Colombaia, he could see Isabella and Franco near at hand, talking excitedly in the driveway.

Slowly and carefully he opened the window. Selecting the high-powered bolt-action Beretta sporting rifle, he took it to the window, knelt on the sill and took careful aim, moving the weapon slightly from the tumbled platinum hair of Isabella to the shorter brown curls of Franco, back and forth, back and forth.

Blam-blam, he said to himself. *Blam-blam.*

CHAPTER 15

▪▪▪▪▪▪▪▪▪▪▪▪▪

. . . that strange, outflowing power of hers . . .
Purgatorio XXX, 38.

Ned Saltmarsh wasn't the only male at the school who was dazzled by Julia Smith. Tommaso O'Toole pursued her with witty insults that were a refreshing change from Ned's adolescent infatuation. The other guys were susceptible too. Among themselves they rolled their eyes and indulged in hilarious fantasies.

As for the girls, they were jealous of Julia at first, but before long most of them succumbed to her amiable good humor. She fixed Sukey's typewriter, she braided Debbie Sawyer's hair, she loaned Debbie Weiss a pair of earrings and admired the pictures of Debbie Foster's boyfriend. She listened and teased and said what she thought. She was comfortable to be with.

But one of the older women, Joan Jakes, couldn't bear the high pitch of Julia's extreme good looks.

"Look at that," she said to her friend Dorothy Orme, watching Julia from across the dining room, "the way the males hang around her. I think it's disgusting."

"The worst is Ned Saltmarsh," said Dorothy. "The poor boy has a terrible crush on her. He's such a child. I suspect he misses his mother."

"His mother?" snickered Joan, adding cleverly, "You mean it's more suck than fuck?"

"More suck than—oh, I see. Well, perhaps. On the

whole I think Julia handles it well. I suspect she had sensible parents.''

Joan snorted. Picking up her dishes, she took them to the serving table, banged them down, and glowered at the men around Julia. Surely something was fishy about the woman. She couldn't be all that perfect. Usually things balanced out. Look at herself, for instance. She might not be beautiful, but she was smart as a whip. Would she rather have been pretty and dumb? Certainly not.

Striding out of the dining room, Joan suppressed for the moment the harsh truth of the daily ordeal of looking in the mirror every morning. At such times she would have given anything, anything, to see a plump young face looking back at her, not the same old sunken eyes and fallen cheeks, the bitter mouth, the mole on the eyelid. What use in all creation was one more homely woman?

They talked about Julia in the kitchen too. Matteo Luzzi remembered Julia from the summertime, when he had seen her at the church of San Lorenzo. Now he made exaggerated shapes in the air, and wondered if Signorina Smith was *frigida* rather than *sensuale*. Franco compared her with the stone goddesses on the lawn. Her thighs were like this one, her shoulders like that one, her breasts—Franco made balloonlike gestures in front of his chest—like Psyche's, halfway down the driveway. And then Isabella whispered that Professor Zibo had drawn a picture of the signorina. It was in his sketchbook, hidden in his desk. And she had found a little pair of panties in the wardrobe belonging to Tommaso, the *ragazzo* from Bergamo. The signorina's name tag was attached to the elastic. These revelations were greeted with raucous laughter, Isabella's high scream rising above the rest.

Julia herself tried to balance good with bad. She was glad to have found the school, glad to be settled, glad to have made up her mind—glad, glad to be learning what she was learning. The emptiness she had felt when she was on her own was gone. The splendors of the city of Florence were no longer a passing show. If she wasn't exactly climbing into a fresco of the Annunciation, or running with a band of marble children across a choir loft, or dwelling among the columns in a superbly proportioned church, at least she was learning about them and talking about them and tying them together with threads of meaning.

Therefore she was grateful to her professors, especially to Zee and Lucretia. It was a gratitude that came very close to affection. Julia had always loved her teachers. Now from long practice she kept her enthusiasm mute in the classroom, only glancing up to register the quick changes on Zee's face, or the rapid strokes of Lucretia's chalk on the blackboard. For the time being she was content to be a container for information, a jar passively filling.

All this was to the good. The bad thing for Julia Smith at the American School of Florentine Studies was the presence of Ned Saltmarsh. Here she was, once again, dragging a clumsy weight behind her, a weird little dog nipping at her heels.

Ned was everywhere. As the regular schedule of courses began in earnest, he established a pattern, right away, of sitting beside her in class. Julia tried to ignore him. She focused on the lectures, she listened intently and wrote everything down. As Zee pointed out the tourist sights of the *Inferno*, reciting the torments of this individual soul or that, making clear the awful rightness of God's justice, Julia assigned Ned to whatever grim punishment was the order of the day. To hell with Ned Saltmarsh!

Work was piling up. Some of Julia's classmates fell behind. They were disappointed to discover that school was school on both sides of the Atlantic.

Lucretia's two courses were especially rigorous.

On Tuesdays and Thursdays she taught Italian. Her method was traditional, moving through the pronouns, the first conjugation, the second. The star student was Tommaso, who spoke the language like a native. All three Debbies were quick, and so was Julia. Joan Jakes was only fair. Dorothy Orme was the oldest member of the class, and the slowest. Homer was not as old as Dorothy, but he too had lost the spongelike powers of youth. Lucretia's words rattled past him. He couldn't tell where one ended and another began.

He practiced with Isabella and Alberto, Franco and Matteo. He could begin easily enough, with some hearty remark—*Buona sera, come sta?*—but as soon as they responded, he was sunk.

Matteo was the worst. He talked too fast.

"Slow down," Homer would urge, *"lentamente!"* And Matteo would grin with contempt and jabber faster than ever, exclusive possessor of the splendors of the Italian language.

Lucretia's second course was the art of the Florentine Renaissance. It was less like an ordinary series of lectures than an exploration of the city, something like their class tours on alternate mornings. Her teaching was a kind of poking around the city streets, dodging back and forth among politicians, poets, painters, grammarians, bankers, goat butchers and dyers of wool. Soon all the notebooks were choked with the names of miscellaneous Florentines whose fortunes were intertwined.

Himmelfahrt's Italian history class was less successful. At first it met at three, directly after the Dante class. But that proved unsatisfactory.

"They fell asleep," reported Himmelfahrt angrily. "They all fell asleep. I insist on teaching first in the afternoon. I didn't come three thousand miles to lecture to people with their eyes closed."

"We'll trade places," said Zee, seizing the easiest solution.

But that didn't work either. Zee's students were just as lively at three o'clock as they had been at two, whereas Himmelfahrt's dozed off in the same puzzling way.

Homer Kelly's class in modern Italian literature fared better than it deserved. On the first day he confessed the thinness of his preparation, the superficiality of his reading. To his surprise the students seemed flattered to be taken into his confidence.

"It's wonderful," Homer said to his wife, "the way ignorance provides a firm foundation. If you admit you know nothing, nobody can take you by surprise or point out your mistakes. It's pitiful, really, that they put up with me."

"Well, of course, dear, most teaching is a sleight-of-hand trick, you know that. You'll be fine. Good God, I've lost my cosmetic case. Have you seen it? Oh, here it is."

Mary's possessions were spread out on the bed. She was packing up, leaving for Rome to begin studying her nineteenth-century Americans abroad.

"I'm leaving too," said Homer gloomily. "This place is too rich for my blood. I'm going to rent one of those little motorbikes and commute to the school from the town. I'll find a pensione somewhere."

"Well, I'll miss you, Homer darling. But all those naked people in Rome are calling me."

Homer gaped at her. "Naked people?" Then he laughed. "Oh, you mean all that white marble sculpture with the plump fingers and pretty toenails."

"Of course a lot of it isn't in Rome anymore. They shipped it home to Boston. I'm afraid a lot of it is stored in the basement of the Museum of Fine Arts. Oh, Homer, they're so bad, all those Carrara marble gods and goddesses. So limp, so feeble. But the Americans who went to Rome to make them weren't limp and feeble, they were fascinating, and I want to find out all about them." Mary snapped her suitcase shut and looked fiercely at Homer. "Whatever you do, be kind to Zee. That man never murdered his wife."

"Of course he didn't. Of course not."

In the days that followed, Homer did as he was told. It was an easy duty. Zee willingly complied with his idea of a late afternoon walk every day. Together they climbed and descended the hill of Bellosguardo, and stared in at the pompous gateways of neighboring villas.

Before long Homer abandoned false courtesy and began asking his usual nosy questions. He remembered the trial in the Suffolk County Courthouse, he said. What the hell was it all about? Boldly he echoed Mary. "You never murdered your wife."

"Oh, my God, I don't know, Homer. My attorneys thought I was—what do you call it?—the fall guy in some big drug deal. But the jury didn't believe it. And if my wife had family connections with Italian dealers in narcotics, she never told me. Of course there were a lot of things she never told me." Zee sounded bitter, and Homer remembered the ugly headlines about his wife's extramarital adventures.

"I thought your motive was supposed to have been jealous rage, or something like that. And how were you supposed to have killed her? There was something about a car—"

"Her car, yes, it blew up in the garage. Afterward they found traces of cocaine in her spare tire. My lawyer thought

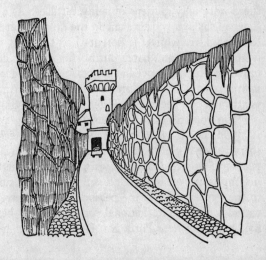

she was killed because she was moving in on the wrong territory. Her connections, he said, had been purely in heroin, not cocaine. But he couldn't prove it, and I spent five years in Walpole State Prison."

The road was steep. They passed a shrine built into the wall, a memorial to a fatal accident. There was a jar of fresh flowers in front of the weathered Virgin. "And afterward," said Homer, "you returned to Florence and got a job at the university?"

"I was lucky. The head of the department was an old friend." Zee glanced at Homer and tossed his hand skyward, a gesture Homer would remember for the rest of his life. "It was like the passage at the end of the *Inferno* when Dante comes forth from the darkness of Hell, *to look once more upon the stars.*"

The next day Zee talked about his childhood. He was amusing on the subject, describing the discomforts of the fortress-like villa on Via Bolognese in which he had grown up. There had been a library with costly editions of Dante and Petrarch, there was a butler who sang like Elvis Presley, there were ugly gardens of spiny cactuses. As a small boy Zee had sat in a wicker chair in the *limonaia* at I Tatti, his feet dangling, while his parents had tea with the shawl-wrapped Berenson. Later during his student days at the university he had moved among fashionable people who remembered the Sitwells and Somerset Maugham. One old gentleman had been insulted by Evelyn Waugh.

"Do you still own the house?"

"Oh, no. It went to pay my attorneys' fees. I wasn't sorry to see it go." And then Zee talked about his last five years in Florence. Coming back to the city of his birth after his imprisonment in the United States, he had not returned to the cypress drives, the peacocks, the parterres and balustrades of the international set. Until now he had been living cheaply near Porta San Frediano. "But here we are again, *grandioso, pomposo.*" Zee turned his back on another magnificent wrought iron gate. "Well, it's a new start."

But the next day Homer was dismayed to learn that Zee's fresh beginning had already been threatened. Professor Himmelfahrt had received a gossiping letter from the United States, relaying the news about Zee's conviction and prison sentence, and at once he spread it all over the school.

Lucretia was furious. "It's envy," she told Homer. "He knows Zee is more popular with the kids than he is, and he can't stand it."

Homer wondered if the revelation would change things. But in Zee's Dante class the students remained attentive. The lovely Julia sat among the rest, her head bent over her notebook, Ned Saltmarsh in worshipful attendance.

Homer worried that Zee's career might be in jeopardy for other reasons. "Listen, friend," he said, "what about the drug connection? Don't you think your wife's involvement might pursue you here? You know, Italian politicians, businessmen, bankers, they're all supposed to be in on it. Are you sure nobody's after you?"

Zee laughed. "You're talking about the Italian underworld, the *malavita*. There's not much of it here in Florence, nothing on a high level. Oh, there are kids who buy the stuff, a few pushers perhaps. But no big wheels. And now there's the pope's crusade against drugs. It seems to be working. *Fantastico!*"

CHAPTER 16

∎∎∎∎∎∎∎∎∎∎∎∎∎∎∎

The wondrous truth outstrips my staggering pen.
                                    Inferno IV, 147.

B y this time the extraordinary success of the pope's
Holy Year Against Drugs was news all over the world.
        In mid-September the holy father flew to New
York City to bless thousands of repentant addicts in Yankee
Stadium. A week later he was in Rio de Janeiro, then Buenos
Aires and Bogotá.

In Rome itself trainloads of grubby pilgrims from the
back streets of all the great cities of Europe kept turning up
without warning, creating monstrous traffic jams. Ordinary
citizens had to make their way through throngs of kids with
backpacks heading for Saint Peter's Square. The kids slept
everywhere, clogging the sidewalks.

It was dumbfounding to the promoters of the campaign
in the Vatican, and their elation was mingled with concern.
The thing was getting out of hand. At any moment it might
change its course and turn ugly. How were they to maintain
control, to keep the ball rolling, to hold these cleansed young
souls in the paths of righteousness?

In other quarters there was a different sort of dismay.
Leonardo Bindo's business had fallen off still farther. Trade
on the street was slack.

But Bindo was by nature an optimist. If things went
badly, one did something about it. All things could be made
to serve, even ill fortune.

When Homer Kelly wandered into the Banca degli In-

Via Fossi

nocenti, Bindo was attracted by his great height and his amiable American face. Waving aside the teller, he went to the window and waited on Homer himself.

Homer needed cash for the rental of a motorbike and for the first month's rent at a pensione. Leaning toward the teller's window he began bravely, *"Vorrei cambiare questi—"*

The smiling man at the window interrupted. He had a round face with shiny rosy cheeks. "You would like to cash your traveler's checks? Certainly, sir. If you would sign them, please?"

Then while Homer scribbled his name across check after

check, the teller introduced himself and made courteous conversation. His name, he said, was Leonardo Bindo, and he was the manager of the Banca degli Innocenti. He was fascinated to learn that Homer was teaching at the Villa L'Ombrellino. "Ah, what a beauty spot! I went to a wedding there in days gone by. It was I, as a matter of fact, who arranged the lease for the new school. Signor Zibo, is it not, is a professor there?"

Bindo failed to mention his connection with the school secretary, although he was in constant touch with Matteo Luzzi. The stupid *ragazzo* was complaining about the inconvenience of taking the bus, whenever there was a letter "from the cardinal" to be carried by hand to Roberto Mori, or an answer written by Father Roberto to be conveyed to His Fictional Eminence. Matteo was pressing for a car. Well, Bindo might have to rent one for him, something cheap, a modest little Fiat.

Homer shoved his signed checks across the counter. "Tell me, Signor Bindo, how does this little bank compete with the big ones?"

"Oh, we are all friends." Signor Bindo laughed. "How do you say it in English? We're in cahoots."

"Hey, fella, are you through?"

Homer turned in surprise. Behind him stood a tall American in a Milwaukee Brewers cap. "Oh, sure. Sorry to keep you waiting." Pocketing his money, Homer nodded at Bindo and moved aside.

The tourist shuffled forward. "Hey, listen, how many whatchamacallums to the dollar?"

But after Homer was safely out of the bank Leonardo Bindo beckoned the man in the baseball cap into his office and closed the door. He was furious. "How many times do I have to tell you to stay away from here?"

"Oh, sure, sure, right. Big deal."

"Big deal?" Bindo stared at him suspiciously. "What is a big deal?"

"Never mind. It's nothin'. I gotcha."

"Gotcha?"

"Oh, for Christ's sake, never mind." And then Earl went on to complain that the kids had disappeared from Piazza Santo Spirito. Hardly anybody wanted to buy.

"Well, it's not my fault," said Bindo. "Blame the Vatican. Blame His Holiness."

"Well, Jesus, why don't somebody blow him away?"

"Blow him away? What is it, to blow away?"

And then Earl demonstrated, holding up a mock handgun and uttering a violent noise.

"Ah, I see," said Signor Bindo, beaming.

Homer found a room in a pensione on the Via Fossi. It was a small high chamber, sparsely furnished, but from his window he could look out on the church of Santa Maria Novella, which dated back to Dante's time.

The proprietor stood waiting while Homer craned his neck out the window and congratulated himself on being where he was. He thought of his mother, who had never been abroad, although she had taught Latin to generations of adolescents in South Boston. Now, leaning on the windowsill, Homer could feel in the palms of his hands the weight of his mother's forty years of teaching. He wanted to push this moment back through his own blood and bones into hers.

"Si, Signore," he told the landlord, "prendo la camera," and handed over a thick wad of ten thousand-lire notes.

It was ten o'clock, time to meet Zee and the Dante class in Piazza del Duomo.

A street sweeper was droning down Via Fossi when Homer came out into the sunlight, a huge machine, vibrating and wobbling from side to side, its brushes whirling, catching up the debris of the street. Ahead of it shopkeepers hurried out of their doorways with brooms, sweeping their premises clean, brushing everything into its path.

Homer galloped across Via Fossi, paused to consult his

guidebook, then made his way in the direction of the Duomo, struggling to ignore the thick life of the street, the shoppers, the people waiting for the bus on Via Cerretani, the chic sportswear in the store windows. Closing his eyes, he tried to imagine the streets as they had been in Dante's time.

In this city, after all, the past had not been emptied out like water from a pitcher whirling down a sink. It was more like a deep well in which all events and all times hung suspended, poised like fish below the trembling surface of the present moment.

Opening his eyes again, the lordly citizen of an everlasting Florence, Homer strode across the street as the light changed. But, whoops! he was nearly run down by a pair of pretty girls on gold roller skates. "Scusi," cried the girls, and they rolled away in their gold tights, carrying gold pocketbooks, their platinum hair streaming behind them, their sandwich boards advertising the perfumes of Estée Lauder. A cavalcade of guys on Suzukis, Yamahas and Hondas thundered in their wake, whistling and catcalling, and Homer's universal grasp on the entire stretch of time and space fell away, and he nipped up on the sidewalk on the other side, glad to be alive.

There was a newsstand near the corner, decked in magazines and big sheets of newsprint with giant headlines. Homer paused to read the news, wondering if his Italian was up to it. The words across the front page of *Il Messaggero di Roma* were clear enough—

IL PAPA PORTA LA CROCIATA ANTI-DROGA A BERLINO

Nothing to it. The pope was taking his anti-drug crusade to Berlin. And Homer could get the gist of the headline of *La Repubblica*, which was wagging its finger at all the women in the world, who, in the opinion of the holy father, would never be priests—

NESSUNA DONNA
SARA UN PRETE
DICE IL PAPA

The local paper, *La Nazione*, was more sensational—

BAMBINI GEMELLI SIAMESI
MORTI NELL ARNO

Good lord, dead Siamese-twin babies had been found in the Arno.

Homer turned away, pleased with himself, and began breasting the crowds of tourists approaching the Piazza del Duomo. Before him rose the cathedral, an immensity of colored marble, a stupendous stone valentine. Homer gaped at it, and stumbled blindly forward, but his way was blocked by an elderly couple, husband and wife in yellow trousers. The husband was fumbling with a guidebook, unfolding a map.

"You know, honey," said the wife, "it's not what I thought it would be. I mean it's so foreign." She was staring at a young couple embracing beside the railing, trying out various interlocking grips they had seen in films.

"Well, Christ, honey," said her husband, "it's a foreign country."

Homer edged past them, aware of himself as a tourist among tourists. Alien hordes were occupying the famous square. Sorrowfully he made his way around the Baptistery to the south door and walked into its shadowy interior, to find Zee with Ned Saltmarsh and the seven women members of the student body of the American School of Florentine Studies gathered in the gloom, staring upward.

In the glowing darkness their faces were white blobs that glanced at him, then looked up again at the glittering mosaic pageantry on the octagonal dome.

Zee was lecturing, directing their attention to Christ the

Baptiste

Judge, the ranks of the blessed, the tortures of the damned souls in Hell. "Dante was baptized here," he said, trying not to look at Julia Smith. Julia had taken off her dark glasses, and he was struck to the pit of his stomach by the way her eyes followed his pointing finger so obediently. "As you travel with him through the *Inferno*, remember the visions he saw here in his infancy."

Sukey Skinner was repelled by the lizards and snakes biting the poor sinners condemned to Hell. "It's barbaric, just incredibly barbaric," she said, almost in tears. "Religion ought to be, you know, sort of inspiring, not scary and disgusting like this."

As they drifted out of the Baptistery, blinking in the sunlight, the bell in the Campanile began to ring. Looking up, they could see it swinging in the tower. Like great wobbling drops the bell notes fell, as though the tower had sucked up into itself the city of Florence and was releasing it now in tears of sound, celebrating the genius of the city, mourning its contentious pride, lamenting the crushing of the republican spirit under the grand dukes, sorrowing for the time when great men had been as thick on the streets as cockroaches.

"Where are the other guys?" said Homer, looking around for Kevin and Throppie and Tom.

"Oh, they all begged off," said Joan Jakes contemptuously. "Not a good sign, I'm afraid."

"Tom, at least, has seen it all before," said Dorothy Orme.

"Then why did he come to the school at all?" exclaimed Joan.

"Time for *gelati*, I think," said Zee firmly, and he led them around the corner for ice cream—*cioccolata, vaniglia, fragola*.

Meanwhile, back at the Villa L'Ombrellino in the absence of most of the students, Isabella Fraticelli was once again making herself at home in the rooms in the dormitory. Her

VIA
DEL SOLE

FI C9115

VOLKSWAGEN

Santa Maria Novella

chambermaid's key was an 'open sesame.' She could poke
around in drawers and cupboards as much as she liked.

In Ned's room she studied the snapshot of his mother.
In Julia's she looked for beauty secrets—facial creams, mascara, transparent negligees. But there were no magical cos-
metics on Julia's dresser, no pretty nightgowns in her
wardrobe, only cotton pajamas and a flannel bathrobe.

It wasn't until she went upstairs to Professor Himmelfahrt's room that Isabella found something interesting. There were pornographic magazines under his bed. Lying down on his tumbled bedclothes, she lit a cigarette and flipped the pages. When she heard Matteo talking to someone in the hall she got up carefully, stuffed the magazines back under the bed, and began wielding her dust cloth.

Later he saw her with mop and bucket, doing Himmelfahrt's floor, and it dawned on him that she had been there all along.

"My God, what did she hear? What were we saying?"

"Nothing. It's all right. But we've got to be more careful."

CHAPTER 17

■ ■ ■ ■ ■ ■ ■ ■ ■ ■ ■ ■ ■ ■

Witness that first proud being, made so bright
He topped creation; yet he fell anon,
Unripe . . .

Paradiso XIX, 46–48.

The important lessons in the use of firearms had begun. Bindo knew of a remote farm north of the city. It had been useful to him in the past. It would be an excellent place to practice.

He had supplied Matteo with a rented car, a little Fiat. It was an insult to Matteo, whose imagination ran so naturally to Maseratis and Lamborghinis. Now Matteo pressed the accelerator to the floor and moved out into the passing lane, trying to zip ahead of a Ferrari. To his shame the Fiat refused to pick up speed, and he had to drop back, cursing.

"Mother of God," said Roberto, frightened.

Roberto was timid with firearms too. Matteo had to teach him everything. Even when the man had the weapon in the correct position, he trembled so much the barrel wobbled and moved in circles.

"*Beh*, he's hopeless," Matteo complained to Signor Bindo that afternoon in the Banca degli Innocenti.

"Don't worry. He'll learn, there's plenty of time. Here, take this to him."

"Another letter from the cardinal?"

"A masterpiece." Bindo grinned at Matteo. "It's an apologia for strong action. I've composed a history of tyrannicides, a list of despots assassinated for the good of humanity—Caligula, Sejanus, Heliogabalus, Rasputin, Czar

Nicholas. Suppose Hitler had been killed in 1939, think how many millions of lives would have been saved." He winked at Matteo. "I'm sure you'll find Father Roberto a better student from now on."

A few blocks away from the bank, in the palace of the archbishop, His Excellency was engaged in another uneasy telephone conversation with the Prefect for the Pontifical Household.

"Nuns from the United States," warned the prefect. "A horde of rebellious women, they're coming, they're coming soon."

"Rebellious nuns?" The archbishop could hardly believe his ears. All the sisterhood of his own experience, whether cloistered within convent walls or active in the world, were strong but gentle women devoted to the sacred traditions of the church. "What are they rebellious about?"

"The opposition of His Holiness to the idea of women priests."

"Women priests!" The archbishop gasped. Of course he had heard of this apostasy, but only on the outer limits of his horizon. "But the ordination of women is impossible. The holy father is right. No sensible person could accept it. There were no women priests in the time of Christ. All of Christ's disciples were men."

"Oh, you don't have to persuade me," said the prefect testily. "But these madwomen in Chicago, this National Federation of Religious Sisters, they're coming to Italy to mount a long campaign. What if they make an outcry at the celebration in Florence next Easter? I think we should change our plans. His Holiness should not leave the Vatican."

The archbishop was flabbergasted. He spent the next ten minutes explaining that the protesting women would be kept away from the cathedral. The Holy Father would never even see them. The plans for the security of His Holiness would be superb, the prefect could be certain of that.

The prefect didn't seem to be listening. Abruptly he changed the subject. The archbishop's head whirled. What was His Eminence talking about now?

". . . the *Anno Sacro Anti-droga*, the holy father's crusade against drugs. You must have heard of it?"

"Oh, yes, Your Eminence, I'm familiar with the crusade. It's been a triumph. You must be very proud of the Holy Father."

"Of course, of course." The prefect brushed the compliment aside. "It's been such a triumph, as a matter of fact, that he wishes to launch a second crusade on Easter Sunday next year. As the first year comes to an end, the second will begin. It's so appropriate, you see, Your Excellency—the resurrection of Christ and the new birth into life of thousands of penitent addicts who have abandoned their degradation during the period of Lent. In fact His Holiness has vowed to carry on the crusade for the rest of his life, until the illegal traffic in narcotics is utterly at an end."

"A noble vow," said the archbishop politely, wondering how his celebration of the seven hundredth anniversary of the cathedral could be combined with this irrelevant crusade.

"The trouble is," said the prefect, speaking solemnly, emphasizing his words one by one, "it isn't only those insane American women you've got to hold in check, it's the young people themselves. Your Excellency, I wish you could see what it's like here in Rome—the crowds, the hordes." The prefect spluttered as though he could find no words to describe the daily tumult in Saint Peter's Square. "You must find a way to contain the enthusiasm of the throngs of pathetic children throwing down their needles like afflicted pilgrims at Lourdes tossing away their crutches. Imagine! Saint Peter's Square littered with used hypodermic needles! We have to pick them up at once with heavy gloves for fear of AIDS! We can't miss a single one!" He was almost sobbing into the telephone. "I beg you, Your Excellency, to discuss this matter with your committee on security."

"Of course I will, of course, of course," promised the archbishop, wincing at these horrifying prophecies, casting about in his head for possible solutions, finding his mind a total blank. As he hung up, his glasses became entangled in the telephone wire, and he had to crawl around on the floor, groping for them blindly.

CHAPTER 18

■ ■ ■ ■ ■ ■ ■ ■ ■ ■ ■ ■ ■ ■ ■

Heaven cast them forth—their presence there would dim
  The light . . .

Inferno III, 40, 41.

Ned Saltmarsh irritated everybody. No one had expected to find a jerk like this so far from home. Oh, yes, they'd all known kids like him back in high school. But he shouldn't have turned up here, having a junior year abroad along with the rest of them.

"Ned, listen," said Julia. "You don't love me. That's just silly."

"Yes, I do," whined Ned. "I love you. Lordy, I do. I'll kill myself, I swear. Lordy!"

Julia winced. *Lordy* was Ned's only retort to the evil in the world. He had obviously never experienced the explosive freedom of a hearty *bullshit*, never expanded his horizons with an *asshole*. "Look," she said in exasperation, "you mustn't take it so seriously. You're not going to do anything so dumb. You're not in love with me, you're in love with all this."

They were sitting in the garden under the cast-iron umbrella. Julia swept her hand over the landscape of domes and towers. Then for a moment she forgot Ned, distracted by the red-roofed city where Dante had loved so greatly, where Savonarola had preached a different sort of passion and gone up in flames. Turning back to Ned, she found it hard to focus on the pink pudding of his face.

But Ned in his callow ardor hungered for her attention. If he didn't get it, he would have to press harder, display his need more clearly, be more forlorn.

He looked at her craftily. "Professor Zee, he's got a thing about you."

"A thing? What do you mean, a thing?" But Julia knew what he meant. And she didn't know what to do about Zee. Everything seemed to speak for him—his face, his voice, his learning, his zestful strength that had survived such terrible things, or was perhaps itself the fruit of trouble. Even the city of Florence was speaking up for him now, there on the other side of the wall. He was linked to it, he was its deputy, its spokesman. How could she care for one and not the other?

But Florence was an Italian city. Perhaps she didn't speak its language well enough to know whether it spoke true or false. She would wait. Julia glanced back at the blue haze lying like a sweet poison over the medieval rooftops and told herself there was pleasure in the waiting.

Ned looked at her jealously. "He's so old. I think it's gross, really gross."

It was time for lunch. Ned stuck fast to Julia as they entered the dining room. Listlessly she filled her plate. She was tired—tired of being grasped at, of having pieces of her flesh bitten off in gobbets.

Lucretia looked at them shrewdly. "Ned Saltmarsh," she said sharply, "would you see me in the office after lunch?"

The office was not a private place. Zee was there, and so was Matteo, typing slowly with two fingers. Both of them pretended not to listen as Lucretia sat down in a corner with Ned and chastised him for pestering Julia.

"Don't you think you're overdoing it? Bothering her so much?"

Ned paled. "You mean," he whispered, "like she said so? Oh, golly, did Julia say that?"

Lucretia made an impatient motion. "No, no, I say it. Anyone can see you never give the poor girl a moment's peace."

"I can't help it," said Ned, sighing gustily. "I admire her so. She's, like, a saint."

"Oh, she is not." Lucretia picked up a flyswatter, whammed at a fly and missed. "Why don't you get interested in the younger girls? They're all very attractive."

"Oh, no," pouted Ned. "They're so immature. Lordy!"

"Immature?" Lucretia was stunned. She held the flyswatter poised in air. "Well, anyway, in the future try not to hang around Julia so much. She'll like you better for it." *Bang*, she swatted the fly.

Ned made a sulky face and went away. Lucretia snorted contemptuously, dismissing all the witless boobies in the world, Matteo snickered, and Zee stood frozen, Lucretia's words ringing in his head. This boy was in love with Julia, and so were all the others, *indubbiamente*, and so was he, just one more lovesick jackass, *un buffone* like Ned Saltmarsh.

Matteo had stopped typing. He was staring out the window.

Zee glanced out too, and saw Isabella Fraticelli sweeping mildewed figs from the terrace far below. Franco Spoleto was nearby, smoking, leaning against a tree, staring at Isabella. His hedge clippers lay on the ground beside him. His arms and shoulders were bare, the muscles of his chest were powerful under his tank top.

The straps of Isabella's little blouse kept slipping off her shoulders, and she flicked them up as she swept. After a while she let them fall. She looked at Franco and stopped sweeping.

Lucretia came to the window too.

It was like a scene in a film. Throwing away his cigarette, Franco began walking heavily up the steps of the terrace. Isabella dropped her broom. Franco reached out and stroked her hair, her bare shoulder. He kissed her throat.

Zee and Lucretia had seen enough, and they turned away, but Matteo went right on gazing, grinning from on high.

Later that afternoon Homer stopped in at the office. He had a book-order form in his hand. At the door he encountered Augustus Himmelfahrt backing out.

"Good lord, don't go in there," whispered Himmelfahrt, hurrying away.

Homer imagined copulation or nakedness or some hideous depravity, but when the door swung open it was only Lucretia on her knees.

"Oh, forgive me," said Homer.

"No, no, it's all right." Lucretia stood up. "You poor Protestants think there's something private about praying, but that's because you don't do it very often. It's a perfectly ordinary human function, like eating and breathing."

"Of course," agreed Homer. "I know that. I was raised a Catholic myself."

When Homer went away, Lucretia went back to the window. The terrace was empty but for a small green lizard scurrying along the wall. Isabella's broom lay forgotten on the stone floor, Franco's hedge clippers were abandoned on the lawn.

She wondered if the two of them were making love right now in some corner of the villa.

Love, it had such terrible, crushing power—no one knew that better than Lucretia Van Ott. She sighed. She knew what would happen. Sooner or later the attraction between the gardener and the wife of the cook would make trouble at the school. It was bound to. And that would be a nuisance, an awful pest.

CHAPTER 19

Florence, within her ancient walls embraced
Whence nones and terce ring still to all the town. . . .

Paradiso XV, 97–98.

The Dante Game began by accident on the next guided tour of the city.

The tours were an extension of the lectures of the classroom. Lucretia's slides came to life on the walls of churches. Zee's pitiful souls condemned to Hell had actually lived in this or that rough-hewn tower.

One cool athletic morning the whole school climbed the long twisting stairway to the top of the dome of the cathedral, then came down and climbed the Campanile. After that they were too ravenous to go home for lunch, so they went to a trattoria and drank more wine and made more noise than they were used to, and took the bus in a state of hilarious exhaustion and got out at Porta Romana, where Sukey Skinner promptly threw up.

Even after a month of city exploration they still weren't used to the Florentine traffic. "You can't cross the street here," screamed Lucretia, as they approached the Piazza del Duomo one morning in October. "Only at the corner, only at the corner."

Poor Sukey was in trouble again. There she was in the middle of the street, huddling and whimpering, caught in a stream of motor scooters. Honking derisively, they dodged around her. A boot grazed her leg, and she had to be rescued by Tommaso, who helped her back to the sidewalk.

Then in single file they drifted past the bulging chapels

Porta Romana

at the east end of the cathedral, stepping carefully to avoid
the tiny feces of little Florentine dogs, making their way to
the Museo del Duomo, buying their tickets and crowding
through the turnstile.

The game was Zee's impulsive idea. He was taking pity
on some of the kids who had obviously seen enough for one
day and were ready to go home.

"Find the pope Dante hated," he said. "The one he
wanted to bury upside down in the Eighth Circle of Hell."

At once they perked up, and began moving around the
big ground-floor gallery, staring at labels. But the pope was
in plain sight. Ned Saltmarsh squealed and ran to the end
of the room, where a marble Boniface the Eighth sat ponderously on his throne, gazing into space, mild and majestic,
as if he had never grasped at worldly pomp and kingly power,
never sold the offices of the church for gain, never conspired
to condemn Dante to lifelong exile.

"*Bravo*," said Zee in congratulation. "Good kid," and Ned beamed in triumph.

Homer Kelly missed the beginning of the Dante Game. He was making expeditions of his own, every evening, exploring the city on foot after skimming back from the school on his newly rented motorbike. It was true that the monuments were best seen in the daytime, but the life of the street was more interesting at night.

It was more Italian, for one thing, less American-English-German-Japanese. Local citizens poured into the city in the late afternoon, teenagers and young parents with small children from the suburbs and the outlying towns. He had seen them crowding the buses, clinging to the overhead railings, clutching babies and folded strollers, tumbling out on

Piazza San Marco or Piazza del Duomo in couples, in families, in hilarious bunches of smartly dressed girls or clusters of grinning high-shouldered boys.

At this hour they filled the streets, boisterous and cheerful, drinking wine and coffee in the brightly lit bars, ambling in shoals past the open shops, admiring the jewelry in the windows, the digital watches, the jaunty clothes, the belts and scarves spread out on the pavement by black men from Senegal.

Even the fruit and vegetable sellers made a bid for attention. On the evening of the first day of the Dante Game, Homer stopped beside the loggia of the Mercato Nuovo to admire a display of fresh produce piled up on a cart by some descendant of Donatello or Ghiberti, a monument of pears and peaches, cherries and apples, broccoli and cauliflower, topped by a spray of leeks like an oriflamme.

He was in no hurry to get back to his lonely room. On Via Calimala he stopped to watch the owner of an enormous Harley Davidson show off his machine in the middle of an admiring crowd.

The skinny kid was completely hidden by a shining scarlet helmet and a tight-fitting racing outfit. He sat on his big glittering bike with his feet flat on the stone street, making the engine roar in menacing flatulent bursts. It was apparent that he was living in a dream, not yet tied down with a couple of kids and a pregnant wife. *Varoom, varoom*—majesty, manhood, power.

Smiling, Homer turned away, but at once there was a shriek, and he looked back. The owner of the motorcycle had lost control. His idling machine had bucked up and knocked down one of the bystanders. The wounded kid lay on the street, rolling in pain.

There was a sudden confusion, a babble of high-pitched voices. The boy on the motorcycle pulled off his helmet, revealing a stricken childish face. Leaping from his machine, he knelt beside his friend on the ground.

Someone else took charge, a big man in a butcher's apron. *"Non lo toccare,"* he said emphatically. Don't touch him, translated Homer—good advice. He watched as the butcher snatched a tarpaulin from a cart and covered the boy and snapped an order to a woman who had popped out of a shop, *"Telefona alla Misericordia, numero due-uno, due-due, due-due."*

Misericordia? What was that? It sounded like mercy. Could you telephone for mercy in the city of Florence? Apparently you could. Hardly a moment had passed before people along the street were making way, moving aside for the approach of an ambulance from the direction of the cathedral square.

"Aha," murmured Homer, reading the name on the side of the ambulance, *Misericordia di Firenze*. He watched as two men in black robes jumped out of the front seat, looking more like monastic friars than medical technicians.

In his best patchwork Italian, Homer asked the butcher about the Misericordia.

"Ah!" The man swelled with civic pride, and explained. Homer caught enough to understand that it was an ancient organization of volunteers. In times past it had buried the victims of plague, now it transported sick people to hospitals. Florentines from all walks of life served in the Misericordia, working a few hours a week, faithful to the organization for their entire lives. The butcher gestured at the black-robed man who was rolling the victim of the accident onto a stretcher. *"Ecco, il Sindaco!"*

"The mayor of Florence?" Homer stared at the mayor, impressed by his lifelong commitment to so ancient a public charity. And then he walked homeward, moving slowly in a thick press of people, hearing the din of voices and the rattle of metal shades being pulled down over shop windows.

As the Baptistery blocked out the soft light of evening he came upon the central office of the Misericordia. Ambulances were parked in front of it, here in the Piazza del Duomo in the very heart of the city.

Homer hurried back to his pensione, floated upstairs in the tiny elevator, entered his room, turned on his forty-watt bulb, and sat down to write all about it in a letter to his wife.

CHAPTER 20

■ ■ ■ ■ ■ ■ ■ ■ ■ ■ ■ ■ ■

Hoarding and squandering filched the bright world's glee
* Away. . . .*

Inferno VII, 58, 59.

Leonardo Bindo too was thinking about his wife, and also about another woman who was an intimate friend. At an expensive furrier on Via Ricasoli he bought a splendid mink coat and a cheaper but more glamorous jacket of butterscotch muskrat.

Against his better judgment he showed them to Matteo Luzzi in the privacy of his office, turning back the tissue paper, lifting out the luxurious furs, lying, "They are both for my wife."

Matteo held the sleeve of the fluffy jacket against his cheek. "Business must be better than you say it is," he said jealously, resenting his own poverty.

"No, but it will improve. And of course I am buying these on time." Hastily Bindo covered up the furs again, and closed the boxes.

Then they began talking seriously about Roberto Mori.

To Matteo, Roberto was still a backward student in the use of the simplest handguns and target pistols on the firing range at the farm. Matteo's awe in the presence of the good-looking priest had waned. Although Father Roberto was unfailing in his courtesy, the lack of sympathy between them had become more and more manifest. In Matteo's opinion Roberto's lofty purpose was *ridicolo, stupido. Porca l'oca!* How could anyone think such things?

"Ah, my friend, be patient. Remember that for us he is a precious jewel, a treasure beyond price. How he sparkles when we hold him to the light! We must guard him, protect him, flatter him, inspire him, stroke him and keep him safe, at least until he accomplishes his task."

"Oh, si, si, I know," grumbled Matteo, and then they sat down to examine the tentative schedule of events for the celebration of the cathedral's seven hundredth anniversary.

"The *Scoppio del Carro*," said Bindo, tapping his pencil on the schedule. "The old Easter tradition of the Explosion of the Cart. Such a lot of noise!"

When Matteo returned to the Villa L'Ombrellino, Professor Zee called him into the office. "Would you be kind enough to type this up?" he said. "I want to post it on the bulletin board this afternoon."

Matteo had been heading for his room, meaning to lie down and leaf through his new copy of *Il Mercenario*. He couldn't help thinking that he himself would have made a better model for the cover picture than the punk kid in leather pants who was standing with his boots spread wide apart against the backdrop of a ruined street, clutching an assault rifle, holding it incorrectly.

Hurriedly Matteo banged away at the typewriter, making a mess of Zee's handwritten list. Slapping the result down on Zee's desk, he galloped away upstairs.

Zee glanced at the garbled page, sighed, and typed it over himself. Then he took it downstairs to the Pleasure Dome of Kubla Khan, where Mrs. Keppel's daughter had once held intimate little dinner parties. Now the miniature domed chamber was a utilitarian room with a public telephone, a table for incoming and outgoing mail and a bulletin board for miscellaneous messages. Zee tacked up his list. It was a set of clues for the Dante Game.

And there behind us I beheld a grim black fiend.
Consider there how vast a world I have set under thee.

The sixth planet, temperate, and of sheen pure white.
He that with turning compass drew the world's confines.
The souls of the unbaptized.
The Garden of Earthly Paradise.
The tree of the knowledge of good and evil.
Dante's portrait.

The Dante Game was an American plaything from the start. No self-respecting Italian, Zee knew, would condescend to such a childish form of instruction. The citizens of Florence needed no game to help them understand their ancient city. They had lived with its monuments all their lives. They didn't walk around with cameras lifted to their faces, they didn't stop to gawk at the Duomo, they didn't line up at the Accademia to stare at Michelangelo's *David*. These wonders were theirs by birthright.

But for the American students the Dante Game was a handle by which they could grasp the city. Already they were familiar with the bus stops at Porta Romana and Via Cerretani and San Marco. Already they felt superior to the newcomers wandering lost on the stony byways, their noses in their maps.

Joan Jakes and Dorothy Orme, leaning from a lofty Gothic window high up on Giotto's campanile, could name the towers and steeples, they could point out to each other the bridges over the Arno. Under Zee's guidance the entire class had been permitted to look at precious Dante editions in the Biblioteca Riccardiana. Venturing out by themselves they had become used to thousand-lire notes, they had bought souvenirs in the Mercato Centrale. The boldest had found a *videodiscoteca*, a club called *Divina*, a couple of piano bars. And now the studious ones were tracing Zee's list of clues, searching out the answers by themselves.

Homer Kelly was enchanted with the Dante Game. He

was beginning to see the city of Florence as a picture book of Dante imagery, a compendium of all the vivid scenery in *The Divine Comedy*. Hell steamed from the manhole covers in its stony streets, Purgatory sprouted from the steep hillsides across the river, Paradise was manifest in the serene perfection of Brunelleschi's lofty dome.

His favorite clue was the devilish fiend from the twenty-first canto of the *Inferno*, because there were devils all over the city.

On the corners of buildings they supported spiky iron lanterns and iron rings for torches. Grinning batlike creatures spread their wings under lofty pedimented windows. Why, he wondered, were angels noncommittal, while devils smiled from ear to ear?

The devils were easy, because they were everywhere. Some of the other queries on Zee's list were more difficult, but three of them were cleared up at once, on the second day of the Dante Game, by a field trip to the Museum of the History of Science.

Homer found the first one. Staring into an exhibit case he shouted, "*The compass that drew the world's confines,* here it is! And, good God, it belonged to Michelangelo."

Julia Smith discovered the next. There on a shelf was the diary of astronomical observations in which Galileo had recorded his observations of the moons of Jupiter. "Look at that," she said. "Is Jupiter the sixth planet?"

"In Dante's heaven it was," said Zee.

Joan Jakes was not to be outdone. Rushing into another room she came upon a gigantic gold orrery displaying the entire medieval cosmos. Hurrying back to Zee she hauled him away to behold her booty. "*How vast a world I have set under thee,*" she cried, "okay?"

It was time to go home. But when they gathered at the bus stop, someone was missing.

"Where's Throppie Snow?" said Tom.

"Oh, don't mind about Throppie," said Kevin. "He'll turn up sooner or later. He's just sort of, you know, restless."

Throppie Snow was really Winthrop Pendleton Snow, scion of a wealthy Springfield family. His father was a wealthy manufacturer of elastic bandages and industrial webbing. For Throppie money unrolled like an endless bandage, wrapping him up so thickly he was incapable of self-generated endeavor.

This was Throppie's first trip abroad, his first taste of independence. He had expected a European orgy of wine, women and explosive music, but it hadn't turned out that way at all. Throppie was disappointed to find himself so completely under the thumb of the faculty and so far from the center of action. Jesus, you had to walk a mile and take a bus, and when you got there everything was closed half the time and the churches were ugly and the museums were boring and the city was full of tourists who looked just like his parents and the Italian kids were really weird. And that Van Ott woman seemed to think she could boss him around. What the fuck business of hers was it if he never came to class? Throppie had paid plenty of money to come to this run-down villa, and he was doing them a favor by being here at all.

It was soon apparent to Lucretia that she had no choice. After talking it over with Zee, she called Throppie into the office and told him he had to go. Throppie shrugged his shoulders and grinned and went off to call his mother. Lucretia called her too, and explained the situation, and offered to return forty percent of his tuition.

"Oh, I understand perfectly," Throppie's mother said. "But don't send the money to us. Give it to Winthrop. He's going to bum around the continent on his own. I think the experience will be so good for him, don't you?"

Lucretia was outraged. "Independent study, she called it," she told Homer. "They just don't want him in their hair, that's all."

"Well, would you, if you were his parents?" Homer had begun to see everything in terms of the Dante Game. Throppie Snow was a living example of slothfulness, and by rights he should be expiating his sin by galloping at full tilt around and around the mountain of Purgatory.

So Throppie went away, but his absence didn't fix everything. There were other irritations. Isabella was listening at the door again. Joan Jakes had been deep in a personal history of her life, confessing everything to Dorothy Orme in Dorothy's room, dwelling on the torrid love affair of her last Caribbean cruise, and she had suddenly thrown open the door to find Isabella on her knees with a scrubbing brush.

"You were listening," cried Joan.

"No, no, Signorina," said Isabella innocently, grinning at her.

But of course she had been listening. Isabella was an insatiable eavesdropper. She loved carrying stories back to the kitchen. Her English was patchy, but she was a clever girl with an instinct for scandal. The idea that the ugly Signorina Joan should have had a lover was hilarious and the others all laughed hysterically, even the melancholy Alberto.

CHAPTER 21

••••••••••••••••

New sport, good Reader! hear this merry prank!
Inferno XXII, 118.

The archbishop was worried about the committee in charge of security. In his opinion it was moving too slowly.

Its members had begun by taking junkets out of town, consulting with police departments in Pistoia, Arezzo, Siena, Forli and Pisa, in order to assemble large numbers of reinforcements, enough to satisfy the Vatican Prefect, who—the archbishop was beginning to think—was deliberately making excessive demands. But until recently the committee had made no move to consult the local police department at the Questura.

Thank heaven for the assistance of the remarkable Leonardo Bindo! Signor Bindo had shown a genius for cutting red tape, for sorting the important from the unimportant, for taking on his own shoulders many duties requiring tact and discretion. The man was a wonder, a kind of ballet master controlling the circling dance of the archbishop's too many committees. When Signor Bindo took over the committee on security, contact with the local police began at once.

What a relief, to hand over the job to someone so capable! Of course it was a heavy responsibility, but Bindo's shoulders were broad, and the archbishop was gratified by his willingness to volunteer for other tasks as well.

"What about the Misericordia?" Signor Bindo inquired at the next meeting of the supervisory committee. "Suppose someone in the crowd faints or has a heart attack? The ambulances of the Misericordia are right there in the square anyway. Shouldn't we involve them in the plan from the beginning? Would you like me to speak to them? The Governor of the Misericordia is a friend of mine, the *Provveditore*."

There were murmurs of agreement around the table. "How sensible," said the archbishop. "I would be extremely grateful if you would do so, Signor Bindo."

"*Prego*. It is my pleasure."

And of course Leonardo Bindo was a man of his word. Next morning he went to work at once, immediately after attending mass in Santissima Annunziata. Walking around to the Piazza del Duomo, he called on the governor in his study in the central office of the Misericordia.

The governor was cooperative. "Of course you can have as many members as you like. There are more than sixteen hundred active brothers and sisters, but surely you couldn't use more than, say, one hundred of them?"

"One hundred would be more than adequate. We will ensure that they will have free access everywhere, past all the check points, without question."

The two shook hands and parted, but not before Leonardo Bindo had asked for application blanks for a friend of his, who, he said, had long wished to become a member of the Misericordia.

"Certainly," said the governor, and at once he opened a drawer and pulled out a blank. "The applicant must of course be a Catholic of good character, recommended by two members of the fraternity, but surely that will not be a difficulty."

"No, indeed. He is a man of impeccable reputation. *Arrivederla, Provveditore*."

CHAPTER 22

. . . .

. . . desire wafts homeward dove with dove
To their sweet nest . . .

Inferno V, 82, 83.

The heat of summer had returned to Tuscany. It was the hottest day of a stifling autumn week. Under the broiling sun Homer Kelly rode to school on his new motorbike.

It was a modest machine called a Bravo, and it was exactly what the doctor ordered, floating him effortlessly along the streets of the city, its little engine purring. Actually it was a trifle small for Homer's great height. His center of gravity was too high and his knees projected sideways. But the larger machines had offended him by making too much noise or by running with ponderous heaviness. On the Bravo he was a bird in flight.

At the villa he parked it in the driveway, mopped his forehead, walked up the stairs and joined the Dante class.

The room was sweltering. Zee's students sat on the sticky folding chairs in shorts and sleeveless T-shirts. Most of them were barefoot. The marble floor was cool, but the air was sultry.

Zee himself seemed unaffected by the heat. Swiftly he wrote on the blackboard the words CENTRAL METAPHORS, and Kevin Banks groaned. Kevin hated abstractions.

But Zee's metaphors were accompanied as usual by nimble little figures cavorting across the board, acting out the images.

Dorothy Orme kept falling behind. "What's that?" she whispered to Joan Jakes.

"A seal. It's a seal."

"A seal?"

"The seal of form," hissed Joan impatiently, "imprinting the wax of matter."

"I don't understand," said poor Dorothy, but Zee soon cleared it up. The human body, he said, was material substance, like a blob of wax, and on it was printed the seal of form, the likeness of God.

"Then why isn't everybody perfect?" complained Homer, speaking up loudly from the rear. "I mean, why are we all such miserable specimens, such wretched misbegotten freakish accumulations of corrupted flesh?"

"Ah," said Zee, "because the wax is lumpish, and doesn't take a perfect imprint." He scrawled another picture on the blackboard, a scrawny little Dante with bow and arrow. "*We are urged to God like an arrow from the bow,* but sometimes the arrow goes astray, *diverted by some false, fair lust.*"

The word *lust* had been uttered aloud in the hot classroom. For Zee it was an introduction to the Second Circle of the Inferno, where the souls of the lustful were blown around and around forever by a terrible unceasing wind. For Homer, looking on inquisitively from the back of the room, the topic seemed highly appropriate for this place, this day and hour.

The whole villa was bathed in a mood of sweet amo-

THE SEAL OF FORM

rousness. What else had undone the drapery clasps of the nymphs and goddesses on the encircling walls? What else had embittered Joan Jakes and engorged with feeble fluid the bloodless organs of Ned Saltmarsh and distracted all the others from the words on the page and cast a spell of enticement around Julia Smith? What else was so manifestly tormenting Professor Zee? Was Julia really a metaphor like Beatrice, one of those cogwheels of Dante's that turned the heart from visible earthly beauties to the worship of an invisible God? Or was she merely an ordinary garden-variety object of sexual desire?

Homer glanced at Julia. She certainly didn't look like a god-bearing image. Merely by sweeping up her hair and baring her back and shoulders she had become lust incarnate. Sukey and the three Debbies were all looking at her furtively. Kevin and Tom shuffled their feet and stared. Matteo gazed at her sidelong. Poor Ned Saltmarsh seemed to sense the ambient lechery, and he stared around angrily, shoving his chair closer to Julia's.

WE ARE URGED TO GOD

LIKE AN ARROW FROM THE BOW

... DIVERTED EARTHWARD BY SOME FALSE, FAIR LUST...

It was obvious to Homer that Zee was hardest hit.

At the front of the room Zee was aware of Homer's piercing inspection, and he tried to control himself. Solemnly he focused on his notes and scrawled rapid pictures on the board. But, *o mio Dio*, he wanted to stride to Julia's chair and gather her up and carry her away. Instead he spoke with a raw crack in his voice of the adulterous lovers Paolo and Francesca, eternally buffeted by the shrieking winds of Hell.

And then in a moment of insanity he asked Julia to read the story aloud. Obediently she began the famous lines about the lovers' fall into sin.

> *As we read on, our eyes met now and then,*
>   *And to our cheeks the changing colour started,*
> *But just one moment overcame us—when*
>
> *We read of the smile, desired of lips long-thwarted,*
>   *Such smile, by such a lover kissed away,*
> *He that may never more from me be parted*
>
> *Trembling all over, kissed my mouth . . .*

Julia looked up in confusion, then finished the stanza—

> *. . . we read no more that day.*

At once Zee abandoned the Circle of the Lustful, and rushed his students further down the precipitous slope of the Inferno into the drenching rain where the gluttonous were perpetually tormented.

But even the downpour of the Third Circle of Hell failed to extinguish the fires of lust in the classroom. Zee dismissed them early, and scuttled hastily away. Homer imagined the poor wretch shutting himself in his room and beating himself with whips, or donning a hair shirt, or inflicting on his sinful flesh some other masochistic punishment to banish lecherous thoughts.

Homer lingered, gathering up his papers, moving slowly in the heat. When he came out into the large hallway running down the center of the villa he found the cook, Alberto, leaning against one of the cloudy painted castles on the wall.

Alberto was sweating and distraught. He stared angrily at Homer. "You see Isabella?"

"No, I'm sorry, I haven't seen her. She's missing? May I help to look for her?"

"No, no. I look allwhere already." Alberto gazed darkly at Homer. "Franco not here also." Turning, he strode away, striking a match with a savage gesture, lighting a cigarette.

Tom O'Toole had witnessed this exchange. "Well, what does he expect?" he said heartlessly. "You put together a good-looking guy like Franco and a cute girl like Isabella, and it's Paolo and Francesca all over again."

"I hope it's not what he thinks," said Homer lamely. Feeling sorry for the cook, he went out into the blaze of afternoon to look for Alberto's missing wife. It would give him an excuse to explore corners of the garden he had never seen.

He began with the east wing, where the tower surmounted a decaying loggia. Below the tower a picturesque stairway ran downhill, entwined with creeping flowers. Walking softly, Homer descended the stairs, which led to a half-smashed greenhouse, while bells began to ring in some distant campanile. Nearer at hand doves were cooing.

Homer stopped. The cooing wasn't doves. Startled, he withdrew a step or two upward, until he could no longer see Franco and Isabella, who were succumbing to the inevitable. There they were, under a blanket, lying on the floor of the greenhouse on scattered shards of glass, protected only by a piece of torn awning.

The awning was not protection enough, apparently, for Isabella gave a sharp little cry, and her hand appeared above the stairway wall, a drop of blood oozing from one finger.

She laughed. Franco laughed. The hand disappeared. The cooing began again.

The bells had stopped. Homer dared not move, fearing the racket of falling pebbles, the shifting stones of the stairs. He sat down cautiously and waited. They were talking now. It was mostly Isabella, babbling eagerly, while Franco interjected an occasional sympathetic remark.

Homer couldn't help himself; he couldn't stop trying to turn the rapid-fire Italian into English. Luckily he was stupid at it, because he didn't really want to overhear. But he understood perfectly Franco's *Tuo marito mi ucciderà*, Your husband will kill me. Well, of course, it was the old melodramatic story, the eternal triangle, the cuckolded husband, the adulterous lovers, just the way Tom had said.

Homer inched himself up another step on the seat of his pants. Now the girl was talking about her father, *il papa*. No possessive with members of the immediate family, Homer reminded himself. Isabella must be saying that her father would kill her too, if he knew.

Slowly Homer worked his way backwards up the stairs, sitting on step after step. As he rose to his feet at the top he was surprised to see a stranger kneeling below the wall in the shadow of one of the stone goddesses.

Both man and goddess were looking down at Franco and Isabella. Stone eyes and living eyes watched the lovemaking with the same silent stare.

The man was splendidly built. He had a youthful face with a strong nose, heavy black brows and a streaked grey beard. As Homer looked at him, the man turned slowly and met his gaze.

What did one say at a time like this? *Buon giorno?* Deciding that no rules of etiquette covered the proper behavior for Peeping Toms, Homer merely nodded and made his escape.

Roberto Mori too moved silently away, slipping through

the trees below the tower to his meeting place with Matteo Luzzi. On the way he encountered no one else. He was in a state of shock. Anxiously he told Matteo what he had seen and heard.

"They said that?" Matteo, too, was astonished. "Are you sure?"

"*Si, si.*" Roberto's fine features were contorted with anguish. "And there was someone else. A tall man, an American, I think. He was watching them. He has a lot of—" Roberto made a gesture over his head to indicate a wild growth of hair. "He must have heard what they said."

"Oh, that was only Signor Kelly." Matteo laughed. "His Italian is a piece of shit. Don't worry."

But later on that day when Matteo encountered Signor Kelly in the dining room, he was shocked by the American's cheery, loud "*Buona sera, Matteo, stare bene?*" It was clumsy Italian, but it was Italian.

Matteo began to have second thoughts.

CHAPTER 23

▪ ▪ ▪ ▪ ▪ ▪ ▪ ▪ ▪ ▪ ▪ ▪ ▪

Onward and downward, over the chasm's rim.
                              Inferno XI, 115.

Next morning, in the corridor of the dormitory wing, someone was crying.

Julia opened her door to find Sukey Skinner sobbing in the hall. "Sukey, Sukey, what's the matter?"

Heads peered out of doorways. "It's in my room," cried Sukey, pointing. "Oh, I can't stand it, I just can't stand it."

A scorpion was crawling across Sukey's floor.

"Oh, ugh," said Debbie Sawyer, "I didn't know we had poisonous bugs."

"Take a good look, everybody," said Tom. "Sukey should consider herself lucky. I mean, Dante must have seen scorpions like this. Nice devilish little creatures to put in the *Inferno*. Living history, Sukey." He ground the scorpion under his shoe.

But Sukey was not to be comforted. She was afraid of other things as well—small noises in the walls at night, little green and yellow lizards basking in the sun. She was especially frightened by the gunshots at dawn. "They were shooting this morning," she said tearfully to Lucretia. "Almost under the window."

"But they're only hunters," Lucretia told her, "firing at birds. Elizabeth Barrett Browning ate thrushes, right here in Florence."

"Well, I think it's just terrible," said Sukey, who had

seen the little bird bodies laid out in pathetic rows in the Central Market.

Sukey was a tender shoot from a wealthy Belmont family. She had never been away from home before. Her whole experience in Florence had been different from what she had imagined.

The final blow was Zee's Dante class in the afternoon, and the sketches he dashed onto the blackboard—the Violent against their Neighbors crying out for help in the river of boiling blood, the Traitors to Kindred gnawing at each others' skulls in the frozen lake at the very lowest pit of Hell.

Sukey wanted to go home.

Lucretia handled it with her usual efficiency. Almost before Sukey knew what was happening she was on a train for Milan, her plane ticket in her hand.

When Lucretia got back from the city it was almost time for supper, and Alberto was missing. The kitchen was bare. No preparations had been made for the evening meal.

Homer Kelly was missing too. He had not appeared for his four o'clock class, and the students had drifted away. When he limped into the dining room at six o'clock, he apologized for not having telephoned.

"Crazy guy lost control of his car, smashed into that fourteenth century cross where I park my little Bravo. Ran into me, bashed my leg." Homer lifted his trouser cuff and displayed the bandage on his ankle. "I had to hobble to a

THE RIVER OF BOILING BLOOD

taxi and go to the hospital of Santa Maria Nuova. I'm fine now, more or less. Nothing serious. My Bravo's okay."

"What about the car that ran into you?" said Zee in dismay. "Didn't he stop? *Gesù!*"

"Hit and run," said Homer cheerfully. "A Fiat, I think, with an American at the wheel. Skinny character with a baseball cap. I was too busy feeling sorry for myself to pay much attention. Car never even slowed down. Hey, what about supper? I could eat a horse."

"Unfortunately the cook has absconded," said Professor Himmelfahrt severely, frowning at the empty tables.

"Hey," said Kevin Banks, "where's the food?"

Lucretia came bursting out of the kitchen with a tray of dishes, exclaiming in Dutch. Smacking down the tray on one of the tables, she said crisply, "I could use, please, a little help."

"Of course." Dorothy Orme hurried forward.

And then there was a terrible cry. Alberto came running into the dining room, wailing. He was sobbing in great gasps, and it took Zee a moment to understand him, while the rest of them looked on, shocked and silent.

Homer snatched at the word *morti*. Someone was dead. No, *morti* was plural. More than one person was dead.

Zee turned to Homer, the color draining from his face. "It's Isabella and Franco. In the greenhouse."

"Good lord," said Himmelfahrt. "This is really the last straw."

Lucretia uttered an involuntary cry. Then she took a deep breath and recovered her composure. "Everyone out," she said brokenly, making a sweeping gesture to clear all the students from the dining room.

They moved slowly, knowing only that something appalling had happened. Tom O'Toole swore in Italian, having understood what the appalling thing was, but he too went away with the others. Julia caught Zee's eye and looked at him gravely. Augustus Himmelfahrt fussed and blustered, but then he moved away after Julia—emotional scenes distressed Professor Himmelfahrt.

"*O madonna mia. O madonna.*" Alberto slumped against the wall with tears running down his face.

Homer wondered if Alberto had seen his wife and Franco making love again in the greenhouse and had killed the two of them, the outraged husband taking righteous revenge. Putting his arm around him clumsily, he said, "Show us."

Wordlessly Alberto led the way, shambling out of the villa with Zee, Homer and Lucretia in his wake. Stumbling across the driveway, Alberto half-fell down the stone stairs.

Homer's guess was grimly confirmed. Once again Franco and Isabella were stretched out on the ground, but now their faces were torn apart and they lay on their backs, fully clothed, beneath the broken metal framework of the greenhouse, with the setting sun striking here a broken shard and there a pane of glass.

Zee cried out with horror, and Lucretia put her hands to her face and began to weep, while Alberto dropped to his knees and clung to his wife's legs, and sobbed, "*Non ha avuto l'ultimo sacramento.*" Homer understood—Isabella hadn't had the benefit of the last rites of the church.

Sickened and shaking, Homer tottered back up the stone stairs to call the police. He was heartsore for Alberto. It was bad enough to have lost Isabella twice—first to Franco and then to death—without being tortured by the thought of her endless suffering in the life hereafter.

There was one thing to be grateful for. The timid Sukey had gone home. She was no longer here to witness a new episode in the Dante Game, this overflowing of the river of boiling blood.

CHAPTER 24

■ ■ ■ ■ ■ ■ ■ ■ ■ ■ ■ ■ ■

. . . When time's last hour shall shut the future's gate.
                                         Inferno X, 108.

Inspector Rossi came at once from the homicide department at the Questura. Rossi was a homely young man of slight build, with an easy buck-toothed smile. At first the smile made him look a little foolish, but Homer soon decided he was smarter than he looked. His English was better than Homer's Italian, but not by much.

Now, getting out of the pale blue cruiser, he introduced himself and his assistant, Agent Piro, and shook hands sorrowfully and said simply, "*Andiamo.* Let's go."

At once Zee led them down the stone stairway to the place where the bodies lay. Homer limped after them, accompanying the stumbling Alberto, and Lucretia came running out of the house, pulling on a jacket.

At the foot of the steps Zee and Homer stood back wordlessly. Alberto pulled out a cigarette with trembling fingers. Lucretia stood silent, looking down at her clenched hands.

"*O mio Dio,*" said Agent Piro. Crossing himself, he fumbled at his camera and began taking pictures.

Inspector Rossi said nothing. Homer guessed that in his short life Rossi had seen worse than this. Kneeling, he gently lifted the heads of Franco and Isabella, then laid them down again.

Alberto, enfeebled by sorrow, moved away down the hillside and sat on the weedy slope with his back to them, taking deep drags on his cigarette and gazing at his shoes.

"*La guardi*," said Rossi, pointing at Franco's right hand. Something lay beneath it on the ground, a slip of paper. Delicately Rossi withdrew it, held it up by its edges, and read aloud a phrase in Italian.

"What?" said Homer, looking eagerly at Zee. "What does it say?"

Zee choked, and whispered a translation, "*Sinners who enslave reason to lust.*"

"Ah," said Homer, the light dawning. "Paolo and Francesca?"

Zee nodded. "*Si*, Paolo and Francesca."

"*L'Inferno*," said Rossi gently, getting to his feet, brushing fragments of broken glass from the knees of his trousers. "*Canto quinto*."

"What a learned inspector," murmured Homer.

Rossi glanced at Alberto, then asked a question of Zee, speaking softly. "*Adulterio?*"

Zee shrugged, and for a moment there was silence. Then Homer cleared his throat and told Rossi what he had seen last week in the same place, the lovemaking of Alberto's wife and Franco Spoleto. He went on to describe the stranger who had also looked on.

"A tall handsome man with grey hair and beard, and a powerful nose with a jog in it halfway down." It was an inadequate description. Homer wanted to explain to Inspector Rossi that there had been an otherworldly quality about the man, something either holy or unholy. He wanted to portray the eeriness of the quiet afternoon. There had been no sound but the twittering birds in the undergrowth, the low chattering of the girl, the answering clucking of the boy, as though they too were birds. "He was quite splendid, in a way."

Rossi nodded. He seemed hardly to be listening. Lucretia joined them solemnly as Agent Piro spread lengths of plastic over the bodies of Isabella and Franco. Then the inspector looked up at Homer and asked, "When they talk, you hear the words?"

"Yes," said Homer. "But I couldn't understand them very well." He paused, wondering if he should report what Franco had said, *Your husband will kill me.* Deciding that Alberto was in plenty of trouble anyway, he repeated the incriminating words aloud. Lucretia and Zee listened, then looked over their shoulders at the crouched figure of the bereaved husband.

Rossi took the news calmly, not bothering to glance at Alberto. "What other things they say?"

"Oh, a lot of things, but the only word I understood was *father.* She mentioned her father."

Lucretia groaned. "Oh, her poor parents. I'll have to call them. No, the telephone is too cruel. I'll go see them myself."

"And Franco lived with his mother in Cerbaia," said Zee quickly. He shivered with apprehension. "I'll go to her."

They climbed the stairs and went indoors. Some of the students were clearing the tables in the dining room. Ned Saltmarsh stopped short with a bowl of fruit in his hand, and stared at Inspector Rossi in fascinated horror. Julia Smith silently swept crumbs off the table. Tom piled dishes on a tray.

Lucretia swung open the kitchen door and called out for Matteo. "Where is he?" she said sharply. "Why isn't he helping?"

"He's gone," said Tom shortly. "We couldn't find him anywhere. His door was open and all his stuff is missing."

Rossi was interested at once in Matteo. He asked questions, and for the first time he took a small notebook out of his pocket and wrote something down. "What he look like, this Matteo Luzzi? You have a picture?"

There was a blank pause, and then Zee reached for the inspector's notebook and made a rapid sketch of Matteo's cherub face, his halo of curly hair.

"Yes, yes, that's Matteo," said Homer, looking over his shoulder. "He looks just like that, like the angel Gabriel."

"*Grazie*," murmured Rossi, taking back the notebook, looking at the picture.

Matteo was missing, but Alberto was present, a prime suspect, front and center. Once again the room was cleared of students. Tom O'Toole protested, then gave in and walked out with Julia. Ned barged after them, the three Debbies wandered off with Kevin, and Joan stalked away with Dorothy.

A chair was pulled out for Alberto, and the questioning began.

It was interrupted by the arrival of three more police agents, accompanied by the medical examiner. Inspector Rossi turned them over to Agent Piro. At once Piro led them outdoors and down the stone stairs to the place where the bodies lay under their plastic sheets. The three policemen began searching the glass houses, exploring the abandoned sheds and cold frames, the rusted pipes and broken chimneys.

In the dining room Rossi explained to Alberto in Italian that he did not have to reply without the benefit of counsel, but then he began at once to ask painful questions, his voice light and courteous. Homer got the gist of the first question—had Alberto known about his wife's lover?

Alberto merely shook his head, and stared at the jars of vinegar and oil in the middle of the table. His eyes were red. He clutched his arms across his chest as if to hold his shivering body together.

"*Lei, è un studente della Divina Commedia?*" In other words, Homer guessed, had he written the words about Paolo and Francesca on the scrap of paper?

Alberto's moist eyes stared in fright at Rossi. He seemed genuinely surprised, as though wondering what this insane question could possibly mean. Was it a trap? "No, no." Alberto turned to the others for confirmation, spread out his hands and spoke in English, "I do not read books," and then he burst out in Italian, "*Sono un tifoso della fiorentina.*" He was a fan of the Florentine soccer team, that was all, not an intellectual, not a reader of books.

But it didn't take Rossi long to discover that Alberto had attended a school in which, as in most Italian schools, two or three years had been devoted to the study of *The Divine Comedy*. Prompted by Rossi, he was able to complete the first line of the *Inferno*.

"*Nel mezzo del cammin—,*" began Rossi encouragingly.

"*—di nostra vita,*" whispered Alberto, his eyes wild. To what was he confessing?

"But everybody knows the first lines of the *Inferno* by heart," said Lucretia, whispering to Homer. "It doesn't mean he knew his Dante well enough to quote the part about Paolo and Francesca."

But Alberto's credibility was sinking still further. He groaned aloud and smote his forehead, as one of Rossi's assistants came into the dining room and laid an object on the table, slipping it from the newspaper in which he had been cradling it.

It was a shotgun. He had found it in one of the greenhouses, leaning against a ruined furnace.

The medical examiner came in too. Bending down over Rossi, he whispered in his ear.

Alberto began to weep. The gun was his, he sobbed. It had been missing for a week.

Zee spoke up suddenly in English, "But we heard the shots. We heard a gun go off early this morning, about six o'clock. Everybody heard it." He turned to Lucretia with a wry smile. "Especially young Sukey." Turning back to Rossi, he explained in two languages, "I thought it was just someone shooting birds."

Rossi looked mildly at Alberto, and asked him when he had got out of bed that morning.

"*Alle quattro e mezzo.*" Alberto had arisen at four-thirty. He had taken his birdgun and driven to the country-side for birds. The shotgun on the table had been missing, but it was not for birds anyway. It was for bigger game, for deer. The projectile was a slug, not a cartridge full of pellets. Sometimes, said Alberto, he went with a friend to the Do-lomites on holiday, to shoot deer. This morning his luck had been bad. He had returned without any birds.

Rossi asked him if anyone could back up his story that he had been somewhere else this morning, not here at the villa.

Alberto cowered, and stroked his bald head helplessly. He didn't know. He didn't think so. He had been alone on a hillside near La Quiete.

The other police agents came in, their tasks completed. Rossi set them to work at once, inspecting the villa.

"I will come with you," volunteered Lucretia, holding up her ring of keys. Homer suspected she didn't want bar-barians blundering around in private places without her supervision.

Rossi turned back to Alberto. He spoke in Italian, but the questions were simple. Homer could turn most of them into English in his head.

"Your wife, was she still in bed when you got back?"

Once again Alberto's eyes looked wild. Homer felt sorry for him. The poor bastard should stop answering questions. "No," said Alberto. "I didn't see her all day. I looked for her everywhere. Only now have I found her." Once again he was close to tears.

Rossi went on. His voice was polite, his questions deadly. "Signor Fraticelli, your wife died this morning at about six o'clock. How do we know you were shooting birds in La Quiete? Perhaps you were here, a jealous husband, killing your wife and her lover." Rossi grinned pleasantly, but his narrow jaw with its prominent teeth was like a fox's muzzle, snapping at Alberto's torn flanks.

Alberto raised his hands to heaven. "I didn't kill her. I swear to you. She was my wife."

Alberto's interview was over. Rossi turned patiently to the others. He questioned Zee.

Homer listened, wondering if Zee would confess his conviction for homicide in the United States. Zee didn't. Well, why should he?

Lucretia had given Rossi a list of the residents of the villa. Looking at it now, he summoned Professor Himmelfahrt. It was apparent that the inspector was going to work his way patiently through the list, one at a time, staff and students alike.

Zee's turn was finished, and he beckoned Homer into the kitchen. Together they scrabbled around hungrily. When they came out again with a tray of sandwiches and a pot of coffee, the interrogation of Himmelfahrt was still going on. Rossi's questions sounded bland enough to Homer, but Himmelfahrt was protesting angrily, threatening to go to the top in the Florentine police department to complain about the way his bedroom had been ransacked. The truth was that Himmelfahrt had been humiliated by the discovery of his collection of sex magazines.

It was Homer's turn. Smugly he informed Inspector Rossi that he had once been a lieutenant detective himself, back in Massachusetts.

"Oh?" said Rossi, smiling courteously.

Homer felt humble under his clear-eyed gaze. "Well, of course," he confessed, "it was a long time ago."

But the inspector was cordial. Getting to his feet, he invited Homer to accompany him on an inspection of Alberto's quarters and the bedroom of the missing Matteo.

Homer was flattered. Apologetically he glanced at Alberto, who was cowering at the other end of the table in the custody of Agent Piro. He seemed lost in his own private misery.

Upstairs they found Lucretia opening doors, displaying

the office and the library to Rossi's assistant policemen. Gravely she led Homer and the inspector to the bedrooms in the east wing.

Matteo's room was empty. The bed was unmade. Hangers lay tangled on the floor of the wardrobe.

"It is strange that the secretary should leave today, *vero?*" said Inspector Rossi, shaking his head, writing tiny words in his notebook.

Lucretia spread out her hands in a gesture of indifference. "He was a very bad secretary. I scolded him today. Perhaps he left in anger. I don't know."

The Fraticellis' room was next door, an untidy chamber, still haunted by the powerful fragrance of Isabella's perfumes. Her pink powder still dusted the floor of the bathroom they had shared with Matteo.

Slowly and carefully Rossi opened the drawers of the cupboard and stirred the contents, dispassionately examining the spidery black pantyhose, the lavender bras, the fluffy nightgowns. There was a pair of jeans on the floor, the two legs standing more or less upright just as Isabella had stepped out of them. Her sparkling T-shirts were scattered around the room.

There was very little evidence of Alberto. His clothes were confined to the wardrobe. His bird-shooting gun leaned in one corner, empty of cartridges. In a picture frame on the table beside the bed was a snapshot of man and wife on their wedding day. The younger Alberto was thinner, his hair thicker. He grinned at the camera, his arm around a slender laughing Isabella in a white veil.

"*Guardi,*" said Rossi. "Look." He had found something in the pocket of one of Alberto's jackets, a little polyethylene bag of white powder.

Homer stared at it. "Heroin?"

"*Si.*"

"Dear God," said Lucretia.

One of Rossi's assistants was at the door, speaking to him in rapid Italian.

They had found something similar in Tom's room. This time it was pills.

Tom was summoned. "I can't sleep," he said, looking at them warily, glancing from Rossi to Homer to Lucretia. "I take them for sleep."

"You have the prescription?" asked Rossi mildly, turning the little bottle over in his hand.

"No, I can't get a doctor to give me another prescription." Tom looked at Homer, who noticed for the first time the circles under his eyes, his air of cynical exhaustion. "I buy them from this guy at Piazza Santo Spirito."

"A dealer?" said Homer. "Does he also sell heroin?"

"I don't buy heroin," said Tom angrily. "All I want is a good night's sleep."

Homer went back to the dining room with Rossi and Lucretia, wondering about this newly discovered facet of young Tommaso O'Toole. He imagined Tom's elemental matter spread out on the ground, a gluey mass of flesh with the bones lying randomly here and there, until God's great whanging stamp had come down to imprint it with the seal of form, impressing the pulpy protoplasm with Tom's essential being, his wit, his bitterness, his flashes of cleverness, and most profoundly, with whatever it was that smoldered inside him now, reddening his eyes and keeping him awake.

The questioning of the students went on far into the night. One by one they were brought into the dining room. All of them claimed to have been asleep at six that morning, except Julia Smith.

"I heard it," she said. "I thought it was hunters." Julia winced as she guessed what it had really been, the murdering shots that had killed poor Franco and Isabella. Dear, cunning Isabella, who always talked so gaily whenever she cleaned Julia's room, gossiping in a charming mixture of English and

Italian, fingering Julia's earrings, her nail scissors, her hair brush, wanting to know if Julia had a boyfriend, if she wanted to get married and have babies.

Ned Saltmarsh had heard the shots too, but he lied to Inspector Rossi. No, he hadn't heard anything, golly! The truth was that Ned had crept out into the hall at dawn, because he knew Julia always took an early shower. The trick was to catch her when she came out, pink and fragrant, her hair tumbling down over her bathrobe as she pulled off her shower cap.

Debbie Sawyer was thrilled at being questioned, but she had heard nothing. Neither had Debbie Weiss nor Debbie Foster. They had all been sound asleep. Kevin Banks too had been zonked out. So had Joan Jakes.

Dorothy Orme had been awake and she had probably heard the shots, she said, but she had been thinking about something else, and had paid no attention. Dorothy, in fact, had awakened very early and stretched out her arm in the dark to encircle her warm husband, but he was not there because he had died a year ago, and after that she had been unable to go back to sleep.

At last everyone in the villa had been questioned. But only Alberto Fraticelli was taken away. The reasons were perfectly clear.

1. The murder weapon had probably been his.
2. By his own confession he had been up and about and using a gun.
3. His motive was overwhelmingly strong.
4. He had no support for his claim that he had been out in the countryside shooting birds.

"What will happen to him now?" said Homer, as Alberto was bundled into the front of the police van. In the back of the van Homer could see a thick package, the wrapped bodies of Franco and Isabella.

Zee grimaced. "He'll be formally accused by a judge, probably tomorrow, then shut up in prison at Sollicciano to await trial." Zee's shoulders sagged. He looked utterly worn out.

They watched as the headlights of the cruiser and the police van swept around the driveway, illuminating the careless goddesses on the wall. The goddesses were still gesturing idly, irrelevantly. The matter was beneath their notice—a breach of divine etiquette.

Lucretia was furious about Alberto's arrest. "The poor man is completely crushed." She looked accusingly at Zee. "You know perfectly well he couldn't possibly have done it. He's a gentle soul. It's not fair, it's not just. And, look here, what are we going to do now for a cook?"

Santi Apostoli

CHAPTER 25

▪▪▪▪▪▪▪▪▪▪▪▪▪▪

Those men do violence to God. . . .
                    Inferno XI, 46.

L eonardo Bindo was thunderstruck by Matteo Luzzi's
   horrifying report. They met in a little alley near the
church of Santi Apostoli. "You ask me to pay you?
For something I never ordered? *Gesùmmaria!* You kill them,
you run away, you're under suspicion?"

"No, no, the husband, *he* is under suspicion. I used his
gun, not mine." Matteo's feelings were wounded. Father
Roberto had witnessed something menacing and dangerous
at the school, he had told Matteo, full of anxiety, and Matteo
had attended to it in the proper way. He had been careful,
he had been resourceful, and this was the reward he got for
it, this ingratitude. "It's true, I was doubtful about the Paolo
and Francesca *stupidità*, but, *merda!* I was there to obey
orders."

"Obey orders? Whose orders? The idealist's? It's my
orders you should be obeying. What was Roberto doing at
the school in the first place?"

Matteo looked sly. "He has a friend there."

"A friend? What kind of friend?"

"He doesn't tell me," lied Matteo.

"Listen," said Bindo, "they'll be looking for you." He
gazed past Matteo's head at the narrow view of the hills
across the river. His head was spinning. The whole thing
had suddenly grown in magnitude and complexity. With his

129

usual quick adaptability he jumped to a solution. "You must go to the farm. You can stay there. I'll arrange it."

"That shitty little Fiat," whined Matteo. "It won't do. Everybody knows it's my car. Rent something more powerful this time—a Mazda, an Audi Quattro."

Bindo laughed. His good humor was returning. "You think of horsepower at a time like this?" They bargained. Bindo gave in, but the new car would be no more expensive than the Fiat. And then against his better judgment he agreed to pay the usual price for the removal.

"But it was two of them, not one," exclaimed Matteo furiously. "A man and a woman. And listen, Signore, another may be necessary. Someone else heard what they were saying. It was one of the Americans. I've already tried to arrange it, but it didn't work. Perhaps we should try again."

Once again Bindo expressed dismay. Removals were all very well, they were often necessary, but they should always be cleared with him first.

"*Allora*, never mind," said Matteo. "*Non importa*. Forget it. The poor fool studies Italian at the school, but he understands nothing."

Then Bindo extracted from Matteo the promise that he would never appear at the bank again. They made arrangements for the next day, and parted.

On the way back to the Banca degli Innocenti, Bindo hardly saw the people on the street, the wheelbarrow rising on a pulley, the men jump-starting a car, the women shoppers, the tourists. He failed to hear the ringing bells, the strong middle note from Santa Maria Novella, the deep vibrating bong from the Campanile. He was thinking hard about Matteo Luzzi.

Matteo was a link between Father Roberto and himself. In the end there should be no link at all. Leonardo Bindo must be surrounded by silence, by emptiness, by a vacuum. Therefore Matteo must eventually be part of the silence. Earl, too, the scum from Milwaukee.

By the time he had unlocked the door of his office, Bindo had made up his mind. He would hire someone else, and hold him in reserve. A professional this time, not another gun-crazy kid. Easy enough! Tossing this heavy decision over his shoulder, Bindo went on to the next thing. Dialing the number of the Misericordia, he asked to speak to the governor. *"Signor Provveditore?* Ah, good morning! Bindo here."

"Good morning, *Cavaliere.* What can I do for you today?"

"I merely called to inquire whether or not my friend has been accepted into the fraternity. You will remember, my friend the civil servant in the Department of City Museums? You gave me his application form last month. It is my understanding that he filled it out and presented it to you at once."

"Un momento. Let me look."

The governor's office was filled with heavy furniture. On a table stood a small figure of Saint Sebastian, patron saint of the Misericordia. The lamp with its green shade illuminated only a narrow circle on the desk. Now he groped among his books and papers, tipped up his typewriter to look beneath it, and at last plucked what he wanted from under a package of Gorgonzola. The application blank smelled slightly of the strong fragrant cheese.

"Oh, yes, Signor Bindo, your friend has been accepted. He will be formally invested next month."

"Invested?"

"It is a religious ceremony. At that time he will receive his vestments in the oratory."

"Oh, I see. Thank you, *Provveditore.* Soon you must drop in at the bank and let me take you to lunch. There is an excellent little restaurant on Via de' Servi. I am deeply grateful."

CHAPTER 26

. . . *My ship of genius now shakes out her sail*
And leaves that ocean of despair behind. . . .
                                        Purgatorio I, 2, 3.

At the American School of Florentine Studies the foundations had been shaken. The violent deaths of Isabella and Franco had slashed a bloody stroke across the daily life of the school.

But classes met the next afternoon, just as usual.

Zee looked around at his students as they sat in their usual chairs in the Drawing Room of the Queen Mother. Perhaps he would leave it to Dante to carry them up and out of Hell.

For to everyone's relief they had finished the *Inferno*. They were breathing the clear air on the surface of the earth, looking up at the pure stars, climbing the lofty mountain of Purgatory, encountering the penitent souls who would become worthy at last of a place in Paradise after centuries of suffering.

"Canto sixteen," he said, forging ahead, "the celebrated discourse on the freedom of the will." Swiftly he made a sketch of Dante pawing through the smoke that billowed around the third cornice of the mountain.

Beyond the classroom windows the real world too was hazy with smoke. Brush burned in a neighboring field. The seasonal agricultural cycle was going on next door as though nothing had happened at the Villa L'Ombrellino, as though two young lives had not been snuffed out only the day before on the hillside where grapes hung heavy on the vine.

132

Zee stood at the front of the room, explaining that most people in Dante's time had blamed their fates on the stars.

"Determinism," said Joan Jakes knowingly.

"People say the same thing now," said Dorothy Orme, "only they blame environmental influences or their genetic inheritance."

Zee permitted himself a glance at Julia Smith, who was looking troubled. Surely she had heard all this kind of thing before? "But Dante," he said, "was eager to stick up for free will, God's greatest gift to humankind."

And then, keeping his eyes firmly fixed on a spot in the middle of the air, he brought the conversation back to love. One could not help loving, he said, his face a miracle of self-control. One loved what one loved, but impossible loves could be overcome by the exercise of free will—

> Granted, then, all loves that wake in you to be
>   Born of necessity, you still possess
>   Within yourselves the power of mastery;
> And this same noble faculty it is
>   Beatrice calls Free Will . . .

Homer had to stop himself from bursting out, "Zee, for Christ's sake, let it out, open up, stop holding back. *Release thy bow of speech that to the head is drawn.*" It was almost

THE POWER OF MASTERY

comic to see Zee displaying the lesson not only on the blackboard but in his own person, in his spasmodic movements, his erect back, his rigidly controlled legs, stepping this way, carefully, then that.

"But how can you tell," said Debbie Foster, "whether you're acting for yourself by free will, or whether you're, like, just programmed to behave that way?"

It was the old, old argument, but since most of them were young, it was not yet hackneyed, and they were still belaboring it at suppertime.

Tom O'Toole professed himself a determinist. "It's like Dorothy said. Your fate is decided by the year you're living in, the country you come from, peace or war, famine or plague. You're helpless in the grip of outside forces."

"Not me," said Julia, and she began dishing up the *spaghetti al sugo* that had been prepared by Tom with the help of Kevin Banks. For an hour or two Tom and Kevin had opened cans and rattled pots and poured oregano into boiling kettles of sauce, leaving the kitchen splashed with sticky spots of red and heaped with dirty caldrons.

"Not you?" Tom laughed. "You haven't got any more choice than a dog, Julia Smith. You'll marry some guy from a certain social class—I could pick him out a mile away. He'll have a certain set of fuzzy liberal values which he'll abandon as soon as he starts working in Daddy's battery-acid factory. You'll have one-point-eight kids and maybe later on you'll go to law school and the two of you will get rich, and you'll buy a second home and a boat, and then you'll get a divorce. It's written in the stars."

"You don't know me very well." Julia looked at him stubbornly, and then almost under her breath she said, "What I mean is, people can make themselves."

Tom snorted, and shook his head with wonder. "Look, if ever there was a human being created by the stars it has to be Julia Smith. Look at you, the stars dumped everything on you. I mean, some people are lucky that way." Tom glanced at Zee, who was sitting down, making a clatter with his knife and fork. "It's the seal of form and the wax of matter, right, Zee? The seal came down, wham! on the wax, and there was this person Julia Smith, everything perfect, and from then on everything happened the way it had to, leading straight to this school, this table, this—" Tom dipped his spoon into his bowl of ice cream—"this dish of *gelato di cioccolata*. Yum, there's nothing like preordained chocolate ice cream."

"No," said Julia. "It's not true."

"Of course it's not true," said Net Saltmarsh hotly, confused, anxious to take Julia's side.

"And the murders, were they preordained too?" murmured Julia.

"Certainly," said Tom.

Zee looked at her and was silent. Inwardly he wondered if sometimes the wax could reject the seal, could become imperious and take some shape of its own choosing. But probably not. Probably Tom was right. Julia would go back to the United States and marry some goofy good-looking young jerk, and they'd move to the country and live in an expensive suburb in Connecticut, and soon she'd forget all about the narrow streets of the city of Florence, and the school for rich kids on the hill of Bellosguardo, and the teacher whose name was Giovanni Zibo.

With an effort he turned his attention back to the conversation, which was taking the course it had followed ten thousand times before, until Tom ended it by recounting a frightful story by deMaupassant about a young man who set out to seek his fortune and couldn't decide which of three forks in the road he should take, so the story had three different endings to show what would happen on each fork, and when he took the first he was robbed at an inn and had his throat cut, and when he took the second he joined the revolution and was run through with a bayonet, and when he took the third a runaway pickpocket put stolen goldpieces in his pocket and the magistrate hanged him for a thief.

"So you see, it's all in the stars," said Tom, and the rest of them shuddered and licked their ice cream spoons and fell silent.

CHAPTER 27

▪▪▪▪▪▪▪▪▪▪▪▪▪

Cerberus, the cruel, misshapen monster . . .
. . . pot-bellied, talon-heeled,
He clutches and flays and rips and rends the souls.
                                        Inferno VI, 13, 17–18.

Next morning Homer went to the Questura on Via
Zara. It was only a few blocks north of Piazza San
Marco. Like everything else in the center of the city
it was an easy journey by motorbike from his pensione.
Homer sped along lightly, his big nose parting the air. By
now he knew how to sway left and right to go this way and
that, and as usual he was floating on a cloud.

The sign in the upstairs hall at the Questura said *Squadra
Mobile*. Homer gave his name to the secretary, then sat down
in the hall to wait. There was a busy hum of voices, a rattle
of typewriters. At the end of the hall someone was hammering. Sunshine fell in dusty shafts on the floor. He could
hear the sound of water rushing into a bucket.

Inspector Rossi seemed glad to see him. Homer was introduced to the Chief Inspector, then taken into Rossi's own
office.

Their conversation was a polyglot confusion. With his
pocket dictionary in hand, Homer struggled to speak Italian.
The Inspector seemed to take pride in struggling with English. "We look for Matteo Luzzi," he said. "At the school,
they not know where is his home. He was in seminary
before. We cannot find the seminary."

"What about the man I saw?" said Homer. "The grey-
bearded *uomo*? Have you tried to find him?"

Rossi shook his head. "We ask people. They do not know such a person."

"Well, what about the handwriting?" Homer made up a word, "*Il scritto?* Do you know who wrote the Dante quotation?"

"We look for a paper with the writing of Franco, and we find it from the time when he was *un soldato*—"

"Doing his military service," said Homer, nodding.

"Franco write like a little child. The paper with the Dante words was more—*da persona istruita.*"

"Written by an educated person," said Homer, nodding again.

"Matteo too. We look also at his writing. It is not like. He is not the person who write the words from Dante Alighieri. Now we will ask everyone to write for us, and then we will compare."

Inspector Rossi went on to report that they had not succeeded in finding anyone who could corroborate Alberto's story that he had been away from the villa that morning shooting birds on a hillside in the neighborhood of La Quiete. "But we try again."

"So Alberto—*resta in prigione*," said Homer.

"*Si.* He stay in prison."

Homer stood up, but the inspector had something more to tell him. "We find something new in this city," he said, gazing at the stapler on his desk, the scissors, the pencils. "There is an inflow of drugs, heroin, not here before."

"I thought the pope was taking care of the drug problem," said Homer jocularly. "*Il Papa*, his *crociata antidroga.*"

Rossi turned his grave attention to the photograph of his wife and children on the wall. "Alberto Fraticelli say someone has put heroin in his room. He say he do not use heroin."

"Perhaps he was not telling the truth."

"Perhaps." Inspector Rossi stood up and smiled and

shook Homer's hand, and then Homer floated away from the Questura on his little Bravo, heading for L'Ombrellino. Masses of students blocked Via San Gallo in the university quarter, and he had to dodge a couple of men brushing litter into the path of a sweeping machine as it came rocking along the street, sucking everything into its maw.

On Via Tornabuoni he stopped at a newsstand to buy a paper. The headlines were as sensational as ever—

> *DUE BAMBINI MORTI*
> *NEL LUOGO DI SCARICO*

Dead babies again, found at the dump this time. Were Italians really as entranced by dead babies as editors seemed to think? Homer bought a copy of *La Nazione* and sat astride his idling bike reading the front page. Americans were all over the news this morning—

> *SUORE AMERICANE*
> *RESISTONO IL PAPA*

Tsk, tsk, American nuns were defying the pope. And what was this?

> *DUE FIORENTINI ASSASSINATI*
> *IN UNA SCUOLA AMERICANA*

Oh, lord, Rossi had released the news to the press. The school was, of course, the American School of Florentine Studies at Villa L'Ombrellino, and the two dead Florentines were Franco and Isabella. Homer stuffed the newspaper into the front of his jacket and buzzed down the street and across the river. At the villa he ran up the grand staircase, threaded his way through the library stacks and confronted Lucretia in the Office of Blue Clouds.

"The bad news is out," he said, flinging the paper on her desk. "Rossi must have told them all about it. If the parents of our students don't know now, they'll soon hear, one way or another."

Lucretia picked up the paper, glanced at it, then dropped it again. "It wasn't Rossi who went to the papers, it was Himmelfahrt. He thought the world had a right to know. He was showing the reporters around last night, after you went home."

At lunchtime Lucretia brought the paper to the dining room and put it on the serving table for everyone to see. Then she stuck her head in the kitchen to see how the new cook was getting on.

Signorina Giannerini was wearing a white coat, tearing a head of lettuce apart with her bare hands. She was a no-nonsense laureate from the Istituto Tecnico Domestico di Firenzi. Lucretia had found her with a single phone call.

"I don't wash dishes," said Signorina Giannerini. Picking up a cleaver she split a chicken in half.

"No, no," agreed Lucretia hastily. "That is understood."

The newspaper made a sensation. Zee glanced at it anxiously, then turned away. Tom snatched it up and flipped the pages and said, "Hey, here we are."

The others crowded around. There they were on page five, the whole student body and Professor Himmelfahrt, standing together in front of the villa, their faces washed out in the glare of the photographer's floodlight. Only Julia and Ned were missing. The beautiful Julia had been urged to stand front and center, but she had backed away and gone indoors. Ned Saltmarsh had eagerly crowded up among the others, but someone had clipped him out of the picture with a pair of scissors.

Ned was humiliated at having been left out. He banged down his plate on one of the tables, dragged up a chair between Julia and Joan, and began talking loudly about the paper he was writing for Zee's class.

The subject was the Wood of the Suicides in the *Inferno*. He had chosen it strictly for the benefit of Julia.

He looked at her significantly, and she knew he was threatening, *If you don't love me, I'll kill myself.* Refusing to take him seriously, she laughed. Ned sulked.

After lunch Inspector Rossi came back to the American school with his assistant, Agent Piro. The two of them stood in the driveway beside the cruiser and looked up at the tower that rose four stories high at the southeast corner of the villa.

"I see inside, please?" Rossi asked Zee.

With Lucretia's help, Zee found the key, but at first it failed to open the door at the foot of the tower. Then Homer leaned against the door, and it opened with an ominous crack.

"Oh, good," he said, starting enthusiastically up the stone stairs, "I love towers. I wonder if this one has an owl and a specter, like Hawthorne's down the road? Twenty-eight dollars it cost him, cheap for a specter, don't you think?"

Room rose above empty room, but the large chamber on the top floor was different.

Here, just under the projecting brackets that held up the roof, they found a laboratory. In the middle of the room on a long table lay a set of metal basins. Glass tubes wound up from three enormous flasks like the apparatus of a mad scientist in a film. On a hanging shelf stood a row of jars with heavily inked labels.

Rossi read the labels aloud, "*Acetone, acetic anhydride, carbonato di soda, acido tartarico, acido cloridrico, alcool puro.*" He bent to examine an unlabelled bottle on a lower shelf, containing a white substance like sugar, then looked around with obvious satisfaction, grinning at Piro. "*Conversione della morfina.*"

"What?" said Zee.

But for Homer the light dawned. "*Morfina?* You mean

this is a laboratory for the conversion of morphine into heroin? Good lord."

Delicately Rossi opened the bottle containing the white powder, careful to hold the stopper by the edges. Sticking in a finger, he pulled it out again and touched it to his tongue. Once again he smiled his ratlike smile. "Heroin."

Zee was stunned. At once he began asking questions in Italian. Rossi answered calmly, and Zee threw up his hands.

"What's he saying?" begged Homer, who couldn't keep up.

"He thinks it's Alberto again. Alberto had heroin in his room, so Inspector Rossi wonders if he's responsible for all this."

"Poor Alberto," said Homer. "Now he hasn't got a chance." He turned to Rossi and spoke up brightly, "What about fingerprints?"

Rossi looked at him and said nothing, and Homer felt like a reprimanded child. Of course, he told himself harshly, Rossi knew his business perfectly well without extraneous advice.

And later that afternoon when the tower was crowded with technicians from the Questura, Homer looked on humbly from afar, and stayed out of the way.

But he was far from satisfied. Mounting his little mechanical pony, he set off for the city. Whenever Homer felt ignorant about something, he went to the library.

In Florence the library was the Biblioteca Nazionale on the north side of the river. The building was an example of Mussolini gigantism, a freakish monument of colored marble and tortured statuary rearing above a tiny parking lot jammed with cars. Homer mounted the steps in a mood of self-confident vanity—the experienced scholar, profoundly skilled in the arcane techniques of wresting information from vast storehouses of knowledge, certain of his ability to pluck from the massed volumes on the shelves the book precisely fitted to his needs.

Lungarno Acciaiuoli

Four hours later, battered and bruised, ground down by bureaucracy, hoarse with argument, exhausted with filling out pink forms in duplicate and blue ones in triplicate, drowsy with waiting, his hands cramped and aching after copying out whole chapters on the backs of envelopes—"No, no, you cannot take home, you must read here; your passport, *per favore*"—Homer climbed back on his bike and struggled through the traffic in a daze, his body shaking with the vibration of the little engine.

There was a public telephone in the tiny lobby of the pensione. Homer popped his *gettone* into the slot and called Zee at the villa. "Listen, it's not good enough. That lab is strictly Mickey Mouse."

"Mickey Mouse?" Zee was bewildered. "Mickey Mouse, you mean Topolino?"

"Topolino?"

"That little cartoon mouse, Topolino."

"Oh, I see. No, no, I don't mean Mickey *Mouse*. It's just an expression. It means feeble. Look here, if that laboratory was going to do an effective heroin conversion, it needed a lot of stuff that wasn't there. Listen." Homer picked up his notes and read aloud to Zee a description of the process of conversion as it had once been practiced in an illegal laboratory in Marseilles.

"I think this one is just a mock-up. They should have had a direct supply of water and a stove and a lot of equipment for safety. The process is so toxic and corrosive you couldn't get along without powerful ventilating machines. You'd need thermometers, because if the stuff boils it destroys the morphine. You'd need measuring devices too, because if you use the wrong proportions it blows up. And those fancy glass distilling flasks were strictly Hollywood."

"Hollywood? You mean, like in the movies?"

"Exactly. That laboratory is a fake. It was all for show, I tell you. Somebody wanted it to be found."

"But why in hell would anybody want to pretend that there was a heroin conversion lab at L'Ombrellino?"

"Damned if I know. Maybe they wanted to ruin the school's good name?"

"Good name?" Zee laughed sarcastically. "We never had a good name. Not with me on the faculty. Wait till they find out my history. We've been in trouble from the beginning."

CHAPTER 28

▪ ▪ ▪ ▪ ▪ ▪ ▪ ▪ ▪ ▪ ▪ ▪ ▪ ▪

. . . through the garden of the world I rove
Enamoured of its leaves in measure solely
As God the Gardener nurtures them above.
                    Paradiso XXVI, 64–66.

I n the Dante class they had arrived at the topmost level
of Purgatory, the Garden of Earthly Paradise, a lush Eden
crowded with allegorical images, including the tree of the
knowledge of good and evil, that sturdy sapling that would
one day provide the wood for the cross of Christ.

Everyone was distracted by the events of the past week.
It was a good time to take an afternoon's holiday.

"We need a little light and air," said Zee to Homer, "a
touch of the Dante Game."

"What's the clue this time?"

"The Garden of Earthly Paradise. It's no secret. They
all know the answer."

"Well, I can guess. The Boboli Gardens?"

"*Bene*, of course, the Boboli Gardens."

The gardens were a famous tourist sight on the hill behind the Pitti Palace, that vast prison of rusty stone where
the wealth of the Medici had grown entirely out of hand.

"We'll skip the palace," said Zee, and they followed him
in a long line as he crossed the rear courtyard and led the
way to a steep shady path running upward between high
hedges.

Homer was amused by the mismatch. There was nothing
of Dante here. As a mirror of his Garden of Earthly Paradise,
the place was a counterfeit. The metaphors were wrong.
These baroque caprices breathed a different air from that of

147

the fourteenth century. The sporting gods and goddesses, the playful grotesques, the stone monkeys—all were careless of any afterlife, although they lived in a fantasy as complex and bizarre as that of *The Divine Comedy*.

But a garden is a garden. The birds sang in the hedges as blithely as if they were singing in Eden.

A very expensive park is a dangerous place for the besotted. Homer pitied Zee. Today the very statuary seemed to whisper, the scent of boxwood added to the conspiracy, the water in the marble pools suggestively reflected the light, the tall hedges gathered themselves into cloudy shapes as if painted by Fragonard.

For the moment, Homer and Zee and Julia and the three Debbies and Kevin and Tom and Ned and Dorothy and Joan were carried into another world. Willingly they submitted to the spell. The three Debbies frolicked up the hill, laughing, with Kevin and Tom loping along behind. Next came Ned and Julia. Homer and Zee strolled along behind them, leaning forward, taking the climb with middle-aged dignity. Joan and Dorothy brought up the rear.

To Homer, looking up, they were like players on a many-leveled stage. He was overcome by the way people were always so consistently themselves. Tom was always Tom, Ned was always Ned. Once again the seal of form had impressed itself relentlessly on the turgid jellylike mass of corporeal matter. He watched as the three Debbies danced apart and swooped together like a chubby version of the three graces. The seal had come down like an old-fashioned rubber printing device, *whang, whang, whang,* turning out three identical girls, the same in substance, the same in form—God in his wisdom producing Debbie after Debbie, for whatever reason known only to the Almighty himself.

Then Homer's attention was caught by Julia. She was stopping, turning to Ned Saltmarsh, saying something, walking quickly away, leaving him standing alone on the steep path.

"Wait," cried Ned.

But she shook her head and walked faster.

Julia's heart was beating hard. *Just this once,* she told herself, *just this once I spoke my mind.* She had been mean, she had been ruthless, but it was about time. She was sick to death of Ned. She couldn't bear him a moment longer.

Her revolt was partly the effect of the awful dreariness of Ned himself, and partly her overwhelming awareness that Zee was walking behind her, looking at her, wanting her.

Poor Ned! Suddenly the golden November afternoon was

turning bitter and unkind. Falling back to the rear, he was rescued by Dorothy Orme, who patted his shoulder and made him one of a threesome—Dorothy, Ned, and Joan.

Dorothy Orme and Joan Jakes were no substitute for Julia Smith. Ned's afternoon was wrecked. He began to sniffle.

"Oh, Ned, for heaven's sake," said Joan.

But Dorothy was tenderhearted. Even though the boy had no outward charm, his glands were surely secreting juices as thick and viscous as anyone else's, gushing forcefully, filling him with yearning. How terrible that his case was so hopeless! The boy didn't have a speck of the average paltry grace that made most children tolerable to their peers. And yet there was a certain sweetness in the poor child, whenever he could be distracted from grabbing and snatching, whenever his attention was turned to something outside himself.

Dorothy wondered if the boy's voracious attachment could somehow be transformed into something better. "Drawn upward and outward, the way Dante said," she murmured aloud.

"What did you say?" said Joan sharply.

"Oh, nothing."

They had come to the crest of the hill. Below them plunged a wide path lined with cypresses and white marble figures. Julia was finished with waiting, she was done with holding back. She turned to Zee, smiling, and took his hand.

Homer let them go ahead of him, and then he too began descending, watching the way the sunlight fell on them in splotches, remembering Beatrice's approach to Dante in the Garden of Earthly Delights—

> In a white veil beneath an olive-crown
>   Appeared to me a lady cloaked in green,
>   And living flame the color of her gown.

Julia had no white veil or green cloak, but her Day-Glo orange padded vest might do for a flame-colored gown. Where did the girl get her clothes anyway? Some flea market, it looked like. Of course, being Julia, she could get away with it. The general effect was always more or less divine. There she was, another Beatrice, leading Zee into paradise.

Tom O'Toole joined them at the foot of the hill. "Another triumph of genetic engineering," he said, pointing at the tall columns in front of the Ocean Fountain, which were surmounted by fish-tailed goats.

Julia laughed. "It's so playful. I love it when they forgot to be grandiose."

"So do I," whispered Zee. He was hardly able to breathe, fearful of upsetting the trembling balance that kept Julia at his side, her hand folded in his, while the same warm rays of the sun fell upon them both, and the same fine spray from the fountain grazed their faces.

Homer went back with them to L'Ombrellino for supper, and there he took poor Zee aside. He had never seen anyone so sick with infatuation. The poor man had no armor, no protection. He was drawn up by love like an arrow discharged from the bow. Every square inch of his face gave him away, even the folds of his shirt, his very shoelaces. Julia must be aware of it. Was she egging him on, getting ready to break his heart?

"Look, my friend, why don't you wear sunglasses or something? Or pull a stocking over your head? Your naked face, it's terrible. Why don't you tell the girl how you feel? I thought all Italian men were womanizers. They've got this sexy reputation for pinching women on the street. What's the matter with you? Why don't you talk to her?"

"Oh, God, I can't do that." Zee swallowed with difficulty. "I've got this miserable past. And now these other horrors have come up."

Homer went brutally to the point. "You didn't kill your

wife. Any fool could see that, just reading the Boston papers. So what difference does it make?"

"Well, I'm so old. I'm ten years older than she is. And she's so—I mean, she could marry anybody, anybody."

"Well, it's up to her, isn't it? Listen, you jerk, for you and me the women worth going after aren't hooked on callow young guys with big chins and thick necks. They're crazy for the Latin ablative and the precession of the equinoxes. That stuff you do, all that high-flown prattle about Dante and Aquinas, they go mad for it. It makes them burn with desire. When you talk about essence and existence they want to tear off their brassieres. You've got it made."

"I don't agree with you, Homer, but thank you anyway." Zee caught at Homer's arm. "The trouble is, I don't know what she's thinking. Usually I know what's going on in other people's heads. In fact I could usually supply both parts of a conversation myself, couldn't you? But what she says is always a surprise."

And that was the bewitching charm of her, thought Homer, feeling sorry for Zee, the poor fool.

CHAPTER 29

▪▪▪▪▪▪▪▪▪▪▪▪▪▪

Dost thou not hear his piteous cries . . . ?
  Dost thou not see death grapple him . . . ?
                    Inferno II, 106–107.

Next day Ned Saltmarsh drooped and dragged around the school. Ostentatiously he exposed his misery. Everyone got the message, especially Julia. Protecting herself firmly, trying to widen the space she had inserted between them, she smiled at him politely and kept her distance.

Ned moped. Sentimentally he thought about suicide. What if he really killed himself? Then she'd be sorry.

When Julia did not appear in the dining room for lunch—she was keeping carefully out of touch—Ned went to look for her. He wanted to present her once again with his pouting face, his accusing gaze.

She was nowhere to be found, indoors or out. Downcast, Ned stood in the driveway and looked up at the ancient tower, attracted by its romantic silhouette. Making his way to the door, he found it broken and ajar. Timidly he pushed it open and stumbled inside. Then with impulsive daring he climbed the stone stairway to the uppermost room where Inspector Rossi had found the laboratory the day before yesterday.

It was empty. Everything had been removed by the police. Turning away, Ned looked back at the stairs. Another flight of steps led to the roof. Breathing heavily, he climbed to the top, pushed back a hinged trap door, and crawled out boldly into the November air.

The roof was made of sloping terra-cotta tiles. There was

no railing. Ned promptly sat down, afraid to go any further, although he would have liked to peer over the edge and imagine himself lying dead, or perhaps only badly injured, on the ground. Before long Julia would find him there, and bend over him, weeping, saying she was sorry.

But now he had no intention of approaching the edge. Instead he gazed out across the valley at the usual landscape of cypress trees and olive groves. Here and there he could see the rooftop of a villa. White ducks were visible in a neighbor's garden, and rows of artichokes and lettuces. Then Ned was surprised to hear voices, quite near.

Looking down into the weedy forest of trees below the tower, he could see three men quite clearly.

One was Matteo, the missing secretary. Ned's heart quickened. The other two were strangers. One of them spoke English with a beautiful Italian accent, the other with the flat tones of the American Midwest. The Italian was good-looking, with grey hair and a dark beard. The American was tall and gangly, with a billed cap and plaid trousers. Ned couldn't see his face under the cap.

But the more he listened, the more frightened he became. Squirming backward on the tiles, he reached back to clutch at the edge of the stairway opening, meaning to lower himself to the steps and close the trap door softly over his head.

But his groping hand jarred loose one of the tiles, and it went clattering down the roof and careened over the edge, falling on a heap of discarded bricks with a sharp little crash.

"Oh, lordy," whispered Ned, as the three faces looked up at him. For a moment they all stayed frozen, the three men staring up from the ground and Ned kneeling on the roof, gazing back at them in horror. Then Matteo and the man in the cap began running toward the tower.

Frantically Ned scrabbled through the trap door. Where could he go? Panting and sobbing, he hustled down the first set of steps. He could hear them pounding up one flight, and then another.

Gasping, he ran into the room that had been set up as a laboratory. Finding no hiding place, he backed into a corner, squeaking with terror.

And there, a moment later, they found him.

As it turned out, the discovery of Ned's body was very much like his own scenario for suicide.

Julia found him, just as he had imagined she would. She had been taking a solitary walk, brushing through tangled shrubbery, going down the hill and still farther down, dreamily losing her way.

The tower was a landmark, and she worked her way toward it, climbing up and up through the rough terrain of an olive grove where a plow had turned up the soil, hurrying because she was late to class.

And there, rounding one corner of the tower, she came upon Ned spread-eagled on a pile of bricks. His shirt had blown up around his neck, exposing his soft pink stomach. His small mouth was open in a soundless cry. He looked very young and pitiful. Julia screamed, then screamed again.

In Zee's class they were beginning the *Paradiso*. Zee had drawn a picture of Dante and Beatrice rising to the light of heaven, accompanied by the music of the spheres. But instead of heavenly chords of music there were only Julia's cries as she came running into the classroom, sobbing that Ned was dead.

Zee tried to hold her, but she tore away. Turning back, she ran down the stairs and across the driveway, with the rest of them streaming after her. Homer and Zee found her on the south side of the tower, kneeling over Ned, weeping in choking gasps, telling him she was sorry. Zee tried to lift her to her feet and soothe her, but she shook her head wildly.

The others gathered around, solemn, tearful, frightened. Himmelfahrt came running up. "Good God," he said, staring at Ned with bulging eyes, "this is too much, it's just too much."

Lucretia was last. She hurried around the corner of the tower with a cooking pot in her hand, stopped short and gave a despairing sob. Then Dorothy and Joan lifted Julia to her feet and helped her back indoors.

Lucretia stumbled after them, weeping. The others trailed in her wake, glancing at each other with stricken faces—Debbie Weiss, Debbie Foster, Debbie Sawyer, Kevin Banks and Tom O'Toole.

Homer was left alone with Zee and the forlorn remains of Ned Saltmarsh. Glancing at Zee's anguished face, Homer put an arm around him, and they went indoors to call Inspector Rossi.

What was going to happen now? Everything had changed. The deaths of Franco and Isabella had been harrowing enough, but the school had pulled itself together and gone on as before. The very heights of Paradise had come almost within their grasp. Now they were right back in the middle of Hell.

CHAPTER 30

▪▪▪▪▪▪▪▪▪▪▪▪▪▪

. . . Why dost thou rend my bones?
Breathes there no pity in thy breast at all?
                              Inferno XIII, 35, 36.

Next day everything was revealed in the newspapers of the city of Florence.

> *SUICIDA ALLA SCUOLA AMERICANA?*
> *SCOPERTO LABORATORIO DI DROGHE*

And it wasn't only Ned's death and the mysterious laboratory in the tower of the Villa L'Ombrellino that had become public knowledge. The Dante Game was part of the story.

> *GIOCO DI DANTE ALLA SCUOLA*

Someone had told *La Nazione* about the game, and passed along a copy of the original sheet of clues. And now, by clever extension, the three deaths at the school had been tied to it in the press. Had there not been a Dante quotation in the hand of poor Franco Spoleto? Was there not another in the pocket of the dead *ragazzo*, Ned Saltmarsh, three lines about the shrieking harpies in the bleeding trees in the wood of the suicides?

The article was gleeful, pouncing. And the worst was still to come. Zee's background as a convicted murderer had at last been exposed—

PROFESSORE CONDANNATO PER OMICIDIO.

Zee read the entire article to Homer, translating it into
English as they sat in the loggia with their backs to the view.

"What sneak told them about your checkered history?"
growled Homer. "What stool pigeon would do a thing like
that? You didn't tell Rossi yourself?"

"No, I didn't tell Inspector Rossi. But it's not exactly a
state secret."

It didn't take long to learn that the blabbermouth was
once again Augustus Himmelfahrt. "He's proud of it, the
ratfink," said Tom O'Toole.

Homer laughed ruefully. "Interesting, the way the man
loves to share juicy pieces of information with all the world.
He'll get his reward in the end. You know what happens to
sowers of discord. They end up in the Eighth Circle of Hell
with axes chopping them in half."

In the newly rented Honda, Matteo Luzzi drove to the corner
where Signor Bindo was waiting for him in his swanky
Mercedes. Matteo beeped, then waited while the Mercedes
pulled out to lead the way.

They were headed for the farm in the countryside where
Matteo was now to take up residence. But no sooner were
they out of the city than Signor Bindo pulled over at a wide
place in the road where a driveway led into a field full of
pottery.

Matteo parked behind the Mercedes and got out.

His employer was enraged. Striding up to Matteo, he
blustered at him, rattling a newspaper, shoving it under his
nose. "What the hell is all this? What the hell?"

Matteo shrugged, and made exclamations in his own
defense. "But there was nothing else to do. *Merda!* The
stupid *ragazzo* heard everything we said. We shoved him
off the roof. It was easy." Matteo swooped his arm to show
the precipitous fall of Ned Saltmarsh, and clapped his hands

for the fatal impact on the bricks below the tower. "It doesn't matter. He was a fool. He won't be missed."

"But, *Gesùmmaria*, what's all this claptrap about a game and the words from Dante Alighieri? Why take such chances? And, *madonna mia*, the laboratory, whose brilliant idea was that?"

"Don't look at me," said Matteo, lifting his palms to the innocent sky. "It's Father Roberto. He likes to add his little flourishes." Matteo rolled his eyes comically and made curlicues in the air. "He's an artist. He's attaching everything to the school. They have this game they play, the Dante Game. His little clues from the *Divine Comedy*, they incriminate the school, the students, the professor. As for the laboratory, he read a book about how it's done. He bought the equipment in Lugano."

"Lugano? In Switzerland?" Bindo stared with open mouth at Matteo, then burst out laughing. "Oh, my friend, it's ironic—we choose Roberto because his motive is so bizarre, so different from our own, and now he protects himself with a false front of dealing in narcotics." Leonardo Bindo couldn't stop guffawing.

Matteo giggled doubtfully.

Turning back the front page of the newspaper, Bindo put his finger on a headline. "Well, Father Roberto is an ass. A lucky ass. He's stumbled on an amazing piece of good fortune. Professor Zibo at the American school was convicted of homicide in the United States. He served a prison term for the murder of his wife. From now on the polizia will think of nothing else, *vero*? And there's more. There was even a drug connection with Zibo's crime. All this, it will keep them so busy at the Questura they'll never notice our humble, inconspicuous, modest little endeavor."

Drivers on the Via Faentina whizzed past them, wondering why two grown men were standing beside the road, slapping their knees, throwing back their heads and roaring with laughter.

CHAPTER 31

▪▪▪▪▪▪▪▪▪▪▪▪▪

. . . pity's sharp assault upon the heart . . .
                              Inferno II, 5.

The response by Inspector Rossi to the sensational news in *La Nazione* was immediate. Zee was brought to the Questura for further questioning.

It was an alarming summons. He knew that Rossi's next move might very well be to send him to prison, *sotto sospettato, non accusato*—suspected, not yet accused—and then a decision about formal arrest would be made by a judge.

Homer Kelly was not invited, but he was permitted to go along in the cruiser that came for Zee. At the Questura he hung around in the hall, pacing from one end of the corridor to the other, peering in at open doors, exchanging greetings with a couple of cleaning women, pausing outside the inspector's office to listen, hearing only a soft mutter of voices.

When Zee emerged at last, Inspector Rossi accompanied him to the office door and nodded courteously at Homer. Then he shook Zee's hand and smiled soberly and said good-bye.

Homer and Zee walked downstairs in silence, and then Homer clapped Zee on the back, and said, "It's okay then? *Va bene?*"

"*Va bene.*" Zee's voice was shaking. "But it was very bad. He built up a case against me. You can guess how it went—my conviction for the murder of my wife, which was probably a drug-related death. The morphine conversion laboratory, which I could have set up in the tower more easily than anyone else. The Dante connection—who more obvious than a teacher of *The Divine Comedy?* His idea was that Franco and Isabella had discovered my lab, and therefore they had to be disposed of. And perhaps young Ned found out something, so I had to take care of him too."

"But Ned's body was still warm when Rossi showed up with the medical examiner, so you had an alibi, right? All of us were with you in the dining room at lunchtime and afterward in the classroom. He must have seen that?"

"Yes, I think I'm off the hook, at least for now."

"Well, thank God." Together they climbed on a bus at Piazza San Marco, and stuck their tickets in the punching machine and travelled across the river. At Borgo San Frediano they got off the bus and walked along the narrow canyon between the houses to the Trattoria Sabatini. Sitting down at a table with a crowd of noisy people, they drank a carafe of wine with lunch, and Zee was soon restored.

But the school was now in serious trouble.

The most painful event was the arrival of Ned's mother. Her journey to Italy had been paid for by the trustees.

Mrs. Saltmarsh was a small dumpy woman, a female version of her son. Her face crumpled into pathetic tears as Lucretia embraced her at the station. "Oh, lordy," she whimpered, "my poor little boy."

Julia Smith tormented herself by accompanying Ned's mother everywhere, making all the arrangements to send his body home, helping Mrs. Saltmarsh pack his belongings. By the time the bereaved mother left for the United States, Julia's face was vacant of expression. She was pale and thin.

"I give us three or four more weeks," said Lucretia glumly. "Until Christmas, no longer. Two weeks for the airmail letters to reach the parents, two weeks for the parents to write and tell their kids to come home for good. After the holidays I'll bet none of them comes back."

But even this forecast was optimistic. The students belonged to a generation of telephoners, not letter writers. They had mastered the technique of calling home from the telephone office on Piazza della Repubblica. Where once poulterers and pork vendors and flax merchants had sold their wares, where moneylenders had built the fortunes of the house of Medici, there was now a lofty arcade where you could change your traveller's checks or mail a package or buy a lottery ticket or telephone to any part of the world.

Debbie Foster was in the habit of calling her boyfriend in Amherst two or three times a week. Even Dorothy Orme regularly called the United States, to keep in touch with her mother, who was in a nursing home in Worcester.

Now all three Debbies made a rush for the phone. And,

as Lucretia had predicted, the natural thing happened. The three sets of parents were horrified, and called the school to insist that their daughters come home at once.

Kevin Banks didn't bother to call his parents, but as he watched the three girls rush into a flurry of packing and embracing and shedding farewell tears, he too began to feel restless. The dormitory wing was half empty, and his sense of connection was fading fast. He told himself he didn't give a shit about Dante anyway.

Dorothy Orme and Joan Jakes would stay on. There was no question about that. For her part Dorothy felt a commitment to the teaching staff, and she had no wish to leave. Joan was writing a learned paper, and she wasn't about to sacrifice Zee's praise.

The new revelation about his past life was of extreme interest to Joan, who suspected that Zee's wife had been a stupid woman who was better off dead. Someday a better wife would come along, one who would truly understand the needs of his intellect, someone genuinely equipped to share his scholarly life.

Nor did Tom O'Toole show any sign of wanting to depart. Tom had become essential to Lucretia. Little by little he had taken over Matteo's duties as secretary, and he was also carrying his weight in the kitchen, helping to clean up the daily mess of dirty pots and pans left by Signorina Giannerini. In gratitude for Tom's helpfulness his second-semester fees were cancelled.

As for Julia Smith, no one knew what she would do. Zee lived in dread that Julia would follow the example of the three Debbies. Any day now she might announce that she was going home. Or perhaps she would go off at Christmas and never come back.

So far she had made no move. Solemnly she listened to his lectures on Dante's *Paradiso*, earnestly she filled her notebook with the things he said. Lighthearted flirtation and handholding were things of the past. In class she sat apart from the others, almost as though she were choosing to sit beside an invisible Ned Saltmarsh, more loyal to the dead boy now than she had been to him alive.

"He didn't commit suicide, you know," Tom told her kindly. "Inspector Rossi says so. Ned couldn't have written that note from the *Inferno*, not in Italian. Rossi says it was another homicide, *certo*."

It made no difference. Ned was dead, and Julia had been cruel and unfeeling. She couldn't forgive herself.

His empty seat in the classroom was upsetting to the others as well, and so were the three chairs in the front row where the Debbies had sat side by side. Sukey Skinner was gone, and so was Throppie Snow. Even more unnerving was the frequent presence at the villa of men from the Questura—Rossi from Homicide and people from the narcotics team.

The police had found no fingerprints in the laboratory in the tower. "But the criminals would naturally be handling all those toxic materials with rubber gloves," said Homer to Inspector Rossi, "so it's not surprising, right?"

Then he explained his theory about the laboratory to the inspector. "It was nothing but a hoax."

Rossi listened carefully, and demurred. "But perhaps it is not all prepared, the laboratory, not finished, no? The stove, perhaps it come later."

Then the inspector showed Homer his Xeroxed copies of the original Dante quotations, taken from the dead hands of Franco Spoleto and Ned Saltmarsh. He spread them out on the dining room table, and Homer bent over to take a look.

One glance was enough. "That's a European *G*, with a long tail. And those *Z*s with crossbars, no American writes them that way." He looked up triumphantly at Rossi.

"*Si?*" Rossi clucked in appreciation. Then he frowned. "But you have Europeans at your school. Tommaso O'Toole, he is part Italian, no? Professor Zibo, Professoressa Van Ott, they are not *Americani*. And Matteo Luzzi, who is not found." Rossi made a wide sweep with his hands, to show that Matteo was still somewhere out there in the vast unexplored regions of the world.

"And Alberto," said Homer. "Don't forget Alberto."

But they both knew Alberto was out of it. At first it had been reasonable to suspect him of murdering his wife and her lover in a fit of jealous rage, but on the day Ned Saltmarsh plunged to his death from the top of the tower, Alberto had been safely imprisoned at Sollicciano. There had been second thoughts in the mind of the judge. He had let him go.

One afternoon Alberto appeared at the school to pick up his things. He was melancholy and dignified.

Lucretia greeted him warmly. "Oh, Alberto, wouldn't you like your old job back?"

But Alberto shook his head. He was through with the Villa L'Ombrellino and its passionate memories. From his room he took his clothes, his bird-shooting gun and the framed picture of himself with Isabella. From the kitchen he removed his own personal set of kitchen knives and his pasta-making machine, and then he left the villa forever to look for a job in some elegant restaurant in Milan.

Lucretia heard later that he had been unable to find anything but a counter job at a *tavola calda*, where the customers ate standing up. It was surely a comedown for Alberto, who was a master at cooking Tuscan specialties, those delicate traditional dishes made with beans or pork livers or tripe, or chicken from Val d'Arno simmered in Marsala.

During the last two weeks before Christmas, Inspector Rossi failed to appear at L'Ombrellino. It wasn't that he had lost interest in the case. During working hours Rossi was diligently pursuing the whereabouts of his favorite remaining suspect, the missing school secretary, Matteo Luzzi. The rest of his time was taken up by his duties as a participating layman in his neighborhood parish in Sesto Fiorentino. Unlike most of his fellow male Florentines, a race of cynics, Inspector Rossi was devout. During Advent his parish priest

ORA PRO NOBIS

Porta San Frediano

called on him to be a lector at morning and evening mass. He had also asked him to offer a daily series of penitential meditations on the O-Antiphons. Both of Rossi's sons were under his tutelage as altar boys, his daughter was preparing her first communion. During this season, he confessed to Homer, he could barely keep up with his official duties at the Questura.

CHAPTER 32

∎∎∎∎∎∎∎∎∎∎∎∎∎

. . . he was a liar and father of lies.
                    Inferno XXIII, 144.

In Dante's *Inferno* there is a terrible city with flaming walls between the levels of upper and lower Hell, the city of Dis. Within it heretics burn forever in fiery tombs.

In Florence most of the city walls were gone, but even there, even now, heretics still blazed. That passionate dissenter Roberto Mori, mildly composing official forms in the Department of City Museums, was surely just such a smoldering renegade against the revealed truth of the church.

Of course no one would ever dream of considering the genial banker Signor Bindo a candidate for the scorching sepulchres of the city of Dis—Leonardo Bindo, friend of the archbishop, supporter of the foundling hospital, the Misericordia, and many another worthy charity.

This morning Bindo glowed with sanctity as he crossed the square. He had just emerged from the church of Santissima Annunziata. Kneeling before the miraculous Virgin he had found something mysterious in the image of the Blessed Mother, something truly divine in the face that had been painted by an angel.

On the way to the bank he ran into Signora Clementi, the wife of one of his principal depositors. He often saw the signora in Santissima Annunziata, wearing a mink coat just like the one he had bought for his wife. This morning she was walking her dogs, a pair of fluffy little Pomeranians.

Bindo knew just the combination of piety and worldly

banter that appealed to Signora Clementi. "Do you know," he said, smiling, "just now on my knees I had the sensation that the miraculous Virgin was about to turn her head and look at me."

The dogs yipped and strained at their leashes, while Signora Clementi tugged and scolded. Turning back to Bindo she widened her eyes. "It's true. I too have felt something extraordinary about her."

"Did you know, Signora, that she is the real one?"

"The real one?"

Bindo laughed merrily. "It is a portrait of the real Virgin Mary. An old woman, a cleaning lady, she told me."

"How charming! Isn't that utterly delicious!"

They parted and Bindo continued across the square, elated by a bubbling sense of optimism. At breakfast he had seen a television report about the anti-drug crusade. It was rumored, declared the newsman, that some of the reformed addicts who had made pilgrimages to Saint Peter's Square were returning to their old ways. They had taken up where they had left off. If the report was true, it was good news.

When the bank closed at one o'clock, Bindo took a cab across the river to Piazza Santo Spirito to check up on the story directly with the scum from Milwaukee. He found Earl crouched on a park bench. Sitting down beside him, Bindo addressed him in English, his voice hushed by caution. "How is business these days?"

"So-so."

"So-so?" Bindo frowned. English was an impossible language!

"The old ones, they come back. You know. They couldn't kick the fucking habit after all. But the new ones, where the hell are they?"

Yes, that checked with the television report. The young were still swearing off, crowding the trains and highways to Rome as thickly as ever, making their crusading journeys to the Vatican. Bindo had seen them on the screen, a swarm of young bodies teeming in Saint Peter's Square like beetles in a jar. Well, give them time. If the earlier ones were backsliding, perhaps the new ones could be expected to do the same. It was enough.

Matteo Luzzi was now firmly installed at the farm.

The place had been rented by Leonardo Bindo once before, when it had been necessary to store a bulky shipment of marijuana, back in his pre-heroin days. It was an ordinary Tuscan farm in the hills north of the city, where the Torrente Mugnone was only a rushing little stream. Vineyards and olive groves dotted the hillside, and the farmer and his wife cared for a small household collection of livestock. Dependable and close-mouthed, they cared nothing for the use to which their buildings were put, as long as the rent was paid.

Soon Father Roberto, too, moved his meagre belongings to the farm. Roberto was fleeing from the landlady of his apartment near the Central Market. To his embarrassment she had fallen in love with him. She was always hanging around his doorway in the hall, she found excuses to knock on his door at night, and once he had come home to find her inside his room waiting for him. What if she were to look in his drawers and find his secret Vatican correspondence, the letters he had been unable to throw away?

But now it was all right. Roberto was delighted to be out of the city. "I grew up on a farm in Switzerland," he confided to Matteo, "a dairy farm, with goats and cows."

"Switzerland?" Matteo was interested as always in any fragment of information about Roberto. "Then you're Swiss?"

"*Si, si*, but my home was only just north of Lake Garda, where everyone speaks Italian." Roberto laughed. "But with an accent, I'm afraid."

And so their joint bachelor life began. As housemates they were not a congenial pair—Roberto's obsessions were too different from Matteo's.

In fact it soon became apparent to Roberto that Matteo's claim to be a priest in layman's dress was highly dubious, and he wondered why the cardinals in the Vatican had chosen him as a go-between.

It was true that Matteo's appearance was beguiling. He looked like an altar boy, a wholesome adolescent in a white surplice carrying the cross in a solemn procession. And only through Matteo could Roberto conduct his correspondence with the Vatican. The boy had rented a box in the local post office. Every day he took away Roberto's letters, and nearly every day he returned with answers—splendid answers, inspiring answers, words and phrases that spoke profoundly to Roberto's every concern. They calmed his fears and allayed his doubts. The deaths of the two servants, the murder of the young American boy, did they trouble good Father Roberto? Ah, he must be assured that there was a higher compassion than a concern for the loss of these simple lives. Think of the multitudes across the world now in bondage to the Holy See!

"Remember, Father, Dante's righteous rage when Pope Boniface VIII sat in the chair of Peter—*Which now stands vacant before God's Son's face!* Remember, and take courage. Remember, and know that you have our earnest prayers, our deepest friendship, our eternal devotion."

Therefore what did it matter that Matteo Luzzi was as unsavory a young man as Roberto had ever known! Matteo must be endured. He brought the letters that were Roberto's life blood.

But of course Matteo's greatest importance was as an instructor in the use of firearms. Since Roberto was still commuting to his job in the city, they could practice only on weekends.

"Bravo," cried Matteo, as Roberto's cluster of hits grew smaller and nearer to the center of the paper target. "You're like a buckaroo in the Wild West."

Matteo reported Roberto's progress to Signor Bindo on

the telephone. "I think he'll be a marksman after all. And, listen, he's worked out a plan of escape. It's very good. I was astonished."

"Escape? You mean afterward?" Bindo did not say that he had no great interest in saving Roberto Mori for a long life lasting into extreme old age.

"*Si*, and it's brilliant. But he needs a hostage, he says, someone to use as a shield."

"A shield?"

"Someone at whom no one will fire. A woman."

"Ah, *capisco*. But where do we find such a woman? Can't he just pluck her out of the crowd?"

"No, no, it must be arranged ahead of time. She must be there from the start." Then Matteo was struck by an idea. "Wait, I know of someone. Yes, she would be perfect. *No one would fire at this woman.* No one, I promise you."

Bindo put down the phone with a mingled sense of misgiving and satisfaction. The whole thing had been simpler in the beginning. There had been less to worry about. But now he was in charge of a real organization. He had a genuine center of operations and a growing staff, like a certain colleague of his in Turin and another in Naples. Here in Florence he, Leonardo Bindo, had become a mover and shaker, manipulating large events that might someday change the world.

CHAPTER 33

▪ ▪ ▪ ▪ ▪ ▪ ▪ ▪ ▪ ▪ ▪ ▪ ▪ ▪ ▪

O you that follow in light cockle-shells . . .
Turn back and seek the safety of the shore. . . .

Paradiso II, 1, 4.

In spite of its troubles the American School of Florentine Studies had not yet foundered completely. Christmas came and went, and all the remaining students returned, including—to Zee's intense relief—Julia Smith. But the trustees back in Boston were restless. One student was dead, and half of the others were gone. What a terrible beginning for the American School of Florentine Studies!

The situation was even worse than the trustees knew. Leaving for the Christmas break, Professor Himmelfahrt announced that he wouldn't be coming back.

"Honestly, Lucretia," he said as he climbed into the cab, "why go on? What's the point? Stop throwing good money after bad."

So Italian history disappeared from the schedule, having ended abruptly with the sack of Rome in 1527. Nobody missed it. The other classes went on as before, with only five students in attendance—Kevin and Dorothy and Joan and Tom and Julia.

Kevin Banks was the only frequent absentee. Sometimes he showed up in the classroom and sometimes he didn't. He had stopped taking notes. He wouldn't last long.

As for Homer Kelly's course in modern Italian literature, the instructor himself was barely keeping up. Homer had meant to do a lot of reading over the holiday, but instead he spent the entire two weeks in Venice with his wife Mary.

Now Homer stayed up every night in his chilly room at the pensione, humped up on his narrow cot, reading Pascoli and Gozzano by the dim light of his tiny lamp.

At the school things were normal through the first half of January, and everyone began to hope that the uproar had died down. But then trouble erupted again.

It was a theft this time. Michelangelo's compass disappeared from the Museum of the History of Science. Left in its place in the glass case was a slip of paper with a quotation from Dante.

"Don't tell me," groaned Zee, when Homer called to inform him. "I know what it said. It's one of the clues from the Dante Game. *He that with turning compass drew the world's confines.*"

"Right. Therefore this vandalism is obviously our fault. Just another example of the diabolical playfulness of the homicidal fiends here at the American School of Florentine Studies."

The connection was farfetched, but Inspector Rossi took the matter seriously enough to send another search party to the villa to look for the missing compass. Once again every-

HE THAT WITH TURNING COMPASS

DREW THE WORLD'S CONFINES..

one's belongings were tumbled and ransacked, but nothing turned up, and Rossi departed with his companions and didn't come back.

To Zee it was apparent that Hell still boiled and rumbled beneath their feet, and might burst up at any moment in fierce fizzing geysers through cracks in the floor.

In class, however, they were officially in Paradise, moving upward from one exalted bliss to the next, rising to the Heaven of the Moon. From the back of the room Homer looked on with compassion as Zee's face became with each ascent more haunted, more cadaverous.

Poor Zee—Homer saw him in a Dantesque light, a man whose intellect was *like a wild thing in its den*, whose arrow shot heavenward but fell to earth, attracted by a *false fair lust*. He was a lost soul whirled by desire in a harrowing wind, *hither and thither, and up and down*.

The tearing and sundering of Zee's nature were almost visible as he stood before them, talking so quietly he was almost whispering. He seemed to grow ever more incorporeal.

It was an odd kind of tortured courtship. But courtship it was, Homer knew that, however one-sided. The object of

THE CAPTURE OF PICCARDA DONATI

Zee's sublimated affection had little to say in class. She wrote in her notebook and looked up only to copy Zee's drawings of the first cantos of the *Paradiso*—Dante and Beatrice on the moon, the story of the virtuous Piccarda Donati, kidnapped from a nunnery.

It couldn't last, thought Homer. One couldn't teeter on a precipice and hold one's breath forever.

As for Julia, she too was suspended, caught between her cruelty to poor doomed Ned on the one hand and her ardor on the other—her unspoken feeling for Zee was a fantasy slowed down, postponed, delayed.

It would be up to her to reach out, she knew that. Zee waited and waited and said nothing. Julia imagined him clasped in a hair shirt like that of a martyred saint. She had seen the one belonging to Savonarola in a glass case in the monastery of San Marco. How it must have chafed and rasped him! Now she wanted to remove Zee's, to tear it off. She longed to soften toward him, to say *Here I am*.

But she couldn't. Not yet. She was too confused, too distraught. Her native caution had returned.

CHAPTER 34

Down must we go, to that dark world and blind. . . .
Inferno IV, 13.

It rained in January for ten days. At last it tapered off
and stopped. On the first clear Saturday morning Lucretia
and Zee piled everybody in the van for a field trip to the
Benedictine monastery of Monte Oliveto. Actually it wasn't
everybody—only Dorothy, Joan, Tom and Homer. Julia
begged off, determined to finish her Dante paper, and at the
last minute Kevin Banks was nowhere to be found, although
Lucretia looked for him everywhere.

The title of Julia's paper was "The Still Center of the
Revolving Wheels," its subject was time and eternity. Time
was water moving in a round vase, it was the perimeter of
the circle of eternity, with God at the center, equidistant
from all points on the circumference at once.

Julia put her tired head on her arms, and thought about
Ned Saltmarsh. If time was a circle, where was Ned? Somewhere on the edge, occupying one small segment of the
perimeter. If one could travel backward along that spidery
geometric curve, one would come to a time when he had
been alive.

Oh, Ned, Ned, she mustn't think about him now. Desperately Julia opened her notebook to the page on which she
had copied Zee's drawing of the capture of Piccarda Donati.

But she was too restless, too troubled to work. Pushing
back her chair, she stood up and put on her coat and walked
out-of-doors into the cool bright air. Crossing the driveway,

she descended the stone steps past the decaying outbuildings and the broken greenhouse where the bodies of Isabella and Franco had been found. Beyond lay a sloping field of wet grass and yellow mud. It was an olive grove, the fruit ripe on the limbs like green cherries. At the other end of the orchard half a dozen people were busy in the trees stripping the olives from the branches, letting them fall on cloths spread over the ground.

When she came back to the house her shoes were covered with mud. Julia stood in the driveway scraping at them with a stick, as Kevin Banks came out the door.

"Oh, hey, Julia, hey, listen, so long, I'm leaving." Kevin hunched his shoulders and shifted his pack. "Jesus, this thing weighs a ton."

"Oh, Kevin, you mean you're really going for good?"

"Oh, right. Like I just got a call from this friend of mine, she's in Venice. You been to Venice? Me neither. Hey, it's fantastic, she says, so why don't you come on up? They've got this extra space because, I dunno, some guy, he left. So I'm on my way." Kevin squirmed to readjust the straps of his pack. "Besides, what's the point of staying here? This place is up shit creek. If my parents knew what was happening they'd have kittens. Like our great professor turns out to be a murderer? Listen, watch out. He's really gone on you. You heard what they said about him, right? He's really bad news, right?"

And with this piece of fatherly advice, Kevin Banks left the Villa L'Ombrellino and the city of Florence and took the train for Verona, Venice and Trieste, shoving his way into the crowded aisle, unable to find a place to sit down. All the compartments were full. Kevin had to sit on his backpack in the corridor for four hours, all the way to Venice.

It was the last any of them saw of him.

Julia went back to her room, feeling sober. Once again she sat down at her desk and tried to collect her thoughts.

She was alone in the house. There was no one to notice

the two cars surging up the driveway, no one to bar the door against the three men who leaped out and came running up the steps.

One of them was the school's missing secretary, Matteo Luzzi. When the phone call came, Matteo had been cleaning his Bernadelli automatic pistol. Swiftly he had reassembled it and thrust in a clip. Now he led the way. "She's supposed to be in her room," he said, running down the staircase to the ground floor in the west wing. Together they threw open Julia's door and pulled her roughly out of her chair.

Julia was tall and strong. Furiously she tugged herself free and tried to dodge past them. When one of them grabbed her by both arms, she struck his face a tremendous blow. He let go, crying, "*Porca madonna*," and nursed his cheek.

But there was no arguing with Matteo's gun. "*Stia ferma un momento, Signorina*," he said angrily. "Stay still, please. Now, quickly, pack your clothes."

"Oh, damn," said Julia. "Oh, damn, damn, damn, damn, damn."

CHAPTER 35

• • • • • • • • • • • • • • •

LAY DOWN ALL HOPE, YOU THAT GO IN BY ME.
                                    Inferno III, 9.

Locked in the back of the little three-wheeled van, Julia
tried to keep track of the turns and twists of the road.
There were no windows, but she could tell when the
three small wheels turned left or right. The back of the truck
was jammed with a mess of electrical equipment, cables,
wires, batteries, battery clamps, wire-cutting tools, all jumbled together. Caught in the seething snarls of wire were
grubby pieces of clothing, greasy paper bags and *panini*-
wrappers, the sports pages of newspapers. At first Julia was
tumbled mercilessly up and down on the metal floor, but
then she managed to rearrange some of the heavy cable to
cushion the shock.

They were passing through the city of Florence, she was
sure of that, circumnavigating the old center, heading gen-
erally east, or perhaps north. Before long the city noises
faded. They were in hilly country. The truck tilted up and
down, moving in long rising and falling curves. At last there
was a sharp turn to the left, and the smoothness of the paved
surface gave way to a bumpy road. The truck slowed down,
and they began climbing more and more steeply, making
violent turns at switchbacks, then rising straight up a precipitous incline. Again there was a sharp turn, and the truck
paused. A gate creaked. The truck moved again, slowed down
and stopped.

There were shouts of greeting, wild whoops. The engine

was turned off and the little vehicle jounced as someone got out of the cab. Julia heard another car pull up and stop. Doors banged. Now someone was scrabbling at the lock of the door that imprisoned her, and Julia turned to face the opening, ready to lash out as she had done when Matteo and the two others dragged her out of the villa.

Light flooded in. Faces were crowded around the back of the truck, staring in at her, grinning. Julia was on them like a tiger.

But there were four of them now, four burly men. They laughed as they subdued her, and one of them thrust his hand inside her blouse.

"*No, no, Raffaello,*" said Matteo. "*Vietato,*" and he shook his finger at him waggishly. Julia was gripped from the rear, but she managed to lunge at Raffaello and kick his shin with all her strength, so that he yelped and hopped in pain. She cursed him, and wrenched herself furiously from side to side, but her heart was beating violently. Good Christ, what was going to happen to her now? She could think of only one use to which she could be put.

They pushed her in front of them indoors. Julia had an impression of yellow stucco farm buildings. In a last glimpse of the little truck she saw the words painted on the back, *ELETTRICISTA MOBILE*

"Upstairs, Signorina," said Matteo. Reluctantly she

climbed the narrow stone stairway, fearful of what might be waiting at the top.

It was a sparsely furnished chamber, a bedroom with a narrow cot and a large barred window. The four men crowded in after her. Julia retreated to the far corner and turned to face them.

But they stayed respectfully beside the door, grinning and staring. The man called Raffaello dumped her canvas suitcase on the floor.

Swiftly she studied the room. The brick walls had once been coated with plaster, but now only scabby patches remained. There was a sink in one corner, and under it a chamber pot decorated with roses. A wardrobe with a missing leg leaned in another corner. There was a chair with a wicker seat. Under the window an old-fashioned cast-iron radiator hissed.

The barred window was large and high. Julia went to it and looked out, turning her back on her captors.

She saw a valley and a hill. There were olive trees like the ones at Bellosguardo, running down into the valley and up the other side, shedding small shadows. Directly below the window a flock of parti-colored chickens and ducks moved jerkily around a farmyard. At one side in another wing of the building she caught a glimpse of a large animal in a pen. The place was clearly a working farm. Perhaps this room had been used for the storage of grain or the plucking of geese. Perhaps generations of farmhands had occupied it, had washed at the sink and fallen exhausted on the bed.

She jumped. Raffaello was leaning toward her, his mop of curly brown hair touching her cheek, his face a picture of jovial hospitality. *"Ha fame?"*

Was she hungry? Some instinct warned her to understand nothing. She backed away and stared at him stonily.

He turned to the others and shrugged. Matteo spoke to her gruffly in English, "We will come back soon."

They went out, and she could hear the door being locked.

She was a prisoner. But at least she was alone. She could fling herself on the bed and weep if she wanted to.

Instead she picked up her suitcase, put it on the bed and unpacked it. Carefully unwadding the shirts and trousers she had stuffed into it so hastily, Julia hung them up in the dilapidated wardrobe as if she were a guest in the Hotel Savoy, arranging her sporty separates and designer gowns and negligees on padded hangers.

She felt a sharp pang of homesickness. Before her rose a vision of Zee looking into her room at the villa, wondering why she had gone off without saying good-bye. Would he see the torn page of her notebook, would he understand the drawing of Piccarda Donati?

But how could he? Oh, how could he? All he would see would be the mess on the floor, the empty hangers, the missing suitcase. Julia's heart sank. He would think she had run off like Sukey and the other kids. He would think she was a cruel, ungrateful bitch.

CHAPTER 36

▪▪▪▪▪▪▪▪▪▪▪▪▪▪

Why must our guilt smite us with strokes like this?
                                    Inferno VII, 21.

"But why would she leave, a girl like that, without saying good-bye?" said Dorothy Orme. "Oh, yes, I can see Kevin Banks taking off without a word, but not Julia. She seemed so responsible."

"I think you misjudged her, Dorothy," said Joan Jakes. "She wasn't what you thought she was. Not by a long shot."

Zee stood in the corridor in the dormitory looking into the neighboring rooms from which Kevin and Julia had departed. Both doors had been left wide open, both rooms were in disarray. It was instantly apparent that the two had gone off together.

Zee closed his eyes in wretched understanding. It was his own fault. He had pressed her too hard. His longing had been unspoken, but it had weighed on her in the same way as Ned's greedy adoration, and Julia had run away, unable to bear it any longer.

With a sinking heart he remembered Tom's prophecy that Julia Smith would settle down in the end with someone just like herself. Well, Kevin Banks wasn't worthy of her, but he came from the same middle-class American background. He must have seemed more appealing to Julia than a lovesick old Italian pedant and ex-convict.

The ice closed around him, freezing his arms to his sides. He was in the frigid depths of the lowest circle of Hell. Speechless, he watched Homer Kelly blunder around in Kevin's room, rummaging through the litter on the floor, the books and papers carelessly tossed aside.

Homer joined him in the hall. He ached for Zee. Curse that woman, Julia Smith. She was a spoiled unfeeling brat, to go off without a word.

Together they walked into Julia's room. Zee went to Julia's desk and looked miserably at her open notebook. She had stayed home from the trip to Monte Oliveto in order to run away with Kevin, not caring enough about her studies to bring her class notes with her. Here they were, abandoned, along with the drawings she had copied from the blackboard so meticulously. Sadly Zee fingered the torn out sheet that lay on top, wondering why one page should have been ripped out so carelessly, nearly torn in half.

While Homer probed in the drawers of Julia's wardrobe, Zee stared at the torn page with its clumsy sketch. At once he recognized his own drawing of the capture of Piccarda Donati.

Picking up the page, he turned slowly to Homer. "Look at this."

Homer glanced at Julia's drawing and grinned in recognition. "Oh, sure, good old Piccarda, snatched from a nunnery by her vicious brother and forced into wedlock with some rich old creep."

"Yes, yes, that's right. Homer, listen, maybe Julia tore this page out on purpose, to tell us what was happening to her."

"What was happening to her? You mean she was snatched away like Piccarda? Kidnapped? Oh, look here, Zee—"

Zee's eyes were alight. "It was Kevin. I'll bet it was. Kevin forced her to go away with him."

"Kevin Banks? Oh, I can't believe that. Not unless he had a gun or something. He just doesn't seem the type. Too feckless somehow."

"Well, then it was somebody else." Zee's wretchedness

turned to agitation. The page from Julia's notebook trembled in his hand.

Homer's compassion deepened. Poor Zee was clutching at straws, trying to persuade himself that the fickle woman hadn't abandoned him, oblivious to the wreckage she was strewing behind her. Zee needed to believe she was different from the thoughtless Debbies, different from Sukey Skinner, different from Kevin Banks and Throppie Snow. But she wasn't. They were all the same kind of kid, spoiled adolescents. Well, Julia wasn't as young as the rest of them, but like them she had followed her whim, careless of the cost. "Yes, I see what you mean. You think she tore this page out of her notebook as a message, while she was being dragged away like Piccarda. Well—"

"But she may be in danger. Terrible danger." Zee took Homer by the arms and shook him. "Those people are murderers. We know that. We've got to tell Rossi."

Homer called the Questura reluctantly.

But Inspector Rossi drove over to the villa willingly enough, although he was distracted from the case that centered around the American school by continuous phone calls about the security forces for the Easter celebration at the cathedral. Rossi had been chosen by the superintendent at the Questura to cooperate with the celebrations committee.

It was a big job. There were so many meetings to attend with the delegates from the carabinieri and the soldati, conferences dominated by the important dignitary, Signor Leonardo Bindo. Inspector Rossi's telephone never stopped ringing.

It was a relief to handle ordinary matters like murder, suicide and kidnapping. Rossi got out of the cruiser in the driveway of the Villa L'Ombrellino, smiled his ratlike grin at Homer Kelly and shook hands.

Then both of them turned and looked at Zee, who was rummaging in the bushes. In mild astonishment they watched him run around the circle of the driveway like a madman, picking up bits of litter from the balustrade, from the muddy tire tracks, plucking a paper cup from the pleated drapery of a stone maiden.

"Zee," shouted Homer, "for God's sake, what are you doing?"

"Look at this. It wasn't here before." Zee's arms were full of trash. He held up a scrap of paper. "Look, a *schedina del totocalcio*. It's a betting form for soccer. This didn't belong to Kevin. It belonged to an Italian."

Inspector Rossi looked at the collection of plastic wrappers, Nazionale cigarette packages, beer bottles and empty Fanta cans. He raised his eyebrows, smiling in disbelief.

"Who else has been here?" demanded Zee, turning to Homer. "Ask Lucretia. Who else? Nobody, I tell you."

"Maybe Kevin and Julia called a taxi," said Homer. "And the taxi driver dumped all his waste paper in the driveway." He took Zee gently by the arm. "How else would they get to the station? They must have had heavy bags."

Zee didn't want to hear the voice of reason. Hurrying after them as they entered the house, clutching his armful of rubbish, he babbled that Julia had been kidnapped and thrust into a car against her will. She had struggled and kicked, and all this stuff had blown out of the car.

It was wildly improbable. Rossi let him rave while he examined Kevin's room, and in Julia's he listened politely to Zee's passionate explanation about Piccarda Donati and the torn sheet of notebook paper. He was more interested in something he found in the back of one of Julia's drawers, folded into a bathing suit. It was a packet of traveller's checks.

"Why she not take?" said Inspector Rossi, holding them up in his hand.

Zee was electrified by the traveller's checks. "Ah, you see? *Meraviglioso!* It proves she didn't leave of her own accord. Otherwise she surely would have taken the money."

Rossi turned away, as if unconvinced. "I must go back to the Questura."

As the inspector climbed into his cruiser, Zee leaned down earnestly to the window. "You will look for her? You will try to find her?"

"Oh, *si, si*. What city she come from in the United States? You have her address?"

Zee looked desperately at Homer. "No, no, I'm sorry. But she went to New York University in the city of New York."

"New York City." Rossi raised his hand in courteous farewell and drove away.

"He won't do anything about it," said Zee bitterly. "He thinks she left on purpose, just like the others."

But Zee was wrong. Next day Inspector Rossi called Homer at the pensione. "The interpreter here at the Questura, she has telephoned the police department in New York. They tell her a young woman who is call Julia Smith was in *difficoltà* in New York at another time. She spend sixty days in prison for possession of *eroina*. She tell them it is not her *eroina*. She store a package for another person."

"I see," said Homer glumly. "It's what we call a likely story."

"What?"

"You know, Inspector, it might have been another Julia Smith. Smith is our most common name, did you know that?"

There was a pause. Homer could hear the little sucking noise made by the inspector's buck teeth. "I tell you something, Signor Kelly. As you know, we have in the Questura here in Firenze a *squadra narcotici*. But the big office for *anti-droga* is in Milano. Heroin in Florence come from Milano. But now it begin to come from Florence too. Your school—"

"Oh, I know, that phony lab in the tower. Pay no attention to that, Inspector."

Sorrowfully Homer passed along the news about Julia to Zee.

Zee was stunned. "It must have been some other Julia Smith. There were probably a dozen Julia Smiths in New York City. Or else it was a mistake. The stuff was planted on her the way she said. People do that. When they're afraid of a search they plant it on somebody else."

"Well, possibly," said Homer.

"Not just possibly. *Certamente!*"

CHAPTER 37

▪▪▪▪▪▪▪▪▪▪▪▪▪▪

To please me at the glass I deck me gay. . . .
            Purgatory XXVII, 103.

"*Ecco il pranzo!*"
        Raffaello was back. He was carrying a tray.
Looking around for a place to put it down, he
raised his eyebrows, then put it on the end of the bed.

"*Grazie,*" said Julia stonily.

Raffaello leered at her. Julia ignored him, and he
went away.

She was starved. Her breakfast had been only a cup of
caffè latte, and it was now early afternoon. The meal was
cold pasta, with a tumbler of red wine. Julia drank the wine
gladly, although it tasted thin, as though it were the pressings
of the local harvest, not yet matured. Not exactly vintage
chianti classico from a famous Tuscan vineyard, but she
drank every drop.

Finished, she put the tray on the floor beside the door.

Before long there was a heavy tread on the stair. It didn't
sound like Raffaello. It wasn't. A woman in a shapeless
flowered dress unlocked the door, entered, and stared at Julia
with expressionless eyes set far apart in her broad face.

"*Buona sera,*" said Julia, smiling at her, glad to see
another woman, relieved to know that the house was not
solely occupied by men. If a woman were part of the domestic
establishment, surely rape would not be the order of the
day? At least it seemed less likely.

Her smile was wasted. The woman made no response.

Stooping to pick up the tray, she went out and closed the door behind her. The key turned in the lock.

Julia felt better. The wine had warmed her, and her hunger was satisfied. She went to the sink and turned on the water. It was rusty, but after a moment it cleared, and she washed her face and hands.

Across the valley the midwinter sun shone on the opposite hill. Julia opened the two casements of the window to the cold air and leaned her head against the bars. In the distance there were other farms, golden buildings set among cypress trees. In the farmyard below, the woman who had taken away her tray was feeding the chickens, crooning at them, tossing grain from a plastic pail. The ducks and chickens came to her in a feathery rush. A dog barked. There was a heavy crashing noise from the pen, and an angry snuffling. Was it a cow?

A car was coming. Julia heard it before she saw it. Holding her head sideways against the bars she could just see the hood of the car as it came to rest on the other side of the farmyard wall. Once again she heard welcoming voices, but this time there was no loud badinage, only a respectful "Buona sera, Signor Roberto."

In response there was a new voice, a man's, low and sharp, asking a question—"L'avete?"

They were answering in a chorus, "Si, si, l'abbiamo."

There was a laugh. "Una combattente." That was Matteo.

Julia guessed they were talking about her, although the only word she could understand was combattente—a "fighter"—and she smiled grimly.

The voices stopped. The men were going inside. Steamy fragrances floated upward. They were eating lunch.

Julia lay down on her bed and stared at the rectangle of luminous sky. When the voices began again, she moved back to the window. A bouncing ball was making a thudding noise and flying above the farmyard wall. Occasionally she could see the heads of the players as they leaped high in the air. They were playing soccer down there between the farmyard and the olive grove.

She took a brush out of her cosmetic kit and began tugging the tangles out of her hair, standing at the window, watching long fingers of late afternoon sunlight streak between the trees on the crest of the hill.

The soccer game was noisy, and she failed to hear new footsteps on the stair. But as she stood with the brush stretched out at arm's length, her hair trailing down from it in loops and swags, she could feel eyes upon her back. Turning, she stared at the door. For the first time she noticed a small round hole in one of the panels. Was someone standing on the other side, looking in?

Julia shivered. Walking boldly across the room, she stood in front of the door and called out, "Who's there?"

There was no sound. For a moment Julia doubted her intuition. Then she heard a key turn in the lock, and slowly the door opened.

A man stood in the hall, gazing at her. He had a shock of grey hair, a strong youthful face and a short grey beard streaked with white. He was wearing a dark suit. He looked like a Florentine businessman home from a day in an office where he ruled, commanding destinies.

Julia was struck dumb. The man said nothing. He merely looked at her—and looked at her.

The cries and lusty shouts from outside continued. Julia came to her senses and slammed the door.

For the first time since she had been snatched from her room at the villa, she felt totally unnerved. As the key turned again in the lock and the footsteps withdrew, she gave an involuntary sob.

Then she went to the wardrobe and opened it to look at the full-length mirror on the inside of the door.

Slowly she began gathering small strands of her hair into
threes, weaving them into braids, long snaky pigtails that
stood erect from her scalp in all directions. The sky was
nearly dark by the time she was done, but she could see the
outline of the scarecrow in the mirror. She was now as
unattractive as it was possible for her to be.

CHAPTER 38

....

Into the hidden things he led my ways.
Inferno III, 21.

The new aspirant to the fraternity of the Misericordia
stood with the others in the oratory, waiting to be
invested.

At this moment they were still novices, but in a few
minutes they would be junior members of the venerable
fraternity. As the ceremony began and the several parts of
the ritual succeeded one another, the newcomers performed
flawlessly.

During the blessing of the vestments they watched the
sprinkling of their new robes with holy water. During the
interrogation they answered the questions of the celebrant—

> *"Do you wish, with the help of God and by the
> love of Christ, to dedicate yourself to the diligent
> service of the brothers and to carry out their works
> of mercy, assistance to the sick and wounded, help to
> the dying and the dead?"*

> *"I desire it."*

During the investment they bent their heads as they
were helped into their black robes. Finally they joined in the
consecration, kneeling in prayer to Mary, the Most Holy
mother of the Misericordia.

At last it was over, and they could rise from their knees
to receive the congratulations of their new sisters and brothers—while four blocks away in the Palazzo Vecchio, a mere

pigeon flight from the Misericordia, Leonardo Bindo walked into another of his everlasting committee meetings.

This time it was the architectural committee for special constructions.

Bindo pored over the plans for the grandstand and the papal platform, following the pointing finger of the architect, listening to his explanations. Then he took off his glasses and smiled in congratulation.

"*Perfetto!* The scheme for the grandstand is just right. But the platform for His Holiness in front of the cathedral—it's too low."

"But the security committee," protested the architect, "they told me it could be no higher than the top step at the west front. The Vatican Vigilanza and the Swiss Guards will be behind him, protecting the rear. They must not be at a lower level than the Holy Father. That's what we were told."

"But the crowds in the square would not be able to see him. All those people behind the barricades, they will have come from far away in the hope of catching a glimpse of the holy father. You must double the height of the platform. I'll make it right with the security committee."

"Well, of course, it's entirely up to you. But twice as high! You're sure they'll agree?"

"Of course. We couldn't possibly allow the supreme Pontiff to stand at such a low level when he's doing us such honor. It would never do, *vero*? Perfection above all."

Across the river at the Villa L'Ombrellino, things were far from perfect. The trustees had notified Zee that the school was to be closed at the end of the semester. Lucretia, Zee and Homer took their usual turns at lecturing, but the student body was now reduced to three—Tom O'Toole, Dorothy Orme, and Joan Jakes.

For Joan it was heaven. She was overjoyed that most of the kids were gone. No longer did she have to compete with a zoo of healthy young animals.

Dorothy Orme felt privileged too. Of course she was

sorry that the school was in such difficulties, but for her it had become the experience of a lifetime. It was like a seminar, or a religious retreat—students and teachers living intimately with one another, exchanging conversation that was sometimes ordinary, sometimes ridiculous, occasionally high-flown in a way that thrilled Dorothy's modest intelligence, and tested it and shocked it.

She was not clever like Joan. She did not have Joan's habit of piping up eagerly with the right answer, the wrong answer, any answer. Yet she could often sum up in simple language the thing everyone was seeking to express, or ask a naive question that left them all speechless.

"Isn't it funny that Dante made such a fuss about the next world, when he was really talking about Florence?"

"Everything you do *means* something, right? Even little things can have"—Dorothy spread her arms—"huge consequences?"

Only Tom O'Toole seemed to get little from the smaller classes. He was carrying on as usual, helping with the daily necessities of running the school, but he was listless, as though the purpose had gone out of things. *He misses the other young ones*, guessed Dorothy, *especially Julia Smith*.

Housekeeping had become simpler. "You know, Lucretia," said Dorothy, "you don't really need that expensive cook. We can handle the food ourselves perfectly well. It's just the six of us, after all."

"You're right," said Lucretia, but she passed the buck to Zee. "You fire her," she told him. "If I do it, there'll be an awful fight."

"*Un idea terrible*," said Zee, but he took on the task. As it turned out, there was a fight anyway. When Signorina Giannerina finally tore off her white coat and stamped out of the villa, she had won two months' extra wages and humiliated Zee.

That was the afternoon when Homer discovered Lucretia

in tears. There she was at her desk in the office, sobbing with her head in her hands.

Embarrassed, Homer didn't know whether to duck out and leave her alone, or put a comforting arm around her. "Can I help?" he said feebly.

Lucretia glanced at him with streaming eyes. "I'm sorry, Homer," she said brokenly, "but please go away."

"Of course, of course." Homer shut the door softly, and went downstairs in a state of shock. Lucretia had been the sturdy engine that drove the school, keeping the rest of them on track in every emergency. If she were to fall apart, so would the entire American School of Florentine Studies.

But that evening she seemed her usual self, supervising the preparation of a scrappy cooperative meal. Next day she conducted her classes with her usual aplomb.

The school routine continued uninterrupted. In the mornings, whenever February granted them a warm dry day, Lucretia continued her field trips to churches and museums, and Zee carried on with a whole new set of clues for the Dante Game.

No longer did they dare to use the van, with the school insignia on its doors. It had become an object of curiosity and suspicion. Fingers pointed at it, faces frowned, one superstitious old woman held up two fingers in the ancient horn sign against the evil eye. Every *fiorentino* knew that the American School was playing a satanic game inspired by Dante's *Inferno*. No doubt black masses were performed at L'Ombrellino, with the fires of hell sending up fiery sparks above the hill of Bellosguardo.

"All we need now is a couple of dead babies on the premises," said Homer cheerfully, squeezing into the back of Zee's little Saab, jamming himself in beside Tom and Joan.

They drove down to Porta Romana and took the bus to Via Cerretani. Today's clue was an impossible one, *The tree of the knowledge of good and evil.*

Only the studious Joan Jakes was ready. She had pounced

on the answer in the notes for the thirty-second chapter of the *Purgatorio*, and she snuggled it to herself, then snatched it out, triumphant, in the reliquary room in the Museo del Duomo.

"The tree of the knowledge of good and evil! The cross of Christ was made from it, right? Look at that!" She stalked across the room and pointed at a glass case containing an elaborate gold reliquary covered with cherubs and jewels.

"I don't understand," said Dorothy.

"I get it," said Tom O'Toole.

"Those little wooden fragments inside the crystal," said Homer, leaning down to peer at them, "they're supposed to be pieces of the true cross."

"Oh, I see," said Dorothy.

And then Zee congratulated Joan mildly, and she gloated. Surely before long he would forget about the enchanting Julia Smith and turn his attention to the most gifted student of them all, a woman who had not gallivanted carelessly off with a silly young boyfriend. With glittering eyes Joan climbed back on the bus with the rest of them, vowing to throw herself even more earnestly at her Dante paper. She would make it longer, still longer, fifty pages, sixty, a hundred!

But Zee did not forget the enchanting Julia. Now that she was gone, now that her physical presence was no longer distracting him, he was aware of something more solid about her, something larger and more lasting. And he couldn't rid his imagination of a repeating vision—Julia locked in some terrible hiding place, being raped, and raped, and raped.

That afternoon, after bringing everyone back to the villa, he lingered in the driveway, staring at the ground, walking slowly around the circle, pouncing suddenly on another piece of litter, then pulling a second out of the rampant vine that tumbled over the wall. Eagerly he took them to Homer and put them down on the kitchen table as if they too were fragments of the true cross.

One was a small electrician's clamp, the other a torn and dirty piece of paper. Homer bent over the paper, which had been ripped in half. It was obviously the remains of some sort of timetable—

ATAF—FIRENZE				**LINEA
ORARIO (F3) No 2121				
VALIDITA: DAL 16-4 AL 24-4				
LA QUERCIOLA	CALDINE			CALDINE N
PARTENZE DA VIA PACINOTTI				
6.12	6.27	6.52	7.10	7
11.10	11.52	12.40	13.12D	13
17.29D	18.25D	19.23D	20.20	21

"It's a bus schedule," explained Zee. "Those places, Querciola, Caldine, they're on the north side of the city along Via Faentina. Which bus is it? We can find out."

"But, good lord, Zee," objected Homer, "how do you know it has anything to do with Julia? It could have blown halfway across Italy. Well, at least it could have blown uphill from the bus stop at Porta Romana."

"No, no, it's part of the stuff from somebody's car. It all belongs together. The *totocalcio* ticket, the cigarette package, the bus schedule—they all blew out of the car when she was taken away. The bus schedule flew up against the brick wall and stuck in the leaves." Zee looked at Homer insanely. "Which way was the wind blowing?"

"I don't know which way the hell it was blowing. It's not blowing now. It's dead calm out there."

"But there's usually some kind of a little breeze. The prevailing winds are from west to east, aren't they? I mean, isn't there a wind that blows around the world from west to east in the northern hemisphere and east to west south of the equator?" Zee looked doubtful. "Or have I got it all wrong?"

Homer wanted to laugh at this cosmic geophysical clue to the disappearance of Julia Smith. Had the winds of heaven, circling the earth, blown the answer into Zee's hand? "Well, I don't know. But let's just suppose you're right, and this bus schedule did come from some vehicle in which the woman was kidnapped. So what? I've got an Italian train schedule in my pocket, but I'm not going to any of those places. What good is a miscellaneous bus schedule?"

Zee folded the schedule tenderly and put it in his wallet. "I don't know, Homer, but Inspector Rossi isn't getting anywhere. At least this is something. And it's all we've got."

CHAPTER 39

How salt the bread of strangers is, how hard
The up and down of someone else's stair . . .
> Paradiso XVII, 59, 60.

At first Julia had nothing to do but stare out the window. She sat on her chair, her arms folded on the sill, and studied the chickens, learning which ones were at the top of the social scale and which had to scuttle away from the others to get their dinner. Some had no feathers on their necks. The six ducks showed wild deviations in plumage. There was a lame dog on a chain. Four orange cats slept in the sun. The animal in the pen was a large pig.

The days were endless and dull, but at least she had not been assaulted. She had plugged the peephole in the door with a sock. Slowly the hours dragged by, punctuated only by breakfast, lunch and supper. The woman who brought the tray was called Tina. She was silent and severe. She brought the meals and took the tray away again. She took away the chamber pot and returned it. To Julia's "*Grazie*," she said nothing more than a solemn "*Prego*."

With the poultry in the farmyard Tina showed more feeling. She called the cats in an affectionate singsong and scolded the pig, screeching its name, *Graziella*.

Every morning a grizzled old man drove a tractor below the high wall of the farmyard, along the road where the younger men played ball. Julia would hear the machine start up noisily and catch a glimpse of it on the road. Later on she might see it in the olive grove, churning up the ground with a disc harrow, loosening the soil. Once she saw the

202

farmer and Tina on the other side of the valley, moving slowly along rows of grapevines. They were cutting and tying, doing winter work, preparing the vineyard for the new growth of the coming spring. Was the farmer Tina's husband? Was this their farm? Or did they work for the distinguished-looking man with the grey hair, Signor Roberto?

On the fourth day of her captivity a new regimen began. Julia was released for a few hours in the care of a couple of the bravos. There were three of them, not counting Matteo—Raffaello, Pancrazio and Carlo.

When they saw her for the first time with her mop of pigtails, they roared with laughter.

Signor Roberto was invisible. He went away every morning before she was released and did not return until she was shut up again in her room. Julia was relieved, but she braided her pigtails every morning just the same.

As for Matteo Luzzi, he was gone too, most of the time. When he appeared one day at noon, surging up the driveway in his rented Honda, Julia confronted him as he got out of the car and slammed the door. "Why am I here?" she cried, shaking him by the arm. "What do you want with me?"

But Matteo only laughed and pulled her to him, and Julia tore fiercely away.

Pancrazio and Carlo laughed too. "*Andiamo*," Carlo

said, grinning at her. *"Vediamo tutto."* And he took her on a tour of the farm.

Together they visited the barn of latticed brick where the tractor was kept. There were rabbits in cages. In another outbuilding plastic baskets were heaped in nested piles, ready for the next grape harvest. Then Carlo unlocked the door of a room filled with terra-cotta jars.

"Olio," he said, beaming at her, removing one of the wooden lids. In an adjoining chamber there were baskets of corks and shelves of dusty bottles. A metal tank stood at one side. *"Vino,"* explained Raffaello, rapping it with his knuckles.

In the farmyard Julia made the acquaintance of the pig. Graziella was a big sow, long and slender like a sausage. She had huge floppy ears, small crafty eyes and a clean pink skin under white bristles. When Julia approached the pigpen for the first time, Graziella made a rumpus, nosing up her heavy dish and slamming it down, demanding to be fed.

"I'm sorry, Graziella," murmured Julia. She found a stick and reached it through the bars to scratch the pig's back. At once Graziella quieted down and stood still, looking at her shrewdly, as if she were thinking, *Never mind, the world is like that. The bastards will get you in the end.* Within a few days she was an old friend.

In the company of Carlo or Raffaello or Pancrazio, Julia explored the hillside, the vegetable garden with the dry stalks of last summer's sprawling squash and tomato vines, the olive grove with its lopped and twisted trees. When Julia spoke, it was in the simplest Italian. She was careful to say no more than *buon giorno, buona sera, ciao, arrivederci, grazie, si* and *no,* and *per favore.* None of them spoke English except Raffaello, who could say only *Pretty girl* and *I love you.* Always she kept a sharp eye on them, hoping for a relaxation of attention.

But they were vigilant. There was never a moment when

she could dart away and make for the distant invisible high-way, where the tires of passing trucks made a high whining noise above the deeper throbbing of their heavy engines.

The time spent in her room was boring. She had nothing to read—until one day Tina brought her a bonanza. The bread on her supper tray was wrapped in newspaper.

As soon as Tina left the room Julia snatched the paper, dumped out the bread and glanced eagerly at the date on the front page. Good, it was yesterday's *La Nazione*. Quickly she studied the bold print. There had been another strike in the city. This time it was *OGGI SCIOPERO ALLA BIBLIO-TECA NAZIONALE*, a strike at the library. She smiled, imagining the rage of all the scholars, stymied in their research.

So much for page one. Tearing off a piece of bread, she turned to page two, and caught her breath. Looking at her was *Il professore, Giovanni Zibo, della scuola Americana a Villa L'Ombrellino*. Jumping off the bed, Julia took the paper to the window and gazed at the picture hungrily.

She struggled with the language of the two columns of print. Something else had been stolen, she gathered, and the authorities had connected it with *il Gioco di Dante*, the Dante Game. There was a picture of the stolen object, a jewelled reliquary containing fragments of the true cross. It had been a treasure of the cathedral museum. Once again the thief had left behind a quotation from Dante, taped to the wall beside the empty glass case.

Below Julia's window there was a sudden screeching of chickens and quacking of ducks. She was too absorbed to pay attention. Oh, God, what was the connection between Zee and the stolen reliquary?

Tina was coming back. Hastily Julia thrust the outer page of the paper under her blankets. Then she wadded the rest into a ball and put it beside her plate. She had just enough time to gobble a few bites of her green beans and pasta when Tina unlocked the door and reached for the tray.

"*Grazie,*" murmured Julia with her mouth full, handing over the rest of her lunch.

"*Prego,*" muttered Tina, and went away.

At once Julia took out the newspaper again. Sinking down on the small chair beside the window, she looked at Zee's picture and suffered bitter remorse. Why had she not allowed herself to say certain things to him? Oh God, it hurt to know so clearly what he must be thinking—that she had gone away on purpose like Sukey and the rest. Yet how could he think she would leave without saying good-bye?

How could he think she would be like Kevin, who had just abandoned everything impulsively and walked away?

Then the truth struck Julia. Zee would think she had gone away with Kevin.

It was too cruel. She put her hands to her hot cheeks. For the second time since she had been dragged away from the villa she began to cry. She sat in the chair with her elbows on the windowsill and sobbed aloud.

At once there was a sound below her, a protesting voice, as if someone were speaking up in sympathy.

Julia jerked her hands away from her face and looked down to see Signor Roberto looking up at her.

Frantically she slammed the inner shutters over the window and bolted them. Then in a wild confusion of feeling she threw herself on the bed, clutching the newspaper, pressing it to her cheek.

CHAPTER 40

▪▪▪▪▪▪▪▪▪▪▪▪▪▪

Like to a hawk, that sits with folded wing,
  Eyeing its feet, and at the call turns swift,
Eager for food . . .

                              Purgatorio XIX, 64–66.

Zee had lost faith in Rossi. The inspector seemed to be making no further attempt to find Julia.

It was true that the poor man was overworked. On the one hand he had to gather security forces for the Easter celebration at the cathedral, and on the other he was harried by the press. Those editors of the Florentine newspapers, *La Città* and *La Nazione*, what did they care about Julia Smith? She was just another dropout. What excited them was the eruption of homicide at the school, the theft of sacred objects, the whimsical connection with Dante Alighieri, the laboratory that might have become the first center in their sacred city for the distribution of illegal drugs.

If anyone was going to find the girl, it would have to be Giovanni Zibo himself—with the help, of course, of that absurd madman, Homer Kelly.

Luckily, thanks to a visit to the supermarket on Via Senese, Zee stumbled on another faint trace of Julia's captors.

He had set out early in the morning, hoping to get to the market before all the bread was gone, but he was met on the driveway by a van full of police officers from the Questura, and had to turn back.

They were looking for the reliquary stolen from the Museo del Duomo. Zee stood by politely while they ransacked the villa once again. It was absurd to think they would find anything. He remembered the reliquary. It was at least a meter tall, not something you could hide in a crack in the wall. After a while they gave up with good grace and went away.

The bread, therefore, was all gone at the supermarket. Zee pushed the little cart up and down the aisles, looking for the other things on Lucretia's list. At the checkout counter he had to wait his turn in line. Three women ahead of him were gossiping among themselves.

Zee listened idly as one of them talked about an accident suffered by a friend of hers in a collision between a truck and a bicycle. "Poor Signor Paschelli!"

"Signor Paschelli?" said Zee, breaking in. "Signor Paschelli of Bellosguardo? The caretaker at Villa Mercedes?"

"Si, si," said the woman, turning to him excitedly. And then she explained that Signor Paschelli had been walking his bicycle up the steep slope of the Via di Bellosguardo when a little Ape, one of those tiny three-wheeled trucks, had come barrelling around a sharp turn and knocked him down.

"Oh, I'm sorry," said Zee, and begged to know if the old man was all right.

The woman rolled her eyes upward and explained that he was in the orthopedic hospital on Viale Michelangelo, and another woman reported indignantly that the driver of the little truck had driven off at full speed, leaving him crumpled on the road.

"When?" said Zee, feeling a stirring of interest.

"Last Friday, a week ago, at noon."

Zee was stunned. Friday was the day Julia had disappeared. At noon the rest of them had all been away from the villa, and they had come home to find her gone.

"Thank you, Signora," he said, picking up his packages and hurrying away. Speeding home in the Saab, he thought about Signor Paschelli.

The old man had been the caretaker at Villa Mercedes for a very long time. The villa was one of the great houses neighboring L'Ombrellino. From the day they had moved in, he had offered Zee and Lucretia good advice. He had instructed young Franco in the pruning of hedges. He had regaled them with tales about the grand old days. He was a mine of information about the international set and the cream of Florentine society.

At the villa Zee dumped the groceries on the kitchen counter, then went looking for Homer Kelly. He found him sprawled on a lawn chair in his winter overcoat on the north loggia, tipped back against the bust of Galileo, reading a novel. Homer was still trying to keep one jump ahead of his class.

He was not impressed by the news from the supermarket on Via Senese. "Listen, my friend, it could have been anybody. There must be five or six hundred cars going up and down Via di Bellosguardo every day."

"Come with me to the hospital," pleaded Zee. "At least we can talk to Signor Paschelli."

The Viale Michelangelo was a broad tree-lined avenue curving high above the river. As they swept along in a sea of traffic the city kept opening out below them, closer at hand than it appeared from Bellosguardo. Rounding a hill they saw the great ribbed shape of the dome of the cathedral rising slowly like a hot-air balloon in majestic ascent.

In the hospital they found Signor Paschelli in the old men's ward. He was sitting up in bed, surrounded by visitors. His daughter stood at one side, tenderly feeding him spoonfuls of a delicacy brought from home. His son-in-law bowed over him solicitously on the other side. The parish priest stood at the foot of the bed holding a rosary.

Graciously they made room for Homer and Zee. The old man was delighted to see them. He beamed. There were introductions, handshakes, nods and smiles. Signor Paschelli was eager to describe the incident in which he had been hurt. He had obviously told the story many times already, and had formed and shaped it into a work of art, a saga with a tumultuous climax and an exciting conclusion in which the hand of God had played a vital part.

For Homer the old man's Italian was too fast, but he had no difficulty in interpreting the whizzing motion of his good arm, the tossing up of his hand to indicate the collision, the collapse back on the pillow to show the way he had been thrown aside.

Zee shook his head in sympathy and asked if Signor Paschelli had seen the driver.

"*Non so.*" Signor Paschelli shrugged his good shoulder. "*Ma penso sia stato un uomo giovane.*"

"A young man," translated Zee.

Signor Paschelli was not finished. "*Un elettricista!*" he cried, rearing up in bed.

"An electrician? Why? *Perché un elettricista?*"

Signor Paschelli smiled in triumph. He explained that while he was lying in agony on the side of the road, he had watched the little three-wheeled truck plunge away down the hill.

His daughter raised her hands in horror to think that the wicked driver had so cruelly left his victim to die on the highway.

"*Abominevole!*" agreed her husband.

"*Assassino!*" protested the priest.

But Signor Paschelli's story was still in midflight. Gazing into space as if beholding a holy vision, he read aloud the miraculous words hanging before him in the air. "*Elettricista Mobile!*" These two words, he told Zee, had been written on the back of the truck in large red letters. He had caught a glimpse of them just before toppling backwards in a dead faint.

"*Meraviglioso!*" gasped his daughter, astounded by this example of her father's amazing powers of observation and recollection.

"*Magnifico!*" said the son-in-law.

"*Splendente!*" murmured the parish priest.

On the way out of the hospital, Zee pummelled Homer's arm. "An electrician, of course. That little electrician's clamp I found in the driveway, remember? It fits."

"You mean Julia Smith was kidnapped by a criminal electrician?" Homer was sarcastic, but Zee was too excited to notice. He rushed to the Saab and tried to wrench open the locked door.

"Look, old pal," said Homer, "before you start investigating all the electricians in the city of Florence, there's something you should do first. You should call some of the other people who live at Bellosguardo. The truck probably belonged to some legitimate craftsman making a house call in the neighborhood, replacing old wiring or installing a new outlet."

"Innocent! A hit-and-run driver? Why was he in such a hurry in the first place?" Zee unlocked the car and groaned, "Oh, God, Homer, of course you're right."

Back at home Zee consulted Lucretia and Tom O'Toole, who were better acquainted with the neighbors. Then with Tom's list in hand, he called the Villa Brichieri, the Villa Bellosguardo and the Villa Mercedes. But no one had used the services of an electrician that particular Friday.

"Are you sure it wasn't a plumber?" asked the British housekeeper in the Villa Brichieri. "We've been having the most god-awful trouble with the drains."

Zee was exultant. "You see?" he said to Homer. "That little truck had no legitimate business in this neighborhood at all. Now all I have to do is find an electrician working along Via Faentina."

Homer laughed. "You mean you're connecting the electrician with that bus schedule you found the other day? Well, my friend, I suppose everything in the world is connected, in a way. I mean, in the cosmic order of things there must be some grand unity—electric guitars and birds in the trees,

hard-boiled eggs and the Leaning Tower of Pisa, bus sched-
ules and electricians. So why not? Carry on."

And then Homer went off to teach his class, and Zee
settled down in the Pleasure Dome of Kubla Khan to consult
the *Pagine Gialle* of the phone book. With his breath steam-
ing in the frosty air he ran his cold finger down the page of
Elettricisti.

What he wanted was a mobile electrician who worked
out of his truck, someone whose home base was one of the
little towns along Via Faentina—Badia Fiesolana, perhaps,
or Fonte Lucente, or Pian del Mugnone, perhaps even Fiesole.

A mobile electrician? Nobody in the phone book described himself as mobile. But there were several establishments with addresses in the towns he was interested in. He
marked them heavily with a pencil, then hurried into the
warm dining room to listen impatiently while Homer lec-
tured about Alberto Moravia, and Joan Jakes interrupted with
fascinating fragments of fact. At last class was over. Zee
hurried forward, pounced on Homer, and showed him the
list. "Look here, an outfit called La Casa on Via Faentina,
and there are five electricians in Fiesole."

"Well, good," said Homer. "That's just fine. Why don't
you show them to Rossi and let him take care of it?"

"Because he doesn't really believe she was captured,"
insisted Zee. "He thinks she just went away like the rest."

Tom O'Toole wanted to ask Homer about Moravia, Dorothy Orme needed to know when the next paper was due,
Joan Jakes was eager to show off. Humbly Zee stood aside
and waited while Homer listened, shuffling papers into his
briefcase, wondering what to do with his insane friend Zee,
who was allowing himself to go so far off the deep end.

The girl had left the school of her own free will, god-
dammit. At this moment she was probably drifting down
Lake Como in a pleasure steamer, or shacked up with Kevin
Banks in a hotel on the Riviera, or drinking champagne on
the Via Veneto in the city of Rome.

CHAPTER 41

▪ ▪ ▪ ▪ ▪ ▪ ▪ ▪ ▪ ▪ ▪ ▪ ▪

I held my tongue; but my desire showed through. . .
                                            Paradiso IV, 10.

In the other part of the house Julia heard the faint ring of the phone. She knew where it was sequestered, behind a locked door in the other wing of the farmhouse. If only she could get at it, if only she could have two minutes alone with it, she could call the school and tell Zee where she was.

But only Matteo and Signor Roberto had keys to the telephone room.

Today the call was for Roberto.

Carefully he shut the door before lifting the receiver. "*Pronto?*"

"Listen, they're looking in the right direction. One of your men lost a bus schedule in the driveway when they took her. It's the schedule for Bus 12, naturally, and now they're going to look along Via Faentina."

"Don't concern yourself. Via Faentina is a long road."

"But it's worse than that. Your driver had an accident on the way. He ran into an old man with a bicycle, and the old man remembers that it was an electrician's truck. Zee has talked to him, and now he's looking for an electrician on Via Faentina."

"*Madre di Dio!*"

There was a pause, then the voice on the line said, "What do you think of the girl?"

"The girl? Oh, the girl Julia. Fortunately she's become docile."

"But beautiful? You think she's beautiful?"

This time it was Roberto who paused before speaking. "Beautiful? What difference does that make? She'll be useful."

In Florence in the Palace of the Archbishop, His Excellency too was picking up the phone. The Vatican Prefect for the Pontifical Household was on the line. "*Buona sera*, Your Excellency. Can you hear me? What's all that racket?"

Rattled, the archbishop cupped both hands around the phone to block out the chanting of the women in the square. They were louder than ever, all shouting in unison. "Nothing, Your Eminence. Only some women. There is some sort of—ah—celebration in the street."

"I see. I only called to inquire how your preparations for the Easter festivities are coming along, and to say that we will be sending our security forces up by train on Holy Saturday, forty officers of the Vatican Vigilanza and forty halberdiers of the Swiss Guard."

The archbishop was stupefied. "But, Your Eminence, you told me thirty. Do you really mean to send fifty more? Is it really necessary? Our people are making their own superb arrangements. There is really no need—"

"I'm sorry, but it is an absolute requirement."

"Do you mean, Your Eminence," faltered the archbishop, "that we must find accommodation for fifty more people for the night of Holy Saturday?"

Out-of-doors the women had started another chant. They were Americans, but they were calling in badly accented Italian for the ordination of women—"*Ordinazione delle donne! Ordinazione delle donne!*"

Hugging the phone closer to his lips, the archbishop raised his voice and pleaded, "Surely, Your Eminence, they are unnecessary, beyond a few ceremonial members of the Swiss Guard?"

"My dear archbishop, I have been leaning over backward to make it possible for the holy father to be present at your

Easter morning ceremony honoring the founding of the cathedral. It is entirely contrary to custom. In my personal opinion he should not be making such a journey at such a time. Therefore, unless we can be utterly certain that he will be surrounded by his usual security forces, we cannot and will not permit him to attend."

"*Allora*," sighed the archbishop. "In that case we will find room for them all."

"And the choir, you must find places for the sixty children in the choir."

"The choir? What choir?"

"The young people who are to sing on the steps of the cathedral. They will be taking the pledge of purity, *il voto di purità*, the promise to abstain from narcotic addiction. A song has been composed for the occasion."

The women under the windows of the palace were screaming another slogan over and over again, *Matrimonio per preti! Matrimonio per preti!* The archbishop wiped his forehead with his sleeve. Marriage for priests, how scandalous. "You mean sixty young children will be standing on the steps of the cathedral with His Holiness? But, Your Eminence, all the places of honor have been assigned. I would have to dislodge people of prominence, officers of the comune, distinguished citizens."

"Then please do so. After all, you must see that the holy father's anti-drug crusade is of paramount importance?"

The archbishop was now completely cowed. "And housing, Your Eminence? All these young people, they too must be housed?"

"Naturally."

The archbishop hung up in a panic, and put his head in his hands. Under his window there were terrible percussive noises. What were those women doing now?

Later on he understood, when the priest who was his secretary brought him a long sheet of paper. Like that quarrelsome person Martin Luther, the noisy women had hammered a list of their pugnacious demands to the door of the palace with carpet tacks.

Demand number one was ordination for women; number two, marriage for priests; number three, birth control for wedded couples; number four—

The hammering had been terrible, as though the tacks were being driven right into his skull. The archbishop had a splitting headache.

CHAPTER 42

....

. . . I—I alone—
Must gird me to the wars—rough travelling . . .
Inferno II, 3–4.

Julia was fascinated by the pig Graziella. She liked her animal innocence and helplessness better than the swaggering *machismo* of Raffaello, Pancrazio and Carlo. And they were alike in being prisoners, Julia and the pig.

She had been a captive for a week. It felt like a month, two months, a year. Julia leaned against the wooden bars of the pigpen door, murmuring nonsense to Graziella and scratching her back with a twig. Grunting with satisfaction, Graziella moved closer so that Julia could reach the remoter parts of her anatomy.

"*Porcellino, eh?*" said Pancrazio, and Carlo made a snuffling noise, the Italian equivalent of *oink-oink*. Idly the two of them crouched in the sunshine against the wall of the brick barn, smoking, watching their prisoner.

Julia could feel their eyes on her back. She was aware that her disfiguring pigtails had not discouraged their lively prurient interest. Raffaello was always finding excuses to touch her, to thrust his body against hers, to sit too close to her on the swaybacked sofa.

In the big ground-floor common room of the farmhouse the men played cards. It was a large dark room with ugly furniture and small windows, hazy with cigarette smoke and soot from the charcoal in the iron stove, clamorous with the din of Carlo's radio and the nearly defunct television set. The next room was the kitchen, where Tina prepared the

meals, keeping up a rapid fire of talk with her husband Egidio.

On rainy days they stayed indoors. Julia sat on one of the folding chairs, flipping through magazines belonging to Raffaello and Pancrazio. With gestures she asked for needle and thread, and mended a sofa cushion. She repaired a loose leg of the card table, after making a twisting motion with her hand to show that the job required a screwdriver—a simple domestic feat that aroused great amusement. Sometimes she leaned back sleepily on the sofa and watched as the men dealt the cards and fanned them out and cursed and laughed like cardplayers the world over.

Occasionally she joined them at poker. No speech was needed. She held up her fingers to say how many cards she wanted, and pushed into the center the pebbles that were poker chips.

But she listened carefully, straining her ears to separate the careless stream of talk into words she could understand. Sometimes she knew they were talking about her. Their eyebrows shot up, they snickered and cast sidelong glances in her direction. Blandly she paid no attention. But when the word *Pasqua* was repeated, she stared at her cards and listened. *Pasqua* was Easter. The word kept coming up. Why were they talking about Easter?

Slowly, very slowly, February became March. The weather turned springlike and mild. Wildflowers sprang up in the olive groves, and the green shoots of *iris pallida*. Tiny pink leaves opened on the grape vines like babies' hands.

Tina and Egidio were busier than ever. With a rotating blade pulled by his tractor Egidio dug up the kitchen garden. Tina planted it. The fertilizing of the vineyards and olive groves went on and on.

Julia envied them their work in the open air. One day she made a dumb show of feeding the chickens, and Tina silently handed her the bucket. Once when Tina came storming into the house complaining about her *macchina da cucire*, her sewing machine, it was Julia who fixed it.

Signor Roberto was gone much of the time. On the rare occasions when he spent the day at the farm, Julia kept her distance. But one day he spoke to her politely, with an old-fashioned formal bow. "Good morning, Signorina. I hope you are feeling well."

Julia looked at him in surprise, grateful to hear her own language. "Oh, please," she said eagerly, "tell me why I'm being kept here. Why can't you let me go?"

He shook his head. "I'm very sorry that I cannot tell you. One day I will explain."

"It's narcotics, isn't it?" said Julia angrily. "And Ned, why did you have to kill poor Ned?" She could feel her eyes filling with tears.

Signor Roberto's face lost color. "Believe me, Signorina, there is a good reason why we keep you here. What is the word? *Una ragione ideale*, a noble reason. Some day you'll understand."

But what noble reason could there be for killing Franco and Isabella and Ned, for setting up a heroin laboratory at the school, for stealing precious objects from the museums of Florence? It was drug-trafficking—it had to be. Perhaps at Easter there would be an enormous delivery of heroin or cocaine. Perhaps millions of dollars worth of illegal narcotics were hidden right here at the farm. Vast amounts of money were stashed away in bulging suitcases, the wine tank was choked with lire, the oil jars were full of coins, a huge pot of gold was buried under the kitchen garden.

One afternoon she made a break for it.

The day was balmy, with a hazy sun halfway up the sky. Pancrazio and Carlo played a ragged kind of two-man soccer in the driveway. They kicked and shouldered the ball, bouncing it off the roof of Matteo's little Honda, chasing it into the shrubbery. They played with an awkward boyish grace. Julia sat watching them on the front step of the house. The ball ricocheted off Pancrazio's head over the wall into the farmyard, and the chickens squawked.

"Where is Raffaello?" said Julia, as they paused for a smoke.

"Raffaello?" said Pancrazio. "*Raffaello è un' elettricista. Lui, sta lavorando oggi.*"

Oh, yes, thought Julia. The little three-wheeled vehicle was an electrician's truck. Raffaello was working today. She should have figured it out for herself. He was an itinerant electrician, a big cheerful slob who left behind him a trail of tossed cigarettes and junk-food wrappers, dropped shirts and shoes discarded in the middle of the floor. Julia smiled at Pancrazio and shrugged slightly, as if she hadn't understood what he said, but never mind.

"*Ah, ecco Raffaello.*" Pancrazio and Carlo called out in greeting as the little truck came bucking up the steep road, turned into the driveway and lurched to a stop.

Raffaello did not return the greeting. Instead he leaped out and began yelling angrily. He stalked up to Carlo, and at once there was a violent argument. Julia couldn't make head or tail of it. She guessed that Carlo had borrowed Raffaello's truck and stolen something.

Now Pancrazio joined in. He and Carlo stood in front of Raffaello, chins thrust out, heads thrown back, forefingers jabbing at his chest. The three of them were all shouting at once.

The little truck stood in the driveway, throbbing slightly. Its motor was running, the door on the driver's side had been left open. Julia looked at it, and stood up slowly.

Someone threw a punch. There was a cry of pain, and then a free-for-all. Silently Julia walked to the truck and slipped into the single seat of the little cab.

No one was looking. Quickly she studied the controls, then shifted into reverse. Taking a firm hold on the wheel, she looked over her shoulder and began backing up. *Watch out, don't jerk it like that. Smoothly, smoothly.* If only she could make it to the steep slope of the stony road, she could be off and away. She could race down to the highway, then jump out and stop a car, or find a house and call the police. In the little truck she couldn't hope to outdistance the Honda on the highway. Julia had seen the swashbuckling Matteo take off in it and tear down the hill, whizzing insanely around the sharp turns.

Softly she backed up to the road. The three men were still furiously rolling over one another in the driveway. Cautiously Julia began the backward turn, but as she twisted the wheel her arm nudged the horn, and there was a loud toot.

Dismayed, she looked out to see three faces staring at her. Frantically she shoved the car into forward gear and began plunging down the hill. In the rearview mirror she could see two of them catapulting after her. Violently she raced the little truck straight down, and then began swerving around the switchbacks, fearful of going off the road. The truck had not been meant for speed on a steep grade. It was tippy on its tiny wheels. Behind her she could hear the loud honking of the Honda. Before she had gone halfway down the hill, Matteo's car caught up with her, forcing her to one side of the road. She had to bump wildly to a stop.

Raffaello was driving. Furiously he dragged her out of the driver's seat, threw her to the ground and fell on her, tearing at her clothes.

Julia fought back, but he was far stronger than she was, and wildly aroused.

Neither of them heard another car grinding to a stop. But in an instant someone was there, jerking Raffaello to his feet, smashing his face with a heavy blow that knocked him flat on his back.

Julia sat up, weeping angry tears, trying to cover herself. Gently Signor Roberto lifted her and helped her into his car. At the house she was handed over to Tina, who grimly shut her in her room.

She had come so close! In feverish disappointment Julia threw herself down on the chair beside the window and listened to the men next door. Carlo and Pancrazio were loud. Raffaello whined. Roberto's voice was threatening.

Soon the younger men fell silent. Julia listened to the deep voice. It was like Zee reading the *Inferno* in Italian. There was the same clear articulation of syllables, the same dire solemnity and awful conviction.

She was worn out. There was nothing to do but sleep.

Dragging her bed across the room, she heaved it toward the door.

She was protecting herself from Raffaello, but not only from Raffaello. In spite of his old-fashioned civility, Signor Roberto frightened her even more.

The bed would be a blockade. Its metal legs screeched across the floor. The headboard hit the door with a crash.

CHAPTER 43

■ ■ ■ ■ ■ ■ ■ ■ ■ ■ ■ ■ ■

Lo, the sweet siren! . . .
> Purgatory XIX, 19.

The rains of early spring fell on the hill of Bellosguardo, pattering on the tile rooftops of the villas overlooking the city, keeping everyone indoors, isolating households from one another, preventing the good sisters of the convent of La Colombaia from sowing their cabbages and lettuces. Only Signor Paschelli's white ducks paid no attention to the downpour, waddling around their little yard at the neighboring villa just as usual, paddling in the puddles.

In the Villa L'Ombrellino the roof leaked on the south side of the central wing. Lucretia and Tom O'Toole put buckets under the dripping ceiling of the Antechamber of the Grand Vizier. Every now and then they had to run upstairs to empty them out the window. Once they forgot, and the buckets overflowed and water poured through the floor into the Pavilion of the Concubines, gurgling down the walls below the barrel vault, making reflecting pools over the huge word *SALVE* on the mosaic floor.

The last quarter of the school year was underway. In June, by the solemn decree of the trustees, the doors would close forever.

Zee felt partly responsible for the failure of the school, and his guilt added to his anxiety.

Homer Kelly too was depressed, his natural cheerfulness at low ebb. Walking his motorbike up the muddy driveway, his shoes caked with yellow clay, he reflected that life was continually in psychic motion, perpetually sagging back toward sadness. One's despondency might be succeeded by a period of liveliness and action, a time that might be called happy—and then melancholy slipped under the door again and climbed the stairs.

His exploratory journeys with Zee were a relief. Together, working their way northward in the Saab, they pooled their anxieties, looking at them from different angles. To Homer, Zee's view of the world was European—subtle and complex—while to Zee, Homer had an American rawness, a fresh vision of reality that was hairy and rough and charged with blood.

For the last two weeks they had been puttering along Via Faentina, talking to the carabinieri in the little towns strung out along the Torrente Mugnone, one of the little streams rushing down to the Arno from the slopes of the Appenines.

The carabinieri were a military police force, often working in tandem with the polizia. Together Zee and Homer visited the Comando Gruppo Firenze on Via Ognissanti, hoping to learn which little towns were served by this branch of the Italian security forces.

"Have you seen this woman?" said Zee, showing his photograph of Julia to the brigadier in San Domenico. The picture showed Julia Smith and Ned Saltmarsh standing in front of the entrance to the Bargello, grinning at the camera. The snapshot was worn at the edges, as though it had been handled many times.

"*Questa?*" said the brigadier, putting his finger on Julia. He showed it to his fellow officer. "Isn't that Giorgio's girlfriend?"

The other officer looked at the picture, then glanced up at Zee. "Is she pregnant? Giorgio's girlfriend is—" he made a huge shape in the air in front of his uniform.

Zee laughed, disappointed, and shook his head.

But in Fiesole they seemed to have hit pay dirt. Yes, yes,

the captain had seen the woman. "She is very pretty, *vero?*"

"*Si, si,*" gulped Zee, his heart beginning to beat.

The captain made an imperious gesture. "*Venite!*" he said, and at once they were herded out-of-doors into the rain. "*Avanti!*"

Down the street they went in a platoon behind the striding figure of the captain. Homer galloped along in the rear, trying to hold his pop-open umbrella over Zee, who kept rushing forward into the downpour. There was a flash of lightning and a sound of thunder like potatoes falling out of a sack.

At the corner the captain made a left-face and threw open the door of a shop. It was a beauty parlor, an *Istituto di Bellezza*. Two young matrons were having their hair clipped and flounced. The two *estetiste* looked up in surprise, and then one of them began chattering at the captain, her red lips smiling, her eyes heavily made up with mascara.

"Speak in English to my friends," urged the captain, grinning at her.

"Hi!" she responded obediently. "You *Americani?* Ah, I love *Americani!*" She rolled her eyes romantically. "Roberto Redford!"

Zee was crestfallen. Homer shook his head mournfully at the captain, who shrugged, raised his eyebrows, kissed the hand of the pretty hairdresser, gazed at himself in the mirror, smoothed his hair, adjusted his captain's hat, and promised to come back for a manicure.

In the car Homer stared gloomily at the drenched houses looming up beside the road, the soggy women and children waiting for Bus 12, the girl in a fur coat whizzing by on a Vespa, and then he explained the incident theoretically to Zee. "The captain is just like Dante, you see, Zee. He looks at the entire universe in the person of the girl he loves."

CHAPTER 44

■ ■ ■ ■ ■ ■ ■ ■ ■ ■ ■ ■ ■ ■

. . . thou hast thy back turned to the thing.
                    Paradiso VIII, 96.

Inspector Rossi had assembled the entire master plan for the security of His Holiness. The thing was finished. Perhaps now he could get back to work in earnest on the pursuit of murderers in the city of Florence—the baby-strangler, the homicidal rapist, the Dante-quoting killer at the American school, and the woman who had finished off her husband with homemade sausage—*sanguinaccio* packed with bread crumbs, blood, candied fruit and strychnine.

The master plan was bound into a folder and sent by messenger to the Banca degli Innocenti. Rossi felt the task of preparation slipping from his shoulders. Now there would be no further duties until the Easter celebration was actually at hand.

But next day he received a note from Signor Bindo, written by the bank manager himself in his small round hand—

Spettabile Ispettore,
Your plan is magnificent. There is another urgent matter I wish to discuss with you. Please come to see me at the bank.

                    Distinti saluti,
                    Leonardo Bindo

229

And that afternoon in the bank manager's office, another burden descended on Rossi's shoulders.

"I appeal to you, Inspector," said Signor Bindo. "You must come to the aid of our saintly archbishop. He's deeply troubled by some of the requirements for the Easter celebration."

"Troubled?" faltered Rossi, filled with awe. "The archbishop? You've been talking with His Excellency, the archbishop?"

"Oh, yes. The archbishop and I are jointly in charge of the festivities."

The inspector goggled at Bindo, his Adam's apple working up and down. It was true that he often felt close to the Archbishop of Florence, whenever he accepted the body of Christ from the old man's own hands in the cathedral. At the same time there was a great distance between them, as though the archbishop floated high above him in the celestial spaces of the great dark dome, while he, Marco Rossi, knelt on the floor, earthbound.

Bindo looked at him shrewdly. "You see, Inspector, the blessed man has been given the task of finding sleeping quarters for the visiting security forces from the Vatican for the night of Holy Saturday. My suggestion to him has been that the Questura should simply commandeer enough spaces in the city—in office buildings near the Duomo, in private houses. It would be like billeting soldiers during wartime. I will give you an official order from the comune. So far we have room for only thirty in the palace of the archbishop. Now there are to be fifty more. Not to mention the Roman schoolchildren. Sixty young people and their choirmistress will need safe and comfortable places to sleep on the night of Holy Saturday. The archbishop has asked particularly that the most talented young officer at the Questura should be given this assignment."

"Do you mean," said Rossi innocently, "that His Excellency asked for me?"

"His Excellency himself." Leonardo Bindo was quick to agree with this misunderstanding. All things could be made to serve. At once he readjusted his line of command. "You will report directly to the archbishop. Shall I arrange a meeting for tomorrow morning?"

"Oh, yes," said the inspector. He went home in a state of excitement and told his wife and children of the great honor that had come to him. Next day he entered the study of the archbishop in a mood of prayerful devotion, and knelt to kiss the old man's ring.

The archbishop was touched by this young man so old-fashioned that he didn't know the *baciamano* was rather out of date. He urged Rossi to sit down, and together they discussed the sleeping arrangements for the security forces from the Vatican and the schoolchildren from Rome.

Inspector Rossi had given the matter a good deal of thought during the night, and he had a number of suggestions—the classrooms of the university, the refectories and sacristies of the nearby churches, the public rooms in the Palazzo Vecchio. And perhaps the children could be put up in local convents where the nuns would look after them.

The archbishop's anguished expression cleared, and he held out his hands to Rossi, a smile illuminating his wasted face. "Then you will take care of the matter?"

"Certainly, Your Excellency. I will find places for them all."

"You will come back and report to me from time to time?"

"Oh, yes, Your Excellency." The inspector knelt again, and the archbishop dismissed him with his blessing.

CHAPTER 45

▪▪▪▪▪▪▪▪▪▪▪▪▪▪

Feed thy faint heart with hope, and calm thy breast. . . .
                                        Inferno VIII, 107.

After two weeks of downpour the sun came out at last. The grass shot up in the L'Ombrellino garden. There were new green leaves on the vine-covered wall and sudden growth on the hedges, blurring the sharp outlines Franco had cut last fall. Along the parapet the naked goddesses were virginal and fresh. Even the planets arching high overhead were moist and swollen in their brightness.

The Dante class was exploring the same planets, floating upward through them one at a time, experiencing Paradise. At the moment they were poised in the Heaven of Mars with warrior saints and images of fortitude.

Zee spent most of the hours outside class in the company of Homer Kelly, visiting all the logical establishments along Via Faentina—the industrial electricians, the electrico-mechanical electricians, the household electricians, the automobile electricians, the suppliers of electrical equipment. All of them had permanent addresses, tiny shop fronts or greasy garages where they leaned over the hoods of cars installing fuse boxes or tracing broken wires. Their vehicles were vans or ordinary automobiles, not little three-wheeled trucks.

Homer Kelly went along on these expeditions partly from his customary sense of adventurous curiosity, but mostly out of a sportsmanlike sympathy for his crazed friend

Zee. But one day Joan Jakes took a phone call that shook things up.

"Hello?" said the voice on the phone. "Hey, who's this? Joan Jakes? Oh, hi, how are ya? Hey, listen, this is Kevin."

"Kevin? Kevin Banks?"

"Right, it's me. You know, like I left last month."

"Yes, we noticed that," said Joan caustically. "Are you coming back?"

"Oh, hell, no. Hey, listen, here's what I'm calling about, like I left my camera behind. Did you find it? I mean did somebody see it on top of the wardrobe?"

"You left a good many things in your room," said Joan acidly. "Are you coming back for them, is that it?"

"Oh, God, no. But my camera, you know, like it cost plenty. I mean it was a high school graduation present. My dad'll be really pissed off if I lose it. So could you mail it to me? I'm in Mykonos, you know, in Greece? Listen, you got a pencil?"

"Kevin, wait, listen. Is Julia there? Would you put her on the phone?"

"Julia?" There was a puzzled silence. "You mean Julia Smith?"

"Of course. Isn't she with you?"

"Hell, no. Why should she be with me?"

"She's not with you? She didn't leave school with you?"

"God, no. Well, I mean, like I said good-bye to her. I mean she wasn't packing up or anything. Maybe she decided I was doing the right thing, and took off herself. I don't know what the hell she did. So listen, could you send the camera right away? Here's my address, okay?"

When she hung up, Joan passed along the news that Kevin and Julia had apparently wearied of the school simultaneously, but had not, after all, gone away together. Afterward she was sorry, when she saw how much the news delighted Zee.

"You mean, she wasn't with him? I knew it, I knew it!"

"I think it's all the more disappointing," said Joan severely, "her leaving by herself without a word."

At once Zee called Homer Kelly, and woke him from a cozy nap in his room at the pensione. Homer had spent an exhausting morning with Zee in the Saab, bouncing up and down on country roads, hitting his head on the ceiling of the car, telling himself it was a wild-goose chase.

Homer was fascinated to learn that Julia had not gone off with Kevin Banks. It dawned on him that Zee was behaving like Dante in the *Paradiso*. No longer was he led by pure reason (in the guise of his kindly and learned friend Homer Kelly). Now he was on the trail of the heavenly Beatrice (in the shape of the beautiful Julia) and the sheer nuttiness of revelation was guiding his footsteps. Well, revelation was supposed to illuminate a higher truth than reason, so maybe the man was right after all.

"You know, Zee," he said, sitting up in bed, "you're wearing me down. All your original assumptions were ridiculous, but your corollaries are impeccable. I mean you've put together a patchwork that's pure piffle, but I'm beginning to believe in it. What's next?"

"Would you call Inspector Rossi? He might take Julia's disappearance more seriously if he knew she didn't just go off with Kevin Banks. Then he might be more cooperative. He's been *un poco* absentminded lately. I don't know what's got into him."

CHAPTER 46

▪ ▪ ▪ ▪ ▪ ▪ ▪ ▪ ▪ ▪ ▪ ▪ ▪ ▪ ▪ ▪

Nay, by another path thou needs must go
If thou wilt ever leave this waste. . . .
                              Inferno I, 91, 92.

Time was growing short. Julia didn't know the date of Easter, but by mid-March she knew it must be soon. Her conviction was even stronger that something appalling was about to happen. There was increasing tension among the younger men at the farmhouse. They were louder than usual, quarrelling and erupting in nervous laughter. Sometimes the arrogance of Matteo Luzzi resulted in furious confrontations. Matteo regarded himself as the social superior of Carlo and Pancrazio, but, lacking the sober authority of Signor Roberto, he failed to command their allegiance. Carlo refused to wash his car. Pancrazio would not even light his cigarettes or surrender to him the best portion of Tina's *pollo arrosto*.

There were passionate exchanges of obscenities. Julia listened with ironic attention, and salted them away as curiosities.

Raffaello was gone, along with his three-wheeled truck. But Signor Roberto now seldom left the farm. He made no demands on Julia, but she tried to avoid him just the same. She told herself that his outrageous good looks made no difference to her, but she was wary of her own vulnerability. She found a way to make her pigtails stand even more fiercely on end. She wore layers of oversized shirts under her burly padded vest and covered it with a drab apron of Tina's.

Her offer to help with the outdoor work had been taken

up with a vengeance. One day Tina opened the door of the pigpen, handed Julia a bucket and scoop, and jerked her head at the pig, saying roughly, "*Faccia pulizia!*"

Clean it up. Perhaps it was a punishment for trying to run away. Julia made no complaint until Tina locked her in the brick shed that was Graziella's pen. Then she looked out in protest at Pancrazio, and said, "Hey!" and thumped on the door.

Sympathetically he peered through the window and spoke rapidly in Italian. Julia shook her head.

Pancrazio acted it out. "*Porcellino scappa,*" he cried, making lickety-split motions with his arms. Then he grasped at the air and fell down comically with an imaginary pig in his arms.

Julia laughed. Apparently she wasn't the only one who

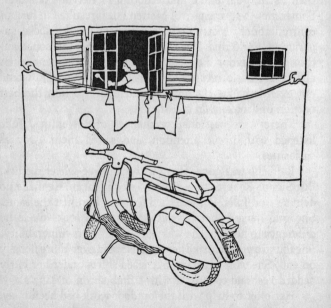

had tried to run away. So had Graziella. Tina had locked the door because the pig could burst through the latch.

The job was vile. Julia swept, scraped, scooped, and spread clean hay.

One day the cleaning of the pigpen led to a discovery. From the rear window she could see a part of the farm that was otherwise invisible, a walled courtyard below the level of the other buildings. There were voices below the window, and the noise of a steady thudding.

Standing up to scatter fresh straw, she glanced out the window and saw Roberto in the lower courtyard firing at a target. Matteo was looking on.

The gun was a small weapon with a fat barrel. Roberto fired again. There was no loud report, only a thud and rattle as the invisible projectile struck the metal target. *Thud-whang. Thud-whang. Thud-whang.* It dawned on Julia that the thick barrel must contain a silencer, a sound-suppressor like the muffler on a car.

She watched as Roberto fired and fired and fired, then replaced the clip and fired again, while Matteo murmured "*Bene,*" and "*Bravo.*"

She should have been distressed, frightened, she knew that. She should have remembered the deaths of Franco and Isabella, the murder of Ned. Instead there was only the crude satisfaction of gazing down at Roberto without being seen. The man had a kind of captivating, unselfconscious grace, even in the performance of a violent act. For once she could drink her fill.

Little by little, Julia and Roberto had begun to speak to one another. Roberto's English was flawless, his vocabulary fitted out with esoteric words and phrases. He was grave and scholarly. He spoke of Dante, and the translation of *The Divine Comedy* by Longfellow that had been imposed on him in an English school in Switzerland. He described the archeological investigation of the ancient church beneath the

Cathedral of Florence. Diffidently he introduced the subject
of the political influence of the Holy See.

His appearance was distracting. Julia couldn't get used
to it. The first overpowering impact always repeated itself.
Zee, she told herself, *remember Zee.*

Remember Zee. One day she snatched at the chance to
write him a letter.

She had no paper, no pen, no stamp, no way of getting
a letter into the mail.

But Roberto, she knew, wrote letters.

Today he was sitting at his desk in the corner of the big
room in the farmhouse, writing one after another. Julia
watched as he folded each letter, thrust it into an envelope,
wrote an address, swabbed a stamp with glue from a jar and
pounded it down with his fist.

He had finished three, and now he was beginning another. Once he glanced up and caught Julia's eye. She flushed
and looked away. He must not think she wanted to look at
him. It was only the pile of letters she was interested in, but
he mustn't know that either.

Julia bent her pigtailed head and looked at her muddy
shoes, aware that she was lying to herself. It was Roberto,
not the letters, she wanted to look at. She was intensely
aware of him as he rose and moved toward her. She glanced
up, and their eyes met, and she knew that hers betrayed her.
He went past her, his trouser leg lightly brushing her knee,
and knelt to open the doors of the stove.

His letters lay on the desk, unattended. Standing up
slowly, Julia glanced at Carlo and Pancrazio. They were playing *briscola,* idly tossing the cards on the table, their attention fixed on the game. She moved closer to the desk, picked
up a stamp and an envelope and thrust them into her pocket,
while Roberto emptied the bucket of charcoal on the
dying fire.

When he rose and went back to the desk she was sitting

once again in her chair, her head bowed over one of Carlo's magazines.

The task was still only half done. Julia waited until the cardplayers wearied of their game. When they sank down in front of the television, trying to coax out of it some kind of picture, she got up and moved past the card table, closing her fingers on the pencil stub and the slip of paper on which they had been keeping score.

Upstairs after supper she got to work at once, pulling the chair up to the window, using the sill for a table. Gripping the tiny pencil, writing very small, she filled every square inch of the scrap of paper with a doll-sized letter. "A farm north of the city, I think. The driveway is a left turn." She spoke of Roberto and Matteo, of Raffaello and his truck, of Pancrazio and Carlo, of Tina and Egidio. Something was going to happen on Easter Sunday, something awful, something criminal, something for which these men were making enormous plans.

There was no room to say anything tender. Wildly she scrawled LOVE across the entire small sheet, and slipped her letter into the envelope. Then very carefully she wrote the address—

> *Professor Giovanni Zibo*
> *Villa L'Ombrellino*
> *Piazza di Bellosguardo*
> *Firenze.*

Lastly she licked the flap and rubbed it tightly closed and put on the stamp. Then she admired the finished product. It was a genuine letter. It would go through the mails like any other letter, and arrive at its destination.

If only an official in the local post office could get his hands on it, and bang down on it the gadget imprinting the name of the town, the seal of form upon the wax of matter.

The *whatness* of the place, its essence, the name that made
it different from all other places in the world, from all other
olive-covered hillsides in Italy, would be solidly imprinted.
Like God, the postmaster would whang down the seal, and
the town would stand revealed, unique and individual for all
to see.

Next morning she ran down the stairs after Pancrazio
with her envelope under her shirt, and glanced eagerly at
Roberto's desk. His pile of letters was still there. Swiftly she
inserted her own at the bottom. Before turning away she
glanced at the address of the topmost letter. It was only a
box number in Florence.

She had done all she could. Now everything would de-
pend on whether the letters were mailed in a bundle—shoved
all at once into a letter box—or dropped one by one into the
slot. Her only hope was a careless mass mailing, not an
inspection of each letter, not a terrible individual holding of
each one in Matteo's hand before he allowed it to fall into
the lovely darkness inside the box.

This morning Matteo was not at the farm. Would the
trip to the post office be delayed until he came back? Julia
watched as Signor Roberto entered the room, smiled at her,
pulled on his long narrow coat and then—good!—swept up
the stack of letters, spoke sharply to Pancrazio, and went
out. She could hear his car starting up outside, grinding over
the pebbled drive, moving out of earshot.

Her letter to Zee was on its way—or else it wasn't.

In reckoning its chances, imagining only two possible
fates, Julia had failed to think of a third. When Roberto
pushed the letters into the mailbox outside the post office in
the nearby town of Caldine, he dropped the entire bundle
at once, but as he thrust it into the narrow slot, the last
letter left his hand a fraction of a second later than the rest.
He saw, just too late, that it had been written by someone
else. In that instant he read the name *Professor Giovanni
Zibo*, and he knew at once what had happened.

Roberto turned and stared at the big glass window of the post office. Through it he could see the clerk behind the counter looking back at him.

The post office clerk in Caldine was a voluble old man with a wild fringe of grey hair encircling his bald head. He took great interest in his work. Officiating behind the counter day after day, week after week, year after year, he had his finger on the pulse of the world. His little office was a nerve center for all Italy. Letters for destinations in all five continents had gone through his hands.

Thus it wasn't surprising that he took a personal interest in the stream of correspondence passing under his nose every day. So great was his curiosity that he regretted the laws governing the privacy of the mails. The stuff of high drama was hidden under those innocent white envelopes—important business matters, high concerns of state, scandalous revelations, family intrigues and secret love affairs—who could tell what impassioned endearments burned beneath the plain envelopes with their simple addresses?

The clerk knew for a fact that the local baker was carrying on a clandestine love affair by letter with a woman in Prato, although he was a married man with six children. And Signora Freschi, who kept a dress shop, wrote to her son at a box number in Rome, but the clerk happened to know that it was the address of a maximum security prison.

This morning the clerk was in for a treat. When he caught sight of the tall good-looking signore with the beard and the handsome head of grey hair, the man was standing outside the post office with his hand on the mailbox, looking irresolute. The clerk watched avidly as the gentleman dropped his hand and walked in the door.

But Signora Mossi was first in line, mailing a package.

"Ah, Signora," said the clerk, "it's for your daughter, who married the artist in Pisa. Has he sold any paintings yet? I thought she was going to marry the *programmatore di computers*, a man with a future. Artists, who knows what will become of them?"

"I told her a thousand times," said Signora Mossi, "she was making a mistake. Her own brother is a *programmatore* in Milano. He's doing very well. He has a beautiful apartment, with a television all over the wall." She made a sweeping gesture to show the immense size of her son's television set.

Behind her the tall man made a slight impatient gesture. The clerk winked at him, said good-bye to Signora Mossi and slapped the counter in welcome. *"Buon giorno, Signore! Dica pure?* What can I do for you?"

At once Signor Roberto took advantage of the clerk's all-embracing interest in the human race. "Forgive me, I'm all apology," he said effusively, "but I've posted a letter by mistake. I shouldn't have done it. I wrote in a hurry, and now I'm sorry. I shouldn't have said the things I wrote in the heat of anger. My letter is in the mailbox outside. Would you be so good as to open the box and give it back to me? I'm so ashamed! The letter would destroy the happiness of my—ah—my sister and my brother-in-law."

"Ah, family quarrels," said the postal clerk, "how well I know them. I too have written angry letters, only to tear them up with the return of reason." Beaming in his forgiveness of the human failings of his customers, he led the way outside.

The key turned in the lock, and the front of the mailbox fell open. It was nearly empty. Only the letters Roberto had mailed himself lay on the bottom. Eagerly he reached for them. "Yes, yes, those are mine."

But the clerk snatched them first, and began running through them inquisitively. "Please, Signore, as soon as they're in the box they're the property of the Italian Civil Service, no longer yours. Which of these letters is it? I see they're all addressed to the same box number, not to a person." Slowly, infuriatingly, he shuffled through them, examining them one by one. "Ah, it must be this last one, addressed in pencil. But perhaps it's not yours. It's in another hand."

"But that's it! Give it to me. The others were written by someone else. I was merely mailing them as a service."

The clerk stared at the controversial letter. "You have a fine hand, Signore. Swift but clear, almost a lesson in calligraphy. Have you had lessons in artistic penmanship? I myself—"

"Please," said Roberto impatiently, "may I have it? It's of the utmost importance that it not go through the mail."

The clerk read the address, savoring the situation, wringing from it the last drop of satisfaction. He was already concocting the phrases with which he would describe the episode to his wife, the story of the distinguished-looking stranger who regretted mailing an angry letter. "*Signor Giovanni Zibo,*" he read aloud from the envelope, "*Villa L'Ombrellino, Piazza di Bellosguardo, Firenze.* Ah, Bellosguardo! I've been there many times, visiting my friend Filippo Lascola. He owns a camera shop on Via Foscolo." Teasingly the clerk held the letter to his breast while he extolled the beauties of Bellosguardo.

At last he handed it over with a little bow. "Hereafter, my friend, we will not write in haste, *vero?*"

When Signor Roberto returned from mailing his letters, Julia looked at him furtively, fearing chastisement. If he had discovered her letter among his own, she would surely be locked up in her room, or punished in some other way.

But he did nothing. His eyes encountered hers, and glided away.

Her spirits soared. Her trick had worked. He had mailed her letter with the rest, and it was now in the impersonal hands of the Italian postal service. Before long she would be rescued. Her heart thumped, and she imagined an invasion of police, a rush of armed men, and Zee looking for her, calling her name.

▪ ▪ ▪ ▪ ▪ ▪ ▪ ▪ ▪ ▪ ▪ ▪ ▪ ▪

CHAPTER 47

What? broken thus, the laws of the Abyss?
                              Purgatorio I, 46.

It was Lady Day, March twenty-fifth, the celebration of
the Annunciation, the day when the unspotted Virgin
had conceived her child.

Leonardo Bindo attended the special services in Santissima Annunziata, where the miraculous picture of the Virgin
was entwined with a garland of lilies.

When he returned to his office there was a fat manila
envelope on his desk. *O Dio mio!* Bindo was sick of the
whole thing. Opening the envelope, he took out a handful
of letters from Roberto Mori. The scum from Milwaukee
had collected them from the post office box as usual, and
sent them on to the bank.

Now Bindo wished he had not been so artful. In the
beginning he had relished the amusing deception. He had
invented a whole set of five imaginary prelates at the Vatican,
every one of them eager to correspond with valiant Father
Roberto Mori. Bindo's collection of stationery had been ac-
quired from a friend in the Vatican Printing Office, and it
was various and wonderful. There were splendid letterheads
for the Congregations for Divine Worship, the Causes of
Saints, and the Evangelization of Peoples. There was a set
for the Sacred Apostolic Penitentiary Tribunal.

"Caution, my young friend," pleaded the grave old cardinal in the Council for public affairs, the one who had begun
the correspondence with Father Roberto.

Ponte Santa Trinita

"Your gallant action will restore the damaged papacy to itself," wrote the political cardinal.

"Your name may never be known to history, but it will live in our prayers of thanksgiving," promised the eloquent cardinal.

"How I wish we could meet and clasp hands in friendship!" exclaimed the affectionate cardinal.

"Even the Vatican cats are with you," joked the witty young diocesan bishop who was Roberto's favorite.

Five distinct correspondences, it was too many! Bindo had burdened himself with the boring duty of writing letters in three different hands and on two separate typewriters. It was tiresome, exhausting his capacity to invent new raffish phrases couched in the dignified language of the Holy See.

Impatiently he tore open the new batch of letters from Father Roberto. They were just like all the others, long handwritten outpourings to the five anonymous prelates with whom the idiot thought he was corresponding. Impatiently Bindo waded through the high-flown language, the protestations of lofty purpose and dedication. The poor *sciocco* thought himself part of a worldwide conspiracy. The man was a fool.

Bindo tore all the letters in two and dumped them in the wastebasket. Thank God he would no longer have to reply. Roberto would expect nothing in return, time was now so short.

But Bindo had a different sort of letter to write. Winding a sheet of paper into his typewriter, he rattled off a command to Matteo Luzzi, and sweetened it by tucking it into a big envelope with a huge wad of hundred-thousand-lire notes. The inflation of the coinage was a nuisance, an anachronism that he, as a progressive man of business, complained about all the time. One couldn't pay anyone a substantial amount of cash without using an attaché case.

Hurrying out of the bank, Bindo trotted around the corner and mailed the envelope to Matteo in Caldine, thrusting it into the mailbox with his own hands.

Matteo received it two days later. He was overjoyed. The money was an advance payment for services yet to be performed, a task so dangerous that he could surely expect a bonus. Now he counted the money and put it into a zippered case.

At once it began to burn holes in the vinyl covering of the case.

Matteo had been warned not to show his face in Florence except for reasons of the gravest urgency, but now the temptation was too great. He put on his mirrored aviator glasses, his sharp new leather-look coat and silver-toed shoes, climbed into the rented Honda and took off.

On the outskirts of the city he was cautious enough to park the car and take the bus the rest of the way to the

Maserati showroom on Lungarno Francesco Ferrucci. Swaggering in, he soon impressed the principal salesman with his obvious intent to buy. It didn't take long. Within half an hour, after leaving a massive deposit, he was test-driving his dream car. It was low slung, scarlet, vicious, magnificent.

Matteo knew a stunning girl with an apartment in the neighborhood of Piazza Beccaria. Why not take her for a ride? Swiftly he zoomed across Ponte San Niccolò and swerved into a parking place in the square. Jauntily he swung open the car door and got out, frowning as became the owner of such an expensive car. Something fell off the front seat as he stood up, a crumpled piece of paper.

It was the letter from Signor Bindo. Bending down to retrieve it, Matteo stood up to find himself looking into the clear hazel eyes of an officer of the polizia.

"Matteo Luzzi?" said Inspector Rossi.

"No, no, you are mistaken. My name is Valenti, Pasquale Valenti." Fumbling in his pocket, Matteo took out one of the phony cards of identification supplied by Signor Bindo.

Inspector Rossi looked at the tiny picture on the card. He had never seen Matteo in person, only in the drawing provided by Professor Zibo, which remained in his wallet at all times. Now he took out the drawing and looked back and forth between the picture and the man who called himself Pasquale Valenti.

"Please, would you remove your glasses?"

He looks like the angel Gabriel, Signor Kelly had said. It was true that this man had a charming boyish face, but there was a slyness about his expression that was far from angelic.

And unfortunately Inspector Rossi was beginning, at thirty-six, to think younger men all looked alike. One *ragazzo* with a dark mustache was very much like another. Reluctantly he handed back the driver's license and watched Valenti swagger away.

A noisy street sweeper was rumbling and coughing along the pavement. Valenti dodged past it, dropped a piece of paper in its path, and turned into a side street.

The sweeper rumbled closer, its brushes whirling. Two merchants rushed out of their shops, vigorously wielding brooms, sweeping trash into the gutter, sending up clouds of dust.

Idly Rossi watched the brushes suck up the debris. The sweepings from the shops disappeared, inhaled by the powerful vacuum within the machine. At the last minute, just as the crumpled paper from the hand of the young man with the Maserati was about to be swallowed, Inspector Rossi darted forward impulsively, snatched it up and leaped back out of the way.

At once the driver of the sweeper slapped open his folding door and shouted at him. Rossi merely returned to him the knifelike grin that sliced his face in half.

Wheezing and growling, the huge machine rolled out of the square. The inspector unfolded the piece of paper and read it carefully.

It was very short—

Luzzi: After Roberto has finished, remove him, during the Explosion of the Cart.

At once Inspector Rossi looked up and stared wildly around the square. The owner of the Maserati had disappeared.

Swiftly Rossi found a phone booth from which he could keep an eye on the car, and called the Questura. Within five minutes a small army of fellow officers drove up, their sirens howling.

He stationed two of them near the Maserati and dispatched the others to search the neighborhood.

They did not find Matteo. Eventually a search of the scarlet car revealed that it had been borrowed from the showroom on Lungarno Francesco Ferrucci. The proprietors of the Maserati dealership were relieved to learn that their valuable fuel-injected twin-turbo convertible had not been stolen after all, nor smashed into worthless fragments in a high-speed collision.

But Inspector Rossi could not forgive himself. Matteo Luzzi had been within his grasp, and he had let him get away. And the message Luzzi had tossed at the sweeper was as menacing as it was mysterious. Who was Roberto? What was he going to finish? What did the word *remove* mean? To Rossi it could have only one sinister interpretation.

The only fully intelligible part of the message was the reference to the *Scoppio del Carro*. Everyone in Florence had an affectionate acquaintance with the Explosion of the Cart. It was an annual custom at the cathedral on Easter Sunday, the noisy setting off of fireworks on the tall ceremonial chariot drawn by white oxen. It was an ancient and beloved

Florentine tradition with roots going back to the crusades, even as far back as the time of the Romans.

Inspector Rossi went at once to the palace of the archbishop. The matter was too important to deal with by phone.

Once again he knelt and kissed the archbishop's ring. His Excellency gave him a tired smile. "What is it, Inspector?"

Rossi rose to his feet. "I may be wrong, Your Excellency. I hope so. We have evidence that something may happen on Easter morning at the cathedral during the Explosion of the Cart. The noise of the fireworks, you see, could mask another sound."

"Another sound?" The archbishop was bewildered. "What sort of sound?"

"A gunshot perhaps." Inspector Rossi explained his understanding of the letter he had snatched from the sweeping machine. His words sounded feeble in his own ears. "So perhaps, Your Excellency, we should cancel the whole celebration."

"Cancel it!" The archbishop was aghast. It was like the moment before death when one's whole life passes before one's eyes. Upon the screen of his mind he beheld in tempestuous review the whole history of his involvement with the celebration of the cathedral's anniversary, the entire chronology of his struggle to persuade the Prefect of the Pontifical Household that His Holiness should attend, the endless catalogue of the committees he had appointed, the multifarious detail of the tasks they were carrying out.

He took the hand of Inspector Rossi and squeezed it. "Inspector, I thank you for your care and concern, but I see nothing to do but go on as before. I trust you totally. My faith in your professional ability is supreme. We are in your hands, as we are in God's. Carry on. I am sure the celebration will be perfect, from start to finish." In the exhausted smile of the innocent old man there was an unaccustomed hint of sarcasm. "Perfection above all."

CHAPTER 48

▪ ▪ ▪ ▪ ▪ ▪ ▪ ▪ ▪ ▪ ▪ ▪ ▪ ▪

. . . Run! run for the pass!
        Inferno XII, 26.

Roberto Mori had given up his job with the Department of City Museums, but he still drove into Florence twice a week to perform his duties as a black-gowned volunteer with the Misericordia. He had begun as an ordinary stretcher-bearer, sitting beside the driver as they went out on calls to transport the sick and elderly to hospitals. But one day when the driver was absent, Roberto took his place, handling the job so well that he was promoted on the spot.

Little by little he acquainted himself with the old building that was the central office of the Misericordia near the Duomo. It was a warren of rooms, spaces that had been used in traditional ways for centuries—the chambers of the *Corpo Generale* and the *Magistrato*, the oratory, the study of the *Provveditore*, the room devoted to archives. There were offices, there was an ambulance garage.

And one day as he explored the building he discovered the right closet. It was full of black gowns. Swiftly he swept two from their hangers and packed them into his briefcase.

The time was very near. Roberto strove to devote himself to details, to practical matters, but the presence of the American girl at the farm was a tormenting distraction.

Daily he tutored her. She listened soberly, as he explained the need for revitalization within the church, the necessity for a massive change in direction. It was very strange. The girl had braided her hair in ridiculous pigtails, but it made no difference. She was half Rubens, half Botticelli. Her silent stubbornness captivated him. She looked at him and glanced away, then looked again with melancholy dignity. Using words that were simple and straightforward, she argued back.

Roberto suffered. Profoundly attracted, he told himself that this was the worst time in all his life for such a powerful diversion of his attention.

Penitently he read and reread the letters he had received from Rome—*Your name may never be known to history, but it will live in our prayers of thanksgiving*—*Your gallant action will restore the damaged papacy to itself*—but the face of the American girl kept blossoming from the pages, it flowered from the dense language of the typescript, it glowed from the spidery handwriting. The remote abstractions inscribed on paper could not compete with the pulsing image of the woman here at hand. Roberto whispered to himself a line from the *Paradiso*, *Love made a noose to capture me*.

Julia too was in distress. A week had passed since Roberto had taken her letter to the post office along with his own. But still there was no rush of cars, no rescuing attack by an army of policemen, no rattle of gunfire below the wall. For a few more days Julia told herself that mail service in Italy was notoriously bad. Then she began to lose hope.

Her disappointment was crushing. She had begun to be terribly afraid of Roberto—not of any cruelty or violence on his part, nothing like that. It was his kindness that was so alarming, his gentle talk, the increasing enchantment of the way he looked at her. She was clinging to the edge of a cliff, her hold slipping and slipping. Now she was hanging by the tips of her fingers.

Matteo Luzzi too was sunk in gloom, furious with his fate. He had not dared to return to Piazza Beccaria to pick up the Maserati, and therefore he had lost both the car and his hefty deposit.

On the morning of Good Friday he strode away up the hill with his shotgun to fire at birds, chickens, dogs, ducks, anything that moved.

It was a fine day, almost hot. Signor Roberto was away from the farm. Therefore Julia could unbraid her pigtails and wash her hair and sit outdoors with her face lifted to the sun. When her hair was almost dry she picked up her bucket, scoop and bushel basket, ready to begin the task of cleaning the muck from Graziella's pen.

Pancrazio had news for her. His eyes widened with excitement. *"Povere porcellino! Oggi l'uccidono."*

"What?"

Pancrazio laughed. Carlo grinned and made a slicing motion across his throat.

Julia gasped. She had forgotten that the pig was kept for a reason. Tears came to her eyes, and she went to the pigpen to look in. Graziella was trampling restlessly within her narrow cell as if she knew there was trouble ahead.

Julia found Tina at the other end of the stony little yard, hanging up wash, briskly snatching wet clothes from a basket and pegging them to the line. *"Porcellino?"* said Julia, making the gesture of a key turning in a lock.

"Un momento." Tina went on hanging towels and sheets with quick furious motions. Patiently Julia helped her, shaking out pillowcases and dish towels and Egidio's trousers, fastening them up with clothespins.

When the basket was empty Tina carried it away, coming back a moment later to open the pigpen door. *"Grazie,"* said Julia, as Tina locked her in.

The pig looked at her with its tiny white-lashed eyes, and welcomed her with affectionate snufflings. She stroked it and scratched behind its ears and ran a hand along its spine. Graziella was fatter than she had been at first, plump and tasty for the cooking. Before long she would be transformed into Tuscan salsciccia and prosciutto, and nothing would be wasted. Julia suspected bitterly that even the pig's head would be boiled and made into sausage.

"Good-bye, Graziella," she whispered. Turning away blindly Julia leaned against the wooden bars of the door, waiting to be released.

But Tina took her time. Carlo went looking for her, but Tina was nowhere to be found, and he came back shaking his head.

After half an hour Julia shook the door experimentally and gave it a shove. It wobbled, but the lock held. She studied the hinges. The pintles were loose. Carefully, using all her strength, she lifted the hinged side of the door and pulled the pintles free. Gently she set the door down again, leaning it upright against the frame.

Carlo and Pancrazio had seen nothing. When Tina came at last to draw the bolt and unfasten the padlock, Julia supported the door with one hand as she went out, then held the heel of her shoe against it as the hasp of the lock was fastened in place.

Tina noticed nothing, and hurried away. Cautiously Julia tugged at the hinged side of the pigpen door until it stood ajar.

Perhaps this was not to be Graziella's last day after all.

Carlo and Pancrazio had invented a new game. They were running around the yard, kicking at chickens. Feathers flew. The black and white ducks and the mottled hens raced frantically this way and that. The dog barked.

"Buona sera," said Julia loudly, wading through squawking chickens, beaming at Carlo and Pancrazio.

At once they stopped horsing around and stared at her in surprise. "Bella, bellissima," said Carlo enthusiastically, gazing at her. In the pigpen her hair had dried completely. Now it poured loosely over her shoulders, curling in ringlets and spirals and fine wires of gold.

Julia made the most of it. Tossing her head playfully, she began to talk boldly in Italian, using more words than she was supposed to know. *"Un bel giorno,"* she said gaily, looking up at the sky. *"Molte nuvole."*

They were delighted. *"Si, si,"* they said together, glancing up too at the white clouds floating in the blue.

Julia tried to think of other things to say, to keep their attention away from the pig. She pointed at the sun shining above the trees behind the house. *"Il sole! Gli alberi!"*

Pancrazio and Carlo were enchanted. *"Si, si! Il sole, gli alberi!"*

She pointed at the farmhouse across the valley. *"Il contadino?"*

"No, no, Signorina," said Pancrazio, laughing at her. *"C'è un podere, non un contadino."*

Julia glanced over her shoulder only long enough to see Graziella's nose emerging from the crack in the door, sniffing at the air. Intelligent pig!

Carlo reached out and stroked her hair. *"Capelli d'oro,"* he said thickly.

And then Graziella took off with a clatter of sharp hooves. They turned to see the pig rushing down the stone steps to the road below the farmyard, her white rump with its curly tail bouncing down the stairs.

"Ehi," shouted Pancrazio, running after her, yelling and waving his arms, followed by Carlo. Tina came rushing out of the house with a rope, shrieking.

Julia saw her chance. Picking up a bucket of kitchen scraps, she raced after them, crying, "Graziella, Graziella."

The pig was already halfway down the hill, dodging and swerving and squealing, scampering through the underbrush.

Julia ran off to one side, calling, "Here, pig, here, Graziella." Then, dropping the bucket, she stopped calling and gave herself up to plunging down the stony little path that was a shortcut between switchbacks. Where was the next shortcut? She found it, a white streak running off the road on the other side, and beat her way along it, down, down, half scrambling, half sliding, shoving her way through scratchy brambles that tore at her clothes, at her bare legs.

Where was the next bend of the road? The shortcut should be leading her straight to it. But the white streak had disappeared, and soon she was engulfed in twiggy underbrush bristling from the steep hillside.

Far away she could hear them shouting at the pig, and for a moment she heard the desperate panting of Graziella, a frantic snuffling, the flailing of her heavy body through the thicket. Good luck, Graziella! Good luck, Julia!

But the sharp branches that thrust themselves across her way were head-high now, entwined with briers and small saplings that tore at her arms and caught in her hair. Good God, where was the path?

In the distance she could hear the sound of a car roaring up the hill, but it was too far away. She was nowhere near the road. She must have taken a wrong turn. She was going away from the highway, not toward it.

Then off to one side all three of Graziella's pursuers shouted and cheered at once.

Poor Graziella! She was back in custody. There were cheerful yodellings and unhappy squealings as the poor doomed pig was dragged back up the hill. Then Julia heard another voice, a single sharp commanding voice calling down the hill, *"Dov' è la signorina?"*

Signor Roberto had come back. He was asking for her. Julia stopped short and listened to the guilty silence. She crouched lower. She was standing in a swampy clump of reeds, her shoes in muddy water. Bending her knees, she sank down until she was huddled near the ground, her loose hair falling all around her.

At the top of the hill they were spreading out again, looking for her. They were no longer shouting, but she could hear the heavy tread of their feet, the snapping of twigs, the whispering of underbrush as their heavy trousers thrust it aside.

Before long Roberto found her. He touched her gently, and knelt beside her. Lifting her hair, he kissed the tears on her cheek and took her in his arms. Julia pressed her face against his coat and sobbed, "Don't let them kill Graziella."

"No, no," he murmured brokenly, "Never, never."

Carlo and Pancrazio came running up, then stopped and grinned at each other, and went away again.

CHAPTER 49

■■■■■■■■■■■■■

Forward! henceforth there's but one will for two. . . .
                                    Inferno II, 139.

It was the Easter weekend, a three-day holiday.

"I'll be back on Tuesday," said Lucretia, picking up her suitcase. "I'm off to Siena."

"Siena?" said Homer Kelly. "Why Siena?"

"Well, it's going to be so crowded in Florence this year, and I've always wanted to see what Easter is like in the Cathedral of Siena. Have you been there?" And then Lucretia launched into a description of the Piccolomini Library, which was part of the cathedral, with paintings depicting the life of Aeneas Silvius Piccolomini, poet, playwright, Bishop of Siena and finally—

"Okay, okay," laughed Homer. "Have a good time."

Dorothy Orme and Joan Jakes were leaving too, taking off for Rome.

"But what for?" said Tom. "You can see the pope right here in Florence. Why go to Rome?"

"Oh, we just want to see what it's like," said Dorothy, "to be in Saint Peter's Square when he appears on the balcony and blesses the crowd."

"The balcony of the Apostolic Palace," said Joan learnedly.

Tom was going away too, spending the weekend wherever the hell he pleased, he said. On Good Friday he set off down the driveway with his backpack, heading for parts unknown.

Zee would have been left alone in the villa if Homer hadn't taken pity on him and moved back in. They had no plans for the holiday except to go right on grinding up and down Via Faentina together.

On Holy Saturday they headed for the last two towns on the bus line.

So far their explorations north of the city had been futile. They had heard no whisper of Julia. They had seen no sign of the electrician's little three-wheeled truck.

The town of Caldine seemed equally bare. They asked their questions in the pharmacy, the fabric shop, the dry cleaner, the grocery and the store that sold plucked chickens, and received only blank looks and shakes of the head. "We might as well go home," said Homer, who was starving.

"Right," said Zee gloomily. Then he cursed politely in English. "Damn, I should have cashed a check last week. Now all the banks are closed until Tuesday."

"How about the post office?" said Homer, pointing across the street. "If you buy a few stamps, they might cash a check."

It was nearly noon. The post office clerk was preparing to leave. But when two interesting-looking strangers came in the door, he grinned at them, showing a mouthful of brilliant false teeth, and went back behind the counter.

He was a cheerful old man with tufts of grey hair standing up around his bald head. At once he poured out a stream of talk, beginning with the weather. It was warm for early April, didn't they agree? How thick the crowds would be tomorrow in Florence! He for one intended to stay strictly at home. Oh, yes, it was true, the price of mailing letters today was *orribile*, was it not? Had they seen the magnificent new stamps in honor of the second year of the anti-drug crusade? No? Then, *ecco*, here they were! But, alas, he could not sell them until the official date of issue.

And then when Zee finished writing his check and handed

it across the counter, the clerk went into a paroxysm of rapture.

He beamed at Zee with all his teeth. "Ah, but you are the professor, Professor Giovanni Zibo, of the family of the handsome gentleman who was here the other day!"

"What?" said Zee.

The clerk was afire to tell his story—what an opportunity for the display of human emotion! He dallied with Zee. "Ah, but I cannot tell you. The discretion of the postal service, *vero?*"

Homer caught enough of this to recognize the clerk at once as a busybody like himself, a brother in meddlesome impertinence. He smiled at him engagingly and worked out a question in Italian. "But perhaps there are two Professors Zibo?"

"Another Professor Giovanni Zibo? No, no!" The clerk winked at Zee. "You have had some disagreement with your brother-in-law, some argument concerning your sister perhaps?"

Zee shook his head, bewildered. "I have no sister, no brother-in-law either."

To the romantic fancy of the clerk this could have only one meaning. "Aha, then it is as I suspected. He said you were his brother-in-law. Perhaps instead you are a rival in love." This time the clerk winked at Homer. "No wonder the gentleman wanted his letter back. And I gave it to him. I unlocked the box and gave it back to him, in order to prevent a lover's quarrel, a confrontation, perhaps an act of violence."

Zee stared blankly at the clerk. Homer had understood most of this frolicsome play of the clerk's imagination, and now he leaned across the counter and formulated another question. "Do you mean that someone mailed a letter and then took it back, a letter to Professor Giovanni Zibo?"

"Yes, yes." The clerk was delighted to be taken seriously. "It was addressed to a villa in Bellosguardo."

Zee gasped. "Bellosguardo? But that's right. That's

where I live, it's where I teach. But the letter, it wasn't mailed? This man, he took it back?"

"Yes, yes, he was so insistent. He had mailed it in haste. He regretted the harsh words he had written in the full spate of his wrath."

Homer's Italian vocabulary included some of the little clerk's words, and his galloping intuition supplied the rest. "Who was he," he said quickly, "this man who wrote the letter?"

"I have not seen him since. But he was unforgettable." The clerk gazed ecstatically at the ceiling. "A god, he was like a god. Or a fallen angel walking upon the earth. He was handsome like a film star, a superstar, a prince of men!" The clerk made a gesture to indicate a splendid head of hair. "His hair so thick, his beard so noble, his nose so magnificent, and, ah, his marvelous eyes, his splendid bearing!" The little clerk strutted proudly, his chest thrust out. Surely he was driving daggers into the breast of this rival for a woman's love.

"Can you describe the letter?" said Zee. "Was there a return address?"

The clerk closed his eyes and shook his head. "No return address. But the hand, ah, it was delicate as a woman's." He smiled seraphically. "I myself have dabbled in the study of handwriting. I couldn't help noticing that the As were neatly closed, and the Os as well. A rapid stroke, upright and precise. Soft and graceful, but displaying a keen sense of purpose." He leaned forward and looked at them significantly. "The handsome signore did not write it, you can be sure of that. It was the letter of a woman, his wife perhaps, written to her lover. He burned with jealousy, he was on fire to read his wife's passionate words addressed to another man."

"That's you," snickered Homer to Zee in English.

"But Homer," said Zee eagerly, "Julia's handwriting was like that, it was just like that. You know, strong but sort of delicate at the same time."

"Mary writes that way too. Lots of women write that way. Maybe it was somebody else who wrote to you. Do you know anyone around here who might have written you a letter?"

"Not a soul." Zee gripped Homer's arm. "It was Julia, I tell you. She tried to write to me, but her letter was intercepted." Zee thanked the clerk and hurried to the door, ready to ransack shops, houses, churches and outlying villages. Homer too said *Arrivederla*, and followed him out.

Left to himself the clerk went to the window to watch Professor Zibo and his tall American friend as they stood on the sidewalk staring uncertainly up and down the street. He was delighted at the dramatic consequences of his tale, most of which he had made up out of whole cloth.

But of course it might be true—the jealous husband, the tormented lovers, why not? Look how seriously they had taken it, the whole story. Ah, he had always prided himself on his understanding of the tortured depths of the human heart!

CHAPTER 50

▪ ▪ ▪ ▪ ▪ ▪ ▪ ▪ ▪ ▪ ▪ ▪ ▪ ▪

While one green hope puts forth the feeblest sliver.
                                        Purgatorio III, 135.

They stood on the narrow sidewalk as Bus 12 whizzed by, then slowed down and stopped. Three small boys leaped out, followed by a pair of old men stepping down cautiously. With a *tootle-toot* the bus started up again, narrowly missing a car hurtling past it the other way.

"It's going up the hill to the end of the line," said Homer, consulting the bus schedule. "Querciola, the place is called. Come on, we'll go there too. You know, Zee," he confessed as they got back into the Saab, "I only came along on this expedition this morning to be a pal. I thought you'd really gone bananas, but now—"

"Bananas?" Zee swerved the car out onto the road and glanced wildly at Homer.

"American expression. Probably out of fashion. I'm always ten years behind the times. Bonkers, how's that? No, bonkers is probably old-hat too. Freaked out? Flaky? Grossed out? Anyway, Zee, the point is, I've changed my mind. I think you're getting somewhere. I recognize that little clerk's description of the man who wanted his letter back. It's the guy I saw at the villa, looking down at Franco and Isabella from above. Handsome, splendid, magnificent—he was all of those things."

"He's got her," said Zee, accelerating too fast, zooming up the hill. "I know he's got her."

At the tiny settlement of Querciola they found Bus 12

parked beside a telephone booth, a dumpster, and a small waiting platform with benches.

Pulling up beside it, they could see the driver lighting a cigarette as he waited for passengers going the other way, heading for the city.

There was a restaurant at Querciola, and a meat market. A housing development burgeoned on the hill above.

"You take the restaurant," said Homer. "I'll try the *macelleria*."

"*Va bene*," said Zee, leaping out of the car.

On this balmy Holy Saturday only a beaded curtain separated the meat market from the out-of-doors. Homer walked in and stood in line behind three women waiting to be served by the white-coated girl behind the counter. Cheeses and sausages hung from the ceiling, and flat round prosciutti. Inside the refrigerated display case fluorescent lamps shone on trays of veal and little carcasses of Easter lamb.

The women looked at him curiously, but when he asked about the *elettricista* and the *bel uomo alto* and the *bella ragazza* named Julia, they shook their heads. One of them said boldly that she didn't know anything about a girl named Julia, but she had a very tall daughter who needed a husband, and then she poked Homer slyly in the chest. It was a joke.

Laughing enthusiastically, he said that to his sorrow he was already married.

By the time it was Homer's turn, three more women had come up behind him. He bought a length of sausage for two thousand lire, and watched as the girl behind the counter swept a square of oiled paper around it. She was laconic and businesslike. *"Nient' altro?"* she said as she handed him the package and the change for his five-thousand-lire note.

She meant, Anything else? *"Sì, Signorina."* Once again Homer inquired about the beautiful girl and the tall good-looking man who was so *dignitoso.*

The young woman shook her head, and then Homer asked a third question in his pigeon Italian. "Oh, Signorina, I am looking for an electrician with a little truck, a mobile electrician. Do you know of one in this neighborhood?"

The girl looked at him and opened her mouth, but the woman behind Homer was already pointing at what she wanted in the glass case. *"Mi scusi, Signore,"* said the girl. *"Sono troppo occupata."*

She was too busy. Homer glanced over his shoulder at the new faces in the line. They were all looking at him

inquisitively. "*Mi dispiace*," he said apologetically. Defeated, he turned away. But then he had an idea, and he came forward again and spoke up urgently.

The signorina, he explained, smiling all over his face, had given him the wrong amount of change.

The girl behind the counter misunderstood. Her face darkened. He thought he had been cheated! The chattering women fell silent. They stared at Homer avidly, expecting a scene.

He persisted, pleading sweetly, "You gave me too much money, you see, Signorina. *Guardi!*" And he held out a thousand-lire note.

The alteration was instantaneous. The women laughed with joy. The girl behind the counter beamed, and took the note. "Thank you, Signore. You are very kind." And then she took pity on him, and did a favor in return. "The electrician parks his little truck in back." She pointed to the rear of the shop.

"*O grazie, Signorina, grazie tante!*" Smiling toothily right and left, Homer made his escape, with the enthusiastic admiration of the women of Querciola pulsing at him from all sides.

He found Zee pacing up and down beside the Saab, dispirited. Homer clasped his hands over his head in triumph. "The electrician's truck, it's right here behind the meat market."

And there it was, waiting for them, when they hurried around to the back of the building—a little three-wheeled truck with the words *Elettricista Mobile* painted across the back in flowing script.

They stood for a moment, gazing at it. Homer repeated aloud a remark of Henry Thoreau's about the strangeness of finding something you have been looking for all your life—*One day you come full upon it, all the family at dinner.*

It was a very small truck indeed, with a one-seater cab and a tiny enclosed rear section like a round-topped trunk.

Cautiously they inspected it. The back was locked. So was the cab. They looked in the window and Zee pounced on the fact that the narrow crannies around the driver's seat were choked with trash. "You see?" he said joyfully. "Every time he opens the door, the stuff must fly out all over the place."

Back they went to the meat market and stood in line, and then Zee asked the girl in the white butcher's apron what she could tell them about the driver of the little truck.

At once she shrugged and made a face. She knew only that he had been living nearby. She did not know his name. He had wavy black hair, she said, a little nose, and he was big and strong. She took a swashbuckling posture, and then said, "*Uffa*," contemptuously. Homer suspected she had been manhandled once or twice.

"*Grazie tante, Signorina*," said Homer again. Zee bowed politely, and they went back to stare at the truck.

"It's the Easter weekend," said Zee. "He may not come back for it until Tuesday."

"But he lives around here somewhere. Now that we know the number on his license plate we can get his name and address. Is there such a thing as an automobile registry in the city of Florence?"

"Of course there is, but it won't be open until Tuesday."

"Rossi will know how to get at it."

It took Homer two hours of hanging around the pay phone at the bus stop while Zee kept watch on the truck. Munching on the sausage from the meat market, Homer called the Questura and persuaded the woman at the switchboard to give him the home number of Inspector Marco Rossi in Sesto Fiorentino.

To his surprise the inspector seemed glad to speak to him. He had information of his own he wanted to pass along. His voice was melancholy. "It is my blame. I find Matteo Luzzi, I lose him again." Then Rossi told Homer about the letter he had rescued from the street sweeper in Piazza Beccaria. "I am very afeared. Someone with the name of Roberto will be killed during the *fuoci d'artificio*—how do you say it? the fireworks, the Explosion of the Cart, the *Scoppio del Carro*. And other things may happen. I must find Luzzi."

Homer had to ask him twice for help in getting in touch with the automobile registry. The inspector seemed distracted. He was just going out, he said, to prepare for his role in the Easter vigil at his local church, and he was already late. "The registry will surely be lock up, nobody there."

"But, Inspector," pleaded Homer, "it's important."

At last Rossi reluctantly agreed to call the director of the registry and persuade him to send an assistant back to the office to look up the name and address of the owner of the vehicle with license plate FIA630021. And then, while Homer leaned against the telephone booth in Querciola, staring at the traffic darting by on Via Faentina, and Zee strolled among the trash cans behind the meat market, Rossi called the registry director at his home in Settignano, and the director called an underling in Pellegrino and ordered him to return to the office in the city.

The poor unhappy file clerk was caught just as he was climbing into a borrowed car to go on holiday with his girlfriend to a swanky hotel near Livorno. He had spent the morning shining his shoes and pressing his beige suit and arguing with his mother and squeezing money out of his brothers, and now in anguish he had to abandon his stunning girlfriend in her flouncy dress and take the bus back into town.

At last the phone in the booth at Querciola rang loudly, and the angry director of the registry barked the desired name and address into Homer's ear and hung up savagely with a fierce click.

Homer winced. "It's important, I tell you," he said to the buzzing phone, and then he went looking for Zee.

The address for Raffaello Biagi was just down the road

in Caldine. "We must have passed it again and again," said Homer, as they climbed into the Saab.

But Raffaello was not at home, and his landlady exploded when Zee asked for him.

"That thief! He left in the night last week with the television set and the clock radio. He owes me two months' rent. I called the carabinieri, but they did nothing, nothing, and then the next night Raffaello came back and took my mother's picture which was in a silver frame, and my husband's toupee, although Raffaello has plenty of hair himself. What was it, a joke? I had to change the lock on the front door. Fifty thousand lire it cost me! But I'll never get my mother's picture back." The landlady stared at them in wrath as though they were Raffaello's accomplices.

"A thief as well as a kidnapper," said Zee grimly, as they drove back to Querciola.

Homer said nothing. He was beginning to get a picture of what had happened. The kid was a common criminal, some kind of low-down rat. He had caught a glimpse of the lovely Julia, had tracked her to the villa and snatched her away, probably at gunpoint. Then he had raped and murdered her and dumped her body somewhere. Perhaps right now she was stuffed in the back of the little truck, a rotting corpse. There had been a bad smell back there behind the meat market, but perhaps it was only the odor of decaying meat in the trash cans.

Back in the parking lot they took another look at the little truck. There it was, still locked, still empty, still silent. Homer took a surreptitious sniff, smelled nothing, then wandered over to the trash bins, inhaled, and was bowled over. He smiled. So much for that repulsive theory.

It was suppertime. Homer was ravenous again. They took turns eating in the restaurant, then spent the night in the car.

It was a ghastly experience. They tried to take turns keeping watch and sleeping. But there was no way Homer could sleep. He folded himself this way and that in the back seat, groaning. Zee was not as cramped as Homer, but he was afraid to close his eyes in case Raffaello should return and drive off while they were both unconscious.

Hours passed. Homer tried kneeling, head down, then wrestled himself onto his back with his feet out the window. Zee hooked his legs over the steering wheel. They were both wide awake at midnight, fully conscious at one o'clock, more or less alert at two o'clock, drowsy at three o'clock, and sound asleep, paralyzed with exhaustion, at four o'clock in the morning.

CHAPTER 51

■■■■■■■■■■■■■■

. . . Through a deep pool a fish slips and is gone.
                              Purgatorio XXVI, 135.

The keepers of the oxen, man and wife, were up early
on Easter morning to prepare the four huge beasts
from the Val di Chiana for the procession to the
cathedral.

First the animals were scrubbed until their white hides
were spotless, then their hooves and horns were painted gold.

The flowers for the wreaths had arrived the night before
from a florist in the neighborhood. Now the wife took the
sprays of irises and roses, tulips and daisies, and wove them
into floral crowns, saying to herself, *The Holy Father will
see them. They must be more wonderful than ever before.*

"*O, ehi!*" cried the husband, urging the oxen up the
ramp into the back of a heavy truck. Then he and his wife
climbed into the cab and drove through Porta al Prato to the
house where the cart was kept.

A few early risers had gathered to see it pulled out of
the high wooden doors. Soon more people came along to
watch the harnessing of the oxen by the handlers and the
crowning of the great horned heads with flowers and the
flinging of purple robes over the broad backs and the tying
of red ribbons to the four tails.

"*Ecco!*" cried the wife proudly, pulling the ribbons into
jaunty bows and stepping back while everyone clapped and
cheered.

In the archbishop's palace, in the anteroom beside His

271

Excellency's bedchamber, a young priest laid out the ceremonial robes—the white cassock and new chasuble. He did not put out the biretta, since the archbishop would of course remain uncovered in the presence of the Holy Father.

Below the archbishop's bedroom a dormitory had been rigged up for the halberdiers of the Swiss Guard. Some of them were already getting out of bed and pulling on their elaborate striped uniforms and sticking their tousled heads out the window to look at the sky.

It was a pearly morning. Patches of blue showed through clouds that were tinted with sunrise colors. One of the guardsmen clipped on the earphones of his little radio to hear the weather report. Rain was threatened, denied, threatened again.

Six miles north of the city, Homer Kelly woke up in the grey light before dawn and moaned pitifully after his hideous night in the back of Zee's car. His knees were rammed against the back of the front seat and his head was crushed down into his left shoulder.

Unfolding himself, he gave one dazed glance out the window, then yelped in consternation.

Zee woke up instantly, sat up and cursed.

They had missed him. Within the last hour Raffaello Biagi had come for his truck and driven it away.

Zee was beside himself. Starting the car in a fury of self-recrimination, he threw it into gear, jerked forward, stalled, started again and lunged across the paved parking lot and around the meat market to the highway.

They were just in time to see Raffaello's little truck come charging up the dirt road across the street and pause while a stream of cars went by on Via Faentina. Blocked on the other side by another stream of traffic, cursing, Zee and Homer got a good look at Raffaello Biagi, a broad-shouldered young goon in a heavy jacket.

"Christ," said Homer, as Raffaello's little truck careened onto the highway and plunged away in the direction of Florence, "look at that."

The hinged door at the back of the truck was open, flapping sloppily up and down, and things were falling out—a sofa pillow, a folding chair. An entire deck of cards fluttered into the air, trailing hearts, diamonds, spades and clubs along the asphalt.

At last the entire highway was empty of traffic. Zee

growled in triumph, and whirled the Saab in a wild circle to follow Raffaello. But Homer caught his arm. "Wait, wait. Stop. It's all coming clear." Idiotically he quoted Dante, "*Then in a flash my understanding clove.* Zee, Zee, forget Raffaello. Let's find out where that driveway goes. What's going on up there on that hillside? We've got to find out. This is the place, I tell you. She's here. She must be here."

Zee gave him a startled glance. Throwing the car into reverse, he backed up insanely without looking, then clashed the gears and turned into the driveway and plunged down the steep incline.

The roadway was littered with a scattering of forks. They collided with a toaster. A lampshade sailed away. And then Zee jammed on the brake and Homer tumbled forward over the back of the front seat and banged his head against the dashboard. Without apology Zee leaped out of the car and ran forward to pluck something from the stony road. It was stuck there upright, its point thrust into the rutted clay as if to inscribe a circle in the dust.

Zee handed it to Homer, the compass that had been stolen from the museum, the one that might have belonged to Michelangelo. Then without a word he started the car again and began racing it up a rugged road of switchbacks and hairpin turns.

Rolling left and right in the backseat, Homer hung on as the car shuddered and climbed. The rough road was a mile long, growing steeper with every turn, twisting more and more sharply. Sometimes the wheels of the Saab failed to grab, and the car slipped back. Then Zee had to shift gears, accelerate and turn furiously at the same time.

Beyond the switchbacks the road went straight up the hill to a group of low buildings, golden in the slanting morning sunlight. To Zee it looked like a typical Tuscan farmhouse surrounded by walls and barns and connecting one-story structures. As they turned into the gate and stopped, they could hear a terrible screaming.

Zee leaped out of the car. "Good God, what's that?"

The noise was very loud, an awful squealing, accompanied by shouting and barking and the terrified squawking of barnyard fowl. "It's an animal," said Homer, uncoiling himself from the back seat, standing up stiffly. "Zee, it's only some kind of livestock."

Boldly they walked toward the noise. Suddenly the squealing ended. There was only the wild squawking and the breathless shouts. Pushing open a gate, they came upon a scene of carnage.

They were within a farmyard enclosure. Chickens and ducks huddled at one side, screeching in a frenzy, fluttering up into the air, flapping their wings. At the other side in the doorway of an open brick barn hung a large pig, its hind feet tied together and slung over a hook. Blood poured from its slashed throat into a bucket. A man with a bloody knife pulled the overflowing bucket out of the way, and a woman shoved an empty pail into its place. Blood spattered on the ground, then poured noisily into the pail.

The man glanced up at them and said roughly, "*Che desiderano?*"

What did they want? Zee stepped forward. He spoke in Italian, but Homer understood it, because it was the simple truth. "We're looking for someone, a young American woman, a beautiful girl with yellow hair."

The man looked down at his bucket, into which the blood was pouring more slowly, and said heavily that he didn't know. The woman, too, claimed to have seen no such person. Turning away, she ran across the yard, seized a chicken and wrung its neck, then snatched up another.

To Homer the slaughter seemed an odd occupation for sunrise on Easter Sunday, but the woman was on a killing spree and couldn't stop. The other chickens skittered away from her, screaming. Ducks quacked wildly and waddled in frantic circles.

"Come on," he murmured. Leaving the noisy blood-spattered enclosure, they walked back to the car. They had left it in front of the largest of the farm buildings. The door of the house swung open and shut, and open and shut. "Look," said Homer, "some more of Raffaello's work."

Once again there were signs of a bungled robbery. A blanket trailed down the stone steps, entangled with a man's overcoat. A broken mirror lay on its back, reflecting the sky.

They walked into the house, and Homer shouted for Julia.

There was no answer. The place felt hollow, with a kind of final emptiness, as if no one would ever occupy it in days to come, as though after they were gone it would never again know the sound of a human voice. It seemed to have no connection with the farmyard, the squealing pig, the farmer and his wife. It existed like an abandoned house in a plague-infested town.

The big ground-floor room was deserted. There was only the furniture—a rumpled sofa, a table, a collection of mis-matched chairs, a desk and an iron stove.

They ran up the stairs, calling Julia's name, and found several untidy bedrooms littered with men's clothing, a bath-room and two locked doors. Zee rattled the handles, and called out, but again there was no answer.

"Let's bash them in," said Homer.

They did. It didn't take long. The doors were old.

When they burst into the first room, there was no trace of Julia. Instead they found an arsenal of weapons.

"What are they for?" groaned Homer. "What the hell for?"

The second was orderly and empty of personal posses-sions, except for shirts hanging in the wardrobe, a few books beside the bed, and a sheet of paper lying on the table.

They looked at the paper. It was a letter. It began, *Eccellenze*, and was signed simply, *R.*

"It's a poem," said Zee, "addressed to some cardinals, I think. That's how it begins, *Excellencies*. It's a kind of farewell. It's quite good, as a matter of fact. Why would anybody write a farewell poem to the princes of the church?" Zee turned a line into English. *"May the common good prevail in the act of my hand."*

"What the hell does that mean?" said Homer.

Baffled, they went downstairs to look in other wings of the farmhouse. They found a staircase leading to three rooms on the second floor of a brick storage shed. One was heaped with potatoes, another was empty except for a tumble of wine bottles. A third was a bedroom with a window looking down on the farmyard and across the valley.

Homer went to the window and looked out. The pig still hung in the doorway of the barn, with blood dripping slowly from its slashed throat. The farmer and his wife were gone.

Zee was exultant. "Julia's room," he said. "Look." In a fever of excitement he reached into the wardrobe and showed Homer the puffy orange vest. "This was hers. And so was this, and this."

Homer snatched something from behind the radiator, and handed it to Zee. It was a yellowed piece of newspaper, a picture of Professor Giovanni Zibo.

Zee barely looked at it. "Hurry," he said. "We've got to hurry. Where are they? They've all gone somewhere. That Raffaello, he knew they weren't coming back."

They clumped down the stairs and found their way back to the car. Then Homer remembered his conversation with Inspector Rossi on the phone. His conscience smote him as he bent double to squeeze himself into the Saab. "Zee," he said, "I didn't tell you, the inspector told me yesterday that somebody named Roberto was going to be killed during the Explosion of the Cart. There was an "R" at the bottom of the poem. Do you suppose it meant Roberto? What the hell is the Explosion of the Cart?"

Zee looked at him and gasped. Wordlessly he started the car and jammed his foot on the accelerator. The Saab leaped forward and plunged down the hill. Homer reared back against the pull of gravity, lurching left and right, while Zee explained with curses that the Explosion of the Cart was an annual event during the Easter celebration at the Duomo. Today, he said, just happened to be Easter Sunday, the pope was coming, and *Gesù*, what were all those guns intended for?

"Oh, God," said Homer. "How much time have we got?"

On Via Faentina they had to slow down. The street was crowded with pedestrians. The inhabitants of the Querciola housing development were walking down the hill to Caldine to attend the first mass of Easter morning.

Homer recognized the girl who had waited on him in the meat market. There she was, arrayed like a lily of the field, walking with a young man in a pale blue suit like a delphinium, heading for the sunrise service. Some of the housewives who had been buying meat for their Easter dinners were on the road too, accompanied by husbands and children, all decked in their Easter finery.

Dexterously Zee piloted the car around them, nimbly he negotiated his way along the main street of the town of Caldine past the church. Homer could imagine the priest at midnight, taking off the black coverings from the altars, pulling down the mourning veils from the figures of the saints, lighting the votive lamps. And now as the Saab rushed by on the narrow street, the bells that had been tied since Good Friday to hush their joyous wrangling were loosed once more and allowed to ring out.

It would not be so in Florence, Homer told himself, as they passed the last of the stragglers on the other side of town and picked up speed. In Florence the pope was coming, and the Campanile bells would not ring until the end of the service in the Duomo. Only when the whole celebration was over would they peal to celebrate the resurrection of Jesus Christ.

And then Homer cursed his own stupidity. In two languages he profaned the sacred joy of Easter morning. Easter morning! Good God, Easter morning, and the pope was coming! The pope was *il Papa*, not *il papà*. The accent was reserved for the father of a family, the ordinary father of an ordinary family, not for His Holiness the pope. Isabella and Franco had been talking about the pope, not about Isabella's father. Lying there in the shattered greenhouse making love, Isabella had not said that her unfaithfulness to Alberto would kill her father, *il papà*. She had been talking about the killing of the pope, *il Papa*.

Homer explained it to Zee, between obscenities. "Oh, Jesus, Zee, what a difference an accent makes. All this time I knew it, I mean it was filed away in my head, only I was too stupid to know it. How can one nation ever understand another when the other guys talk so funny? It's the everlasting curse of Babel. Listen, remember Isabella's habit of listening at keyholes? Well, this time she heard what she shouldn't have heard, and then she passed it on to Franco. But unfortunately someone else was listening this time, the mastermind with the grey hair, the man who looks like a film star. So he had to kill the two of them, or perhaps Matteo killed them for him, because they had found out what he was up to. It was a plot to assassinate the pope."

Zee had to shout above the clashing of the bells in the next little town. "But why Julia? Mother of God, why did they take Julia?"

"I don't know why the hell, Zee," said Homer, but in the teeming confusion of his own mind as they raced along Via Faentina, across the bridge at Badia Fiesolana, past Pian del Mugnone, through Calderaio, slowing down behind tour buses, coughing in the diesel fumes, rushing on into the choked traffic of the city, he couldn't help wondering whether the beautiful Julia had really been the victim of a kidnapping after all. Perhaps she had been part of the conspiracy from the beginning.

CHAPTER 52

· · · · · · · · · · · · ·

. . . I saw entire
The threshing-floor, whereon fierce deeds are done. . . .
Paradiso XXII, 150–151.

The archbishop was beginning to tire, although he had only begun to work his way through the schedule for the day—

7:30 His Excellency the archbishop greets His Holiness and the Cardinal Prefect as they descend from the Vatican helicopter.

7:45 The sacred procession gathers in the Baptistery.

8:00 Easter mass is celebrated in the cathedral.

9:00 The recessional begins.

9:15 The Explosion of the Cart is witnessed from the steps of the cathedral.

9:25 His Holiness blesses the cathedral. School-children perform a choral celebration of the second year of the anti-drug crusade.

10:00 His Holiness departs for Rome.

So far things had gone without a hitch. The archbishop was grateful to the Cardinal Prefect, who was, he knew, responsible for the prompt arrival of the little party from the Vatican. Now as they gathered in the golden gloom of

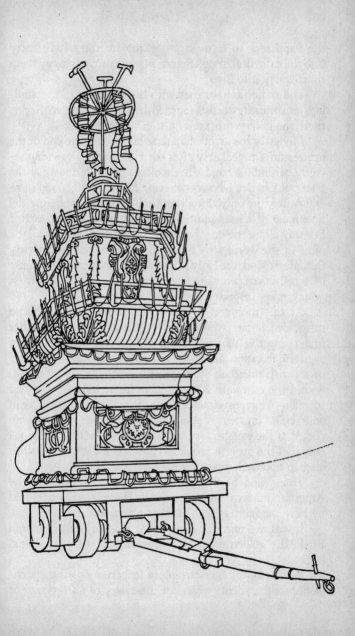

the Baptistery to form in procession for the stately entry into the cathedral, it was Signor Bindo's turn to chivvy them courteously into line.

The archbishop watched with admiration as Bindo, smiling, murmuring softly, touched here a white lawn sleeve, there the golden brocade of a silken chasuble.

Modestly the archbishop took his place at the end of the procession, immediately after the Holy Father, yawning secretly behind his hand. He shook his head graciously at the Sister of Charity who was offering him a little glass of mineral water, the only thing that could pass his lips before the first mass of Easter morning. Watching her as she carried her tray along the line, he couldn't help wishing that all the nuns in the world were as gentle as the Sisters of Charity. But, please God, the Holy Father would never catch a glimpse of those obstreperous women from Chicago. That earnest young man, Inspector Rossi, had seen to that.

At this moment, if all went according to plan, those misguided women were three blocks away, crowded together under a festive tent on Piazza San Marco, the guests of a special delegation of clergy and laity from the inspector's own parish church in Sesto Fiorentino. There was a platform within the tent with a microphone for anyone who wished to make a preposterous address, tables were heaped with delicacies, courteous policemen and policewomen were posted at the exits to assure any restless American religious lady that the press of people in the street made it impossible, alas, to approach nearer to the cathedral.

Thus, God be praised, the rebellious banners of the American nuns would not be seen by His Holiness, nor would he hear the faintest echo of their screams of protest.

It was five minutes to eight. At a signal from Leonardo Bindo the golden doors were opened and the processional began.

Remembering the warning of Inspector Rossi, the archbishop said a silent prayer for the safety of all servants of

San Marco

God taking part in the Easter celebration, especially the holy
father, and then he walked bravely out into the sunlight,
which was now pouring over the square through a hole in
the clouds.

Eight blocks away on Via il Prato another procession
began its march to the cathedral. Cheers went up along the
narrow street as the mounted policemen urged their horses
forward and the band struck up with its drums and horns
and fifes. The doublets of the musicians were red and blue,
their trousers were slashed with scarlet and yellow, their
hats were crowned with feathers. The noise was deafening,
battering back and forth between the stone facades on either side.

Behind the band strode the flag bearers, each with one
jaunty arm akimbo. Tossing their banners high over their
heads, they caught them one-handed on the way down and
tossed them up again.

The pride of the parade was the *Carro del Fuoco*, pulled
along the street on its iron wheels by the four white oxen
from the Val di Chiana. They were taller than their handlers.
Their golden horns sparkled, their golden hooves stepped
heavily on the sprinkled sawdust. Behind them wobbled the
lofty festival cart, swaying from side to side like a drunken
man. Emblazoned with the lily of Florence, wound around
with fireworks, crowned with Pazzi dolphins and a gilt co-
ronet, the tall cart lumbered forward in the direction of the
Piazza del Duomo, while the music tweedled and thumped
and the spectators along Via il Prato and Via Palazzuolo
applauded and shouted, *"Eccolo! Evviva!"*

It was even noisier on Via Cavour, as Homer and Zee
shouldered their way frantically in the direction of the
square. They had been forced to abandon the Saab at Piazza
della Libertà. Around them now the street was jammed,
thickly blocked with Florentine citizens and tourists and visitors from the Tuscan countryside, from Siena and Prato,
Pisa and Carrara, Pistoia and Lucca and Arezzo, all pushing

steadily forward in the hope of catching a glimpse of the
Holy Father.

At San Marco the din was increased by the amplified
voices of the sisters from Chicago, proclaiming the dawn of
a new age for Catholic women. Their only listeners were
Inspector Rossi's patient fellow parishioners from Sesto Fiorentino and the sculptured saints on the facade of San Marco,
lifting their stone hands in wonder. Balloons floated over
Via Cavour in clusters like bunches of grapes, hawkers sold
rosaries and medallions with pictures of the Holy Father,
babies screamed, teenagers laughed and shouted, and two of
them barged past Homer Kelly, their elbows prodding his
ribcage.

"Explain it to me, Zee," whimpered Homer, "this exploding cart. What's it got to do with Easter, for
Christ's sake?"

"Light—the return of light to the world with Christ's

resurrection." Zee shouted in Homer's ear and hauled him urgently through dense crowds of tourists bristling with cameras. "It goes back to pre-Christian times in Florence, when the Romans brought fire from the altar of the gods to every hearth."

"Well, what's this about the dove? What dove?"

"*O Signora, mi dispiace.*" Zee maneuvered past two mothers, two babies, two strollers decked with infant baggage. "It's a toy dove carrying a flint. At the right moment it flies along a wire from the high altar of the cathedral all the way down the nave and out the door to the cart covered with fireworks. The flint strikes a spark and ignites it. Or else—*scusi, Signorina!*"

"What? Or else what?"

"Or else it doesn't, and then the farmers of Tuscany can expect a bad harvest. Listen!"

They craned their necks. From far ahead came the beat of drums and the eerie one-note blasting of horns. Cheers went up in the square. "*I can't see,*" cried a child, tugging at her father, who picked her up and hoisted her high on his shoulders. Homer was tall enough to see above the choked throngs in the street the high-flying banners of the flag tossers. Miraculously they floated in air, then dropped out of sight and floated up again.

"Where's Rossi?" shrieked Homer. "We've got to stop the whole damned thing. He's got to call everything off."

But there was no Inspector Rossi, no uniformed officers of the polizia, only a row of Vigili Urbani in white helmets along the sidewalk and a double file of soldiers in khaki uniforms lining the barrier around the open space between the Baptistery and the cathedral. Beyond the black berets of the soldiers Homer could see the halberds of the pope's traditional household defenders, the Swiss Guard, and beyond the guardsmen rose the grandstands where the important people sat in rising tiers. Homer had read the list in the paper—the prime minister of Italy was there, along with the

President of the Republic and miscellaneous royal personages from Great Britain and Monaco, a clutch of Kennedys from the United States, and a scattering of famous athletes and film stars.

Then Zee jogged Homer's arm and pointed up at the uniformed sharpshooters on the rooftops. "How do we know they're legitimate?"

"Oh, they're legitimate, all right," exulted Homer. "Look, there he is, there's Rossi."

Inspector Rossi was recognizable at once, silhouetted against the sky, a slight figure among the tall men with rifles. He was turning slowly, looking down with an anxious face at the crowded street, sweeping his gaze over the multitudes thickly crushed together in the square and crowded against the barrier.

"Inspector Rossi," cried Zee, throwing his arms in the air. "Hey, hey," hollered Homer.

One of the sharpshooters nudged Rossi, and he shifted his attention and looked in their direction.

"Here we are," shrieked Homer, making huge beckoning gestures. "Come down!"

The inspector nodded and moved out of sight, while Homer and Zee struggled to the side of the street, plunging through a surge of eager Florentines. "*Scusi, Signore*," cried Homer, "*scusi, Signora*," while from a thousand throats a cheer went up, "*Il Papa, il Papa!*"

CHAPTER 53

■ ■ ■ ■ ■ ■ ■ ■ ■ ■ ■ ■ ■ ■

Behold the beast with stinging tail unfurled. . . .
                                    Inferno XVII, 1.

On the other side of the square three people in the black robes of the Misericordia worked their way through the crowd at the barricade. Pausing a moment at the checkpoint, they were waved through by an officer of the carabinieri in a cocked hat.

"Look," said an old man, standing in the front row behind the barrier. He bent down to his grandson, who was squeezed into the circle of his arm. "Do you see the black robes? Those are the good people of the Misericordia. See? There they go with a stretcher. Someone must have fallen ill inside the Duomo."

The music of the service poured out of the cathedral, and the sound of five thousand voices chanting the responses. A stream of schoolchildren in blue choir robes mounted the cathedral steps. The choirmistress hissed at them and pointed *there* and *there* and *there*, and lined them up in three perfect rows.

In single file behind the children came the three people in black gowns, their hoods tied tightly around their heads like kerchiefs. With solemn tread they walked in front of the important people, they passed the tall ceremonial cart as the oxen were unharnessed and led away, they moved up the cathedral steps as a man walked down them carrying a wire.

"Look," said the old man, leaning down again to his

grandson, "the wire is for the dove. You see, the man is attaching it to the fireworks so that they will blow up, BAM, when the dove makes a spark."

BAM," cried the child eagerly. "BAM, BAM."

Inside the cathedral the organ began to thunder a tremendous recessional, and the papal procession started down the central corridor of the nave. Its progress was delayed whenever the holy father paused to bless kneeling members of the congregation or kiss an occasional child. Behind him the Cardinal Prefect murmured, "Holiness, we must hurry."

Benignly the pontiff smiled and walked faster, keeping his eyes forward. As he emerged from the shadow of the lofty central door, the Porta Maggiore, the crowds in the square began to cheer again. Waves of reverent clapping beat against the marble facade and echoed around the square.

Mounting a tall platform, the Holy Father raised his arms and cried, "Christ is risen! Alleluia!"

There was a roar of response, "He is risen indeed! Alleluia!"

Lost in the general clamor was a single defiant whoop from one of the Chicago sisterhood, a stray nun who had escaped the concentration camp at Piazza San Marco. Unrolling an impertinent sign, she held it high over her head and shouted "Priesthood for women!" But only the archbishop, of all the clergy massed on the cathedral steps, witnessed this sacrilege, and he was thankful to see her hauled off at once by a couple of soldiers in khaki.

The great morning was nearly over. The archbishop's heart thumped with foreboding. It was time for the Explosion of the Cart. What was it Inspector Rossi had said? "The noise of the fireworks could mask another sound."

Now, as Signor Bindo leaned toward His Holiness and pointed out the remote control device that would start the little dove on its journey down the wire, the old archbishop let his gaze rove around the square. Hundreds of soldiers encircled the enclosed space between Baptistery and cathedral, scores of policemen with sharpshooting rifles stood ready on the rooftops, dozens of Swiss Guardsmen and officers of the Vatican Vigilanza surrounded the Holy Father, and a thousand carabinieri were scattered among the crowd.

And there was His Holiness, high on the ceremonial platform, ready to begin. The archbishop's eyes widened. Surely the platform was higher than it had looked on the architect's original plan? Had there been some mistake in construction? There was no denying that His Holiness was now a clear and conspicuous target. Closing his eyes, the archbishop told himself that nothing could possibly happen, that they were in God's hands, and that all would surely be well. Opening them again, he whispered, "Amen," and forced himself to look on calmly as the Holy Father pushed the button.

At once a breathless silence descended on the square. A balloon sailed up out of reach, but the child who had been clutching it did not cry. On the cathedral steps Leonardo Bindo moved humbly away from the platform and took his place loyally beside the archbishop. Then the grandfather standing behind the barricade squeezed his grandson's hand and whispered, "Here it comes, the little dove."

The wire thrummed, the toy dove flew out of the doorway, rushed at the cart and struck it, and the fireworks began. There was a puff of smoke. A spitter-spat began at the bottom of the cart, and the noisy explosions circled upward.

Throughout the square there was a simultaneous release of breath, "Aaaah, there it goes! *Ecco!*" Torrents of sparks showered down, and white smoke billowed. There was laughter and applause. His Holiness beamed, and in spite of himself the archbishop smiled broadly, enjoying the din, the overwhelming uproar. It was a happy noise, auspicious and safe and joyful, the sign of a prosperous harvest.

For Inspector Rossi, emerging from the narrow channel of Via Cavour into the open square, it was the moment he had been dreading. At the same instant Homer Kelly caught sight of someone pressing and shoving his way toward the

railing, and he pointed and shouted above the bang and
thunder of the exploding cart, "Look, Inspector, it's Raffaello
Biagi. I told you, he's part of it."

"*Avanti*," shouted Zee. Vaulting over the barricade, the
three of them began to run along the north side of the
cathedral, urged on by the excited cries of the spectators.
What was happening? "Stop, thief!"

The cries alerted Raffaello, who looked back in surprise.
He had come to the Easter celebration to indulge in his
favorite sport of purse-snatching. Now he too leaped over
the railing and took off, while smoke billowed over the square
and the fireworks erupted around the corner in front of the
Duomo.

The man and the two women in the black robes of the
Misericordia witnessed the festive explosion from a vantage
point just inside the high central portal at the west front of
the cathedral. Behind the rows of Swiss Guards and the men
of the Vatican Vigilanza they stood like dark columns in the
shadows, black against black, ready at a moment's notice to
attend a fainting child or an aging prelate overcome with
fatigue.

By this time the sun had crept around to the south, and
it raked across the facade in a blaze of light, illuminating
here a marble apostle, there a virgin and child, dazzling and
blinding the multitude in the square, throwing into total
darkness the deep jambs of the central door.

Julia's hair was hidden under her black kerchief. As the
innocent shield and protector, her place was in front with
Lucretia. Behind them Roberto Mori waited quietly, listening to the machine-gun fusillade from the Carro del Fuoco.

As the cannonade of firecrackers raged in smoke and fire
the whole tidal thrust of Roberto's life was cresting, spilling
over in waves of glory and power. His eyes were moist, his
heart was bursting out of his body. Gazing up at the man
on the high platform, he studied the back of the hand-
embroidered chasuble with its Latin cross, gold on white—

the work, it would be, of Gammarelli, the finest ecclesiastical tailor in the city of Rome. Slowly Roberto lowered himself and knelt on the marble floor. Reaching under his gown with a gloved hand, he withdrew Matteo's .22-calibre American automatic, the one with the thick sound-suppressing barrel. Softly he inserted it between the hanging folds of the robes of the two women in front of him and aimed it at the center of the cross on the chasuble, while the fireworks burst and thundered, mounting swiftly to the summit of the lofty cart, burning through the string holding the three little flags at the top, which now unrolled in sprightly fashion and whirled merrily around and around, displaying the dolphins of the Pazzi family, the lamb of the woolen guild, the lily of Florence.

It was a matter of simple geometry. The long lines running straight across the calendar from Easter to Easter were at last converging. Roberto fired.

But the convergence failed. At the last instant Julia's hand reached down and struck the muzzle aside, and the cartridge spanged into the carpeted step.

The slight noise of the explosion was lost in the last merry snap of the firecrackers at the very pinnacle of the tall cart, above the uppermost coronets and lambs and lilies and dolphins. *Spitter-spat*, rattled the tag end of the squibs and crackers, and then the little flags stopped whirling and the smoke began to clear, and the spectacle of the exploding cart was over. The Holy Father lifted his hands to clap over his head, and everyone cheered.

Trembling, Roberto lowered his weapon and rose to his feet. And then there was a last unexpected pop of fireworks, and everyone laughed. No one saw the tallest of the Misericordia volunteers slump and drop out of sight. But across the square in one of the windows above the open loggia of the Bigallo, Matteo Luzzi lowered his rifle and stepped back into darkness.

Roberto, falling, brushed against the back of Julia's

gown. Turning her head, she saw the blood drenching his black robe. With a sob she bent to take the gun as it slipped from his fingers. Then Lucretia too glanced down, and tore the weapon from Julia's hand.

Julia turned and ran away. The immense empty volume of the cathedral opened around her, and around Lucretia, who was running too.

Only then did one of the Swiss halberdiers on the cathedral steps look back and elbow the guardsman beside him, as the children of the choir began singing and the choirmistress pumped her arms up and down and grinned at them and mouthed the words, *"Mai, mai, mai!"* In the stands there were cooing murmurs of appreciation. "Angels, cherubs."

On the platform His Holiness smiled politely at the singing children and looked down at his prepared speech and cleared his throat, while two Swiss Guardsmen detached themselves from the ceremonial row, moved up into the doorway of the cathedral and bent down over something on the floor, showing the backs of their shining helmets. Now one of them was outside again, nudging a comrade, and in a moment half a dozen had disappeared inside.

Leonardo Bindo remained standing beside the archbishop. His face was flushed and smiling, but inwardly he cursed all the theological idealists in the world and Roberto Mori in particular. At least the fool had got what was coming to him.

Bindo had seen Matteo Luzzi at the window above the loggia of the Bigallo. Well, God be praised for lesser miracles. The wild-eyed idiot from Switzerland had been found wanting—never trust an idealist!—but the thug was worthy of his hire.

CHAPTER 54

- - - - - - - - - - - - -

Too fair to die . . .
        Paradiso V, 71.

T he Cathedral was nearly empty. The crowds that had filled it during the service had poured out-of-doors onto the north side of the square. This morning even the usual parking spaces for motorbikes had been cleared to make room for the five thousand worshippers as they left the church and came out into the open, to be herded out of the way into the narrow channel of Via de' Servi.

The floor of the cathedral was like a marble plain from which rose pillars like mighty towers. The rubber soles of Julia's shoes made no sound as she fled from Lucretia. Light blazed across the floor in radiant stripes from the narrow windows in the south wall, and hung in dusty shafts in the glowing darkness, flung from the round orifices in the clerestory, making great blobs on the opposite wall. Far away in the east end of the church the soaring banners suspended above the high altar rippled in the little winds that wandered from west to east, zephyrs that rose to circle the inverted bowl of Brunelleschi's dome, carrying with them the scent of the altar flowers, descending to escape from the cathedral by the Porta del Campanile, the Porta dei Canonici, the Porta della Balla. Even the distant altar boys were phantoms, moving among the candles in a haze of incense.

Julia ran past the five thousand chairs and the painted horsemen of Castagno and Uccello, blindly she ran past the portrait of Dante Alighieri standing between the city wall of Florence and the gate of Hell. With Lucretia in pursuit Julia ran like a hare, making for the Porta della Mandorla, which stood open on her left hand.

But there she stopped short. Raffaello Biagi was blundering into the dim cathedral, running toward her. Terrified, she gave one glance over her shoulder at Lucretia, who was after her with Roberto's gun in her hand, her black gown streaming behind her, her face contorted and streaked with tears.

There was nowhere to turn. Desperately Julia veered away from the high doorway and bounded up a set of little steps. In an instant she was hidden behind a curving wall, her heart thudding against the cold stone.

She had fled from Raffaello, but she had not escaped Lucretia, who darted after her up the stairs. Raffaello was not interested in Julia, he was not interested in Lucretia. Artfully he dodged along the north aisle. Catching sight of the Swiss Guards running down the nave, he ambled toward them like an inquisitive tourist, then drifted easily across the floor to vanish through one of the portals on the other side.

Lucretia had failed to see Raffaello. She failed to see Homer and Zee and Inspector Rossi running after him through the Porta della Mandorla. She had eyes only for Julia Smith. Pursuing her up the circling stairs she could feel the solid weight of the automatic weapon in her hand, ready to destroy the girl who had twice robbed her of Roberto, who had stolen him from her and killed him. Oh, she had warned Roberto, she had begged him not to trust the girl! What good was it, what good, that they had waited so long and worked so hard?

Lucretia leaped up the stairs, her body limber and strong. Above her she could hear the patter of Julia's hurrying feet. The climb was long and steep, but sooner or later the

stairs would come to an end and the girl would be trapped. Up and up Lucretia ran, her breath coming easily from her lungs, her strong heart powerfully beating.

Homer and Rossi and Zee saw Julia in her black gown run up through the door in the wall. They saw Lucretia lunge after her with the gun in her hand.

Homer was nearest. With a shout he changed direction and hurled himself up the steps and through the door. Inspector Rossi came leaping up behind him, and Homer shrank to the side to let him by. Zee too shoved Homer aside, then thrust past Rossi, mounting the stairs two at a time, sailing upward like an arrow from the bow, calling on a strength that did not come from the muscles in his legs or the breath in his lungs.

Behind them bounded the first of the Swiss Guardsmen, shouting, hampered in his ascent by the weight of helmet and breastplate, the awkwardness of running in pleated pantaloons. Once again Homer had to pull over and cling to the wall.

The stairs were steep and narrow, worn by thousands and thousands of climbing feet. Homer had climbed them before, last September, last October, in the company of Zee and the rest of the Dante class. They had been playing the Dante Game, accepting the athletic challenge of ascending to the very top of the dome, enjoying at the same time the playful notion of mounting through all the realms of Paradise from one heaven to another. But, oh God,—Homer collapsed on a stone windowsill to catch his breath—the play was deadlier this time. Had Zee seen the gun in Lucretia's hand? God help the man! No amount of loving fervor could balance Lucretia's unfair advantage in this last round of the Dante Game.

Up and up, keep going. Homer struggled to lift one foot and then another. Clinging to the railing, he brushed his shoulder against the herringbone bricks of the inner wall, which curved farther and farther inward as he climbed higher and higher toward the pinnacle of the dome.

The last flight of stairs no longer spiraled in a rising curve—it went straight up. The challenge to Homer's exhausted lungs was intolerable. Grasping the two railings he heaved himself from step to step with the feeble strength remaining in his arms.

Far below the dome at the west front of the cathedral His Holiness began to read the last page of his speech in honor of the seven hundredth anniversary of the great church of Santa Maria del Fiore—*that sacred edifice which is itself the very heart of this historic city, dear to all Florentines, dear to Christians throughout the world.*

Loudspeakers carried his voice to the thousands of listeners gathered in the square and thronging the side streets.

As Julia tumbled out onto the platform at the top of the dome the booming amplified syllables filled the air around her—*precious to God himself.*

Lucretia was right behind her. Gasping, the two of them stood alone on the platform, here where there could be no more running away. Caught, exhausted with climbing, Julia remembered a television image of a monkey in frantic flight turning at the last instant to face a lioness. Setting her back against the railing, she faced Lucretia.

Seven hundred years, seven hundred years since Dante Alighieri witnessed the foundation of this cathedral—

Lucretia's drawn cheeks were grey, her eyes were terrible. Cautiously Julia moved away from her to lean against

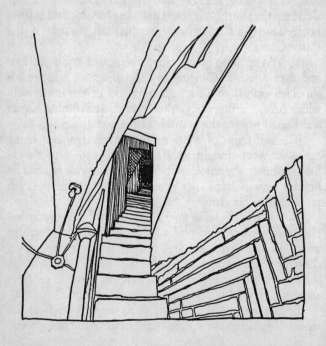

the marble wall of the lantern, which rose from the platform like a little church. She whispered to Lucretia, "He shouldn't have trusted me."

His Holiness had finished speaking. Once again the children began to sing. Their massed voices overloaded the speaker, and five thousand people covered their ears. "What did you say?" said Lucretia.

"I said, he shouldn't have trusted me."

"I told him so, I told him so." Lucretia could hear Zee shouting, she could hear his footsteps on the last steep flight of stairs. "But it isn't only that." Moving closer to Julia she pointed the gun at her face. "We were married in the sight of God."

"I'm sorry, I'm very sorry," murmured Julia. Turning her head away, she closed her eyes and put her hands over her face.

Lucretia said something else, and fired past Julia's head at the wall. The shot pierced an ancient hole, a narrow cavity drilled long ago for the insertion of rods and pulleys, for the ratchets and gears that lifted the marble blocks from the ground and hoisted them high in the air—carved stones with shell-like niches and flowers and scrolls like unfolding ferns.

Half-fainting, Julia slumped to her knees. But Zee was there, his arms gathered her up and held her, while Inspector Rossi grasped the gun and wrenched it from Lucretia's hand. When the guardsman burst lustily onto the platform, ready for combat, he was astonished to see one tall black-gowned woman in the custody of a police officer and the other in a man's embrace. What sort of craziness was this?

On the steps of the cathedral the children had finished singing. There was a massive burst of applause, rising to the top of the dome and dissipating around the lantern like a dissolving cloud.

"The van from the Questura is parked beside the Campanile," said Inspector Rossi to the Swiss Guardsman. "Turn this lady over to Agent Piro."

Then Rossi grinned as Homer Kelly staggered up beside him and clung to the railing.

"Oh, my God, Lucretia," wheezed Homer, moving out of the way as she was herded down the stairs. He gaped at the spectacle of Zee and Julia locked tenderly together. "Rossi, is it all over? What the hell happened?"

The inspector took him by the arm. "Come, my friend. We will wait for them below."

"But—" Homer stared greedily at the broad view of the city of Florence beyond the railing, once again he gawked at Zee and Julia, and then he turned to look with horror at the stairway he had just ascended. "Oh, well, what the hell," he said, starting down again like a good sport, his knees buckling beneath him.

Zee and Julia were left alone at the top of the cathedral. Around them stretched the city in a wide circle to the horizon of green hills, like the great wheel of eternity whose center they knew themselves to be, at least for this moment. Below them rose the domes and towers of the city of Florence, a thousand red rooftops cocked at every angle, with television aerials leaning insanely and drainage pipes wandering from building to building, and pocket-sized terraces with lawn chairs and potted shrubbery. Under the tile roofs the women of Florence were preparing their Easter dinners, roasting the lambs butchered earlier in Holy Week, now to be resurrected in glory, flavored with garlic and rosemary, garnished with onions and new potatoes and tiny wedges of lemon.

A wind rushing down over the countryside from the Italian Alps had cleared the air, and the bells in the Campanile began to ring. Julia and Zee stopped clinging to one another and turned to see them tossing in the bell chamber, and soon the bells of Santa Maria Novella, Santa Croce, San Lorenzo and Santo Spirito were all joining in the jangle, clashing in the brazen harmonics of bells, neither major nor minor but half savage.

Far below them the pope and the Cardinal Prefect stepped

lightly into the Vatican helicopter on the south side of the cathedral. As it rose, tipping slightly forward, its rotary blades beating the air, His Holiness had a momentary glimpse of a pair of lovers on the platform at the top of the dome, and he smiled at them and waved his hand.

But they were aware only of the light of morning pouring down on them on every side, flooding them with *the love that moves the sun and the other stars.*

CHAPTER 55

▪▪▪▪▪▪▪▪▪▪▪▪▪▪

I . . . begged her draw the shuttle's thread
Right through, and all the patterned web unmask.

Paradiso III, 95, 96.

Lucretia turned her face away from Zee. She would not speak to Inspector Rossi or Homer Kelly.

Luckily Mary Kelly had come back to Florence. When Homer brought her to the women's prison, Lucretia was glad to see her. She gripped Mary's hand and talked feverishly. She couldn't stop. Homer waited for hours in the visitors' room, where he had nothing to do but study a torn poster from the first year of the Vatican's great anti-drug crusade.

They had borrowed Zee's car. On the way back to Florence from the prison, Mary took the wheel. Moving in and out of the rapid flow of traffic on the highway, she whizzed around rotaries and dodged into the fast lane and ducked back.

"You've got to keep up with everybody else," she told Homer. "Italians aren't bad drivers. They're terrifically skillful, so they go a lot faster than we do at home."

"Oh, is that it?" said Homer, cringing and closing his eyes in terror.

"Lucretia was a nun. I'm surprised we didn't guess it. Since girlhood she had been a member of a Catholic order in Amsterdam. She met Roberto Mori when she went to study in Rome as a graduate student. He was a priest from Switzerland, teaching Christian archeology at the same uni-

Piazza Donatello

versity. Pretty soon teacher and student fell in love, and wanted to marry."

"A priest and a nun?"

"Oh, of course they knew it would be difficult. It wasn't so hard for Lucretia. The Mother General of her Dutch order recommended to her bishop that she be released, and that was all there was to it. But Roberto had to ask to be dispensed from his vows by one of those big important Vatican congregations, I forget which one."

"And I suppose he ran into trouble? His request was denied?"

"That's right. He couldn't simply ask to be released because he wanted to get married. He had to claim that he had serious doubts about his vocation. But his desire to marry was common knowledge in Rome, and it wasn't considered a sufficient reason. And then he was told that he had to remove himself from temptation by living in a different city from Lucretia."

"And they couldn't bear it?"

"Oh, they tried. Lucretia was hired by the University of Florence, Roberto went on teaching in Rome. But it was no good. Pretty soon they were meeting in Siena, in Viterbo, in Assisi. So he applied a second time and a third time, but the answer was always the same. So at last they got mad, and then both of them began to work for liberalization within the church—for easier dissolution of marriages, for optional celibacy for the clergy, for the acceptance of birth control, for the ordination of women."

Homer whistled. "Pretty strong stuff."

"Too strong for their own good. Before long Roberto was officially silenced by the Congregation for the Doctrine of the Faith. That meant he couldn't write or speak in public anymore."

"So he had to stop teaching?"

"Yes, and for a respected scholar like Roberto it was a

terrible blow. By this time Lucretia and Roberto had long since regarded themselves as man and wife. So in order to be near her Roberto moved to Florence and got a job in the Department of City Museums."

"City museums? Oh, I see, because he was a specialist in Christian archeology." Then Homer threw up his hands in understanding. "That explains how he was able to lay his hands on Michelangelo's compass and the reliquary of the True Cross. Does Lucretia know where it is, the missing reliquary?"

"I didn't ask her. Pay attention, Homer, I'm just getting to the important part." Mary swerved to avoid a DONALD DUK ice-cream cart. "It was around this time that they began to fear for the future of the Catholic church, the whole church—they weren't just thinking about their own problems anymore. They were worried that the trend of new papal appointments in the College of Cardinals would change the balance, making it more conservative. Thus the popes elected by the college in the future would also be more conservative, far into the next century. Whoops! What's that kid doing?"

Homer gripped the dashboard as a boy on a noisy Vespa swooped in front of them. "Ah, I see. So they began to think about violent action. It seems so insane. There they were, a couple of unworldly scholars, turning criminal. Well, it's just like Dante again. They lost the good of intellect."

"They what?"

"*Inferno,* canto three. You remember—the ones who lay down all hope as they enter the gate of Hell, *those who have lost the good of intellect.*"

Mary laughed, and darted into the fast lane to pass a truck loaded with wobbling tanks of compressed air. "It's what my grandmother used to tell me, *Be good, sweet maid, and let who will be clever.*"

They were entering the outskirts of the city, moving

along broad avenues lined with trees and apartment houses where middle-class families lived above shop fronts. The traffic was fast and thick.

"I can see how they might vaguely decide something had to be done," said Homer. "But how did they go on from there? I mean, how did they get down to actually doing it?"

"It was Matteo Luzzi. Julia told us, remember, he was one of the men who kidnapped her from the school. Lucretia said he was in collusion with Roberto almost from the beginning. He turned up in Roberto's neighborhood and introduced himself. He had heard of Roberto's situation, he said. He had been a seminarian himself, and he shared Roberto's views. And then he told Roberto that there were powerful forces in the Vatican who felt the same way, who were looking for an agent of change—"

"An agent of change? That's what Lucretia called it? A murderer, in point of fact?"

"Well, of course they didn't call it that. But pretty soon these great cardinals, these anonymous liberal forces in the Vatican, had presented them with a working plan, to be put into action on Easter Sunday in Florence during the old ceremony of the Explosion of the Cart."

"Well, I must say, it wasn't a bad plan. It very nearly worked. What I don't understand is how Roberto thought they would get away afterward. Did he accept the fact that they would all be shot? I mean, good lord, you should have seen the armies of soldiers and Swiss Guards, and all the policemen collected by Inspector Rossi. They were all over the place."

"Oh, but Roberto had figured it out so cleverly." Mary stopped at a traffic light and waited for the green *Avanti*. "As soon as Roberto fired at the pope they were going to hurry forward in their compassionate black gowns and pick him up on their stretcher and carry him off to one of the Misericordia ambulances and rush him to the hospital around the corner. Whether he lived or died, they would have been thought of as angels of mercy, not murderers."

"Good lord," said Homer, "that's diabolical. I mean it's such a brutal desecration of the long history of the Misericordia. And what about the gun? What about that .22-calibre Ruger automatic with the silencer? It wasn't about to vanish into thin air."

"Right," said Mary. "I asked her about that. She said Roberto intended to drop it somewhere, easy enough in all the confusion. He was wearing gloves. He didn't think there was any way it would ever be associated with him." Mary glanced at Homer. Her face changed. "It's Julia I don't understand. Oh, Homer, Lucretia is bitter about Julia."

"I'm not surprised," said Homer drily.

"Apparently it was Roberto's decision to use a hostage, and Matteo's to take Julia Smith. Lucretia didn't like it much, but she telephoned Matteo on a day when Julia was going to be alone at the villa, a time when all the rest of you were going out."

"I remember. We all went off to that monastery near Siena." Homer held up a cautionary hand. "Watch it, dear."

Mary slowed down behind a fleet of motorbikes tearing along the street three abreast. "So they took her to that farm in the country, and hired two or three guys to keep an eye on her. And then I can imagine what happened. You know how men are around Julia. Roberto was no different from anyone else, no matter how grandiose his motives were. You talked to Julia, Homer. What did she say?"

"Oh, she was very candid. Truthful. She told me she gave up resisting, the last few days at the farm. There had been an attraction between them, and she had fought against it, but at last it was just too overpowering. For a couple of days they were lovers, there at the end."

"Captor and captive," murmured Mary. "Oh, lord, poor Zee."

"And at the same time he instructed her in what she was supposed to do. I don't know how the girl kept her head, in the midst of all that. Julia told me she decided to go along with the whole thing, and play her part, hoping she could do something to stop it at the last minute."

"And she did," said Mary. "She really did."

Homer stared at the fast-moving traffic. "Did Lucretia know about Julia and Roberto?"

"Matteo told her. What a little rat. He called her up on Good Friday and told her. And she couldn't bear it. She had to find out if he was telling the truth, so she hurried off to the farm to see. And when she got there she couldn't find Roberto in the house, and one of the men pointed up the hill, so she went stalking up there and found them together." Mary looked at Homer, her face reflecting Lucretia's wretchedness.

"Keep your eyes on the road, dear," warned Homer, as a truck labeled BEVETE COCA-COLA rattled past them on the wrong side. "But if that's true, why did she go on? I should think she would have said, *Go to hell*."

"Don't forget, she was a woman of intense conviction. And the cause was no longer personal. It had become a matter much larger than her own case."

"So she nobly clung to her original lofty purpose, the assassination of the supreme head of the Catholic church." Homer gave his wife a sardonic glance. "Bully for Lucretia."

CHAPTER 56

▪▪▪▪▪▪▪▪▪▪▪▪▪

. . . We have won beyond the worlds, and move
Within that heaven which is pure light alone:

Pure intellectual light, fulfilled with love . . .
                              Paradiso XXX, 38–40.

Inspector Rossi was skeptical about Julia Smith. He summoned her to the Questura. His warrant for her arrest was already made out. He had it in a drawer.

Homer and Zee sat with her in front of Rossi's desk. Homer glowered self-righteously. Zee clasped Julia's hand.

"You were an accomplice," Rossi told Julia. "And Signorina Van Ott says you kill Roberto Mori with Roberto's gun. How can I know you not try to kill the Holy Father?"

"No, no," said Julia. "It wasn't like that at all." She looked around the inspector's office, which had the usual complement of typewriters, calendars, in-baskets, outbaskets and wastebaskets. A humming fan turned slowly on the windowsill. Pictures of the inspector's family hung beside his desk on the wall. Julia took courage from the pretty wife and three pretty children. "The shot that killed Roberto came from somewhere else."

"Listen, Inspector," protested Homer Kelly, "for God's sake, give credit where credit is due. Julia didn't kill Roberto Mori. She saved the life of the pope. Roberto tried to kill him, and she knocked his gun aside. Look here, Inspector, she deserves a medal, not an appearance in court. Even if she did kill Roberto, which she didn't, it would have been an act of heroism."

They all looked up as the door opened. Agent Piro came in with a folder in his hand. Staring at Julia he blundered into a chair, then walked around it to put the folder on the inspector's desk. *"Grazie,"* said Rossi, and Piro went out again. *"Mi scusi,"* murmured Rossi, opening the folder. In a moment he handed it to Homer without a word.

It was a dry report from the medical examiner and the ballistics department at the Questura. Roberto Mori had been fatally wounded by a six-point-five millimeter projectile entering the left pectoral on a downward path and striking the heart.

"Six-point-five millimeter?" Homer put his finger on the significant number and showed it to Julia. "That's a rifle, not a handgun. It was probably a sharpshooter on the roof of one of the buildings around the square, using a weapon with a telescopic sight." Homer looked up at Inspector Rossi. "Are you sure it wasn't one of your own men?"

"Certamente. I am sure."

"So Julia had nothing to do with Roberto's death," said Zee triumphantly. "She was there under duress anyway. *Mio Dio,* she was very nearly killed herself."

Inspector Rossi turned solemnly to Julia. "That is true? Signorina Van Ott, she try to kill you, *vero?"*

"Well, not really," said Julia. "I mean not when the moment actually arrived."

"Come on, Julia," said Homer, "tell the inspector what you told me. Tell him what Lucretia said."

Julia looked calmly at Inspector Rossi. "It was Dante."

"Prego?" said Rossi, bending forward politely.

"The *Purgatorio,"* said Homer, butting in happily, unable to restrain himself. "The discourse on free will. You remember, Inspector, when Dante describes the inborn counselor in all of us? Well, that's what she said."

"I do not see," said Rossi, shaking his head, bewildered. "Signorina Van Ott, what do she say?"

"You still possess within yourselves the power of mastery," explained Julia. "That's what she said. And then she didn't fire at me, she fired at the wall."

"Ah, *capisco!*" Inspector Rossi grinned with delighted understanding. "*La nobile virtu,* the noble faculty! Signorina Van Ott, she choose not to kill. It is a *Divina Commedia* we are having here now, seven hundred years after Dante Alighieri."

"The seal of form," cried Homer in a state of transport, "and the wax of matter, giving way to the will, the free deliberate will, choosing to transform itself. Brilliant, Inspector, you've got it, I'm proud of you, you are a true scholar. Now can she go, *la Signorina Julia?*"

And then Inspector Rossi, in a rare moment of self-pride and vainglory, taking pleasure in the aesthetic balance of the case, the harmony of then and now, the miraculous geometry of the squaring of the circle, the obvious presence in the room of Dante's pure intellectual light, let Julia go, and she went out into the hall to fall into Zee's arms and go home to the Villa L'Ombrellino.

But the long months of captivity had not left Julia unscathed. She couldn't put aside forever the memory of Roberto Mori and the two warm April days in which they had given themselves up to each other. It was true that even in capitulation she had maintained a small cold center of balance. She had figured out what to do, and then at the moment of crisis she had done it. But Roberto's face, his voice, his carriage, the loving murmur of his talk—no, she could never put him away forever.

Zee understood, and suffered, and made no reproach.

Homer Kelly did not go home with Julia and Zee. He still had a terribly important question to ask of the inspector.

He settled back into his chair in front of Rossi's desk. "What about all those big cardinals in the Vatican? I mean, if there's really a conspiracy against the pope, shouldn't somebody be looking into it?"

Inspector Rossi grinned, and showed his ratlike teeth. "Perhaps, but I do not think they are real, those big important cardinals."

"Not real? But Lucretia said—"

"Has she ever seen them? No. Nor Roberto Mori? No. He also never saw them. Matteo give Roberto letters from them, but these letters, they have no envelopes from Rome, no names. Roberto too send letters, but only to a box number in Florence."

"But you saw the letters in Roberto's room at the farm, the ones he received from all those cardinals. You think they were phony?"

Rossi looked puzzled. "Phony?"

"Oh, sorry. You think they were not genuine, not real?"

"*Si*. They were not real. I think Roberto and Lucretia were—what is the word you call it—dupes, the dupes of professional criminals. The princes of the church know nothing, the members of the Curia in Rome, no, no. They are *innocenti*."

"You've looked into the box number in Florence?"

"*Si*. It belong to a false name, *probabilmente*, but the clerk in the post office on Via Barbadori, he say it is an *Americano*."

"An American!"

"He look like a criminal, says the clerk, not like a messenger from the Vatican. Something is, like you say, phony." Proudly the inspector produced another American word, "Screwy."

"So right now you're looking for Matteo Luzzi and Raffaello and the other two hoodlums, right?"

"And the rifle that kill Roberto Mori. We explore all the buildings around the cathedral, the top of the roofs. We look especially for Luzzi. You remember the cook, Alberto Fraticelli? We find him in Milan. He tell us Matteo know much, very much about guns."

"How did Alberto know that?"

"One day he tell Matteo he like to shoot birds. Matteo, he is interested. Alberto show him his shotgun. Matteo tell him it is in bad condition. Show him how to clean it, talk about guns."

"Those must have been his, then, that room full of fire-arms at the farm." Homer had one more question. "Tell me, Inspector, how was this whole affair hushed up? Does the pontiff know he was the target of an assassination attempt? What about the archbishop in charge of the Easter celebration here in Florence, does he know?"

Inspector Rossi clasped his hands as if in prayer. "The body of Roberto Mori, it was carried into one of the sacristies of the cathedral by the guardsmen. We tell them, *Stai fermo e zitto*, you must keep still until we find Matteo and the others. We want that the missing ones feel safe and think it is over. His Holiness, he do not know. The archbishop" —Inspector Rossi shook his head sorrowfully—"I cannot make myself to tell His Excellency. He is happy. He think the *anniversario* go well."

"You've been to the farm in Caldine?"

"Oh, *si*. We turn it up-goes-down. We talk to the farmer and his wife."

"Oh, yes." With distaste Homer remembered the slaughtered pig, the murdered chickens.

"They say they know nothing. They rent their *podere*, that is all."

"Julia says they knew she was a prisoner."

"They say they think her a madwoman, *una pazza*." Rossi shrugged his shoulders.

"Hey, what about the stolen reliquary? You know, the one with all those pieces of the true cross inside it? I don't suppose you found it there at the farm?"

"No," said the inspector sorrowfully. "We look there. We do not find. That bad *ragazzo*, Raffaello, I think he take it away, along with the compass of Michelangelo Buonarroti." Inspector Rossi looked severely at Homer. "The compass, you have returned it to the museum?"

"Of course we've returned it. And I'll bet you're right about the reliquary. It must have been in Raffaello's little truck when Zee and I saw all those things falling out of it all over the road. I'll bet he's still got it. Can he sell it? Look here, Inspector"—Homer burst out impulsively with a confession of his lapsed faith"—I'm a delinquent Catholic, *una pecora perduta*, a lost sheep, but even I couldn't sell a holy relic. I'd be afraid of bad vibrations."

Inspector Rossi looked puzzled. "Vibrations?"

"Oh, sorry. I mean it might bring me bad luck. I'd be afraid the heavens would fall on me. What about a kid like Raffaello? Wouldn't he be afraid of the consequences? I mean, to sell the very cross of Christ?"

Rossi turned pale, and held up his hands to repel the sacrilege.

And as it turned out, Homer was right. The reliquary was too hot to handle, too sacred for Raffaello's rudimentary conscience. During the first morning mass on the Sunday after Easter it appeared on the high altar of the cathedral, its golden *putti* shining, its jewels winking in the light of the candles, its sacred relics clearly visible within the four great crystal arms.

No one noticed it at first, among the tall candelabra on the altar. It was only after the Communion, while one of the deacons was placing the unconsumed hosts in the tabernacle, that the archbishop noticed the dazzling object half-hidden by a giant vase of flowers.

In his astonishment he dropped the lid of the ciborium, and had to stoop to pick it up, fumbling for it with one of the altar boys, who rushed forward to lend a hand. When it was time for the recessional, His Excellency murmured in the ear of the assisting priest, who obediently put his hands on the heavy reliquary and lugged it into the sacristy, making an effort to hold the precious object upright, as befitted its legendary value and sacred dignity.

But the bolt-action Beretta sporting rifle with the high-resolution telescopic sight was never found, because Matteo Luzzi carried it down to the rear of the Bigallo and handed it to the American tourist, the man called Earl. Earl was ready. Like a peace demonstrator from the 1960s, he thrust a spray of roses into the barrel, then wrapped the whole thing in florist's paper with the roses sticking out at the top. Walking carelessly to the river in the homegoing crowd, he ambled across the Ponte Vecchio to the open loggia in the middle—one tourist among many—and dropped the package over the railing into the mud at the bottom of the Arno.

The roses fell out on the way down and floated on the yellow surface of the water, heading for Pisa and the open sea, a pitiful memorial to Father Roberto Mori.

The Arno did not release the rifle, but a few days later it returned another unwanted thing. At a narrow place in the river, just beyond the bridge where the A-1 crosses to the other side, a child throwing stones in the water discovered a body washed up on the shore. It was the bullet-ridden remains of Matteo Luzzi.

Earl, too, ran into a spot of bad luck—at noon directly in front of the ancient church of Santi Apostoli.

"He was walking in the middle of the street," the priest explained, shouting above the blasting horns of the furious cars trapped behind the Misericordia ambulance. "The car came, smack! and knocked him down and drove away."

"American tourists, what do they come here for?" said the mayor of Florence, who happened to be on ambulance duty that day. "They don't walk in the middle of the street in New York City. Why do they do it here?"

That week the number of deaths in the city of Florence was a little higher than usual. The name of Raffaello Biagi turned up on the list, and when Inspector Rossi saw it, he uttered a pious curse. He was also suspicious of a couple of items at the bottom of the page, a pair of *sconosciuti*, unknown men.

In the company of Julia Smith, he went to the morgue

to take a look. Julia recognized them at once as Carlo and Pancrazio, and her eyes filled with tears, remembering their awkward grace at the game of soccer, their laughter, playing cards.

So they were all gone—Roberto Mori, Matteo Luzzi, Raffaello Biagi, Carlo and Pancrazio. Frustrated, Inspector Rossi went back to the Questura, wanting to reach out his hand beyond them to someone else, someone more competent, more powerful, more clever. It was like groping behind a curtain, trying to touch the flesh of a person you think is there, a hidden figure manifest only as a break in the hanging folds or a slight motion of the filmy cloth.

Inspector Rossi had a few small pieces of evidence to examine. There was the crumpled note Matteo Luzzi had dropped in front of the street sweeper, the one the inspector had snatched up at the last minute before it was devoured. It had been written in a neat script that looked familiar to Rossi. He was sure he had seen it before. And there were Roberto's letters from "the cardinals." Some of them were typed, but some had also been written by hand. Perhaps a study of all these pieces of paper would reveal something useful. Rossi was eager to begin.

Fumbling among the papers on his desk, he began looking for something he vaguely remembered. Failing to find it, he turned to the fat folder on the shelf behind him, the folder labelled *Pasqua*, Easter. In it there were letters from His Excellency, the archbishop. Surely the note had not been written by that saintly hand? No, of course not. The archbishop's writing was large and quavering, altogether different.

Then Rossi came upon a letter that began, *Spettabile Ispettore, Your plan is magnificent . . .*

The script was small and precise. Thoughtfully he withdrew the letter from the file and laid it on his desk beside the crumpled note.

But at that moment his examination was interrupted.

Agent Piro came running in with a sweeping new order from the Questore himself. The entire apparatus of the polizia was in crisis. The alarm had begun with the *squadra narcotici*, but now it was to consume the attention of every other section as well, and every office of the polizia in the city of Florence. The matter was too big, too frightening to be handled by a single department.

Drug trafficking had returned with a vengeance. At every level, from the powerful men giving orders at the top to the miserable addicts and dealers on the street, the thing had escalated out of control. Demand had suddenly rocketed. The price of a half kilo of Turkish heroin or Colombian cocaine was right back where it had been before the beginning of the first Holy Year Against Drugs.

Even among the hordes of young people in Saint Peter's Square—those very same young men and women who had sworn off, who had come to Rome to declare their commitment to the papal crusade—forbidden substances were circulating. The crusade had gone sour. The worldwide fit of youthful repentance was passing as suddenly as it had begun. It was an embarrassment to the Vatican.

Inspector Rossi was not surprised. One of the police officers on duty on the rooftops on Easter morning had witnessed something shocking as the Vatican helicopter circled above the square and headed south on its way back to Rome. He had seen joints passing from hand to hand among the young people of the choir, the same pretty boys and girls who had sung their promises of purity so sweetly on the cathedral steps, *Mai, mai, mai!* Never, never, never!

It was very sad.

CHAPTER 57

■ ■ ■ ■ ■ ■ ■ ■ ■ ■ ■ ■ ■

Florence, my Florence, laugh!
> *. . . for it galls thee not,*
> *Thanks to thy citizens, so wise, so zealous!*
> Purgatorio VI, 127–129.

It was the first of June. Homer had turned in his rented
Bravo, and therefore he had to walk to the Banca degli
Innocenti. He was glad to find the manager himself be-
hind the teller's window.

Signor Leonardo Bindo seemed even pinker and more
shining than Homer remembered. He laughed joyously
when Homer apologized for withdrawing his small account.

"Ah, we don't worry our heads about that." Bindo
couldn't resist the temptation to brag. "We have good luck
with our investments." He pointed a fat finger at the ceiling.
"They go up, straight up to the top of the sky."

"To the tenth heaven," exclaimed Homer happily, "and
the throne of God, right?"

Bindo threw back his head and roared. "*Si*, Signor Kelly.
To the very throne of God." Smiling radiantly, he ushered
Homer out of the bank and watched him wander away across
the square.

The poor ignorant *sciocco* was leaving. The American
school had completed its year and closed its doors and gone
out of business. The Villa L'Ombrellino was back in the
hands of the comune.

It wasn't Bindo's fault that the school had failed. Per-
sonally, he had wished it well. It was the idealist who had
destroyed it with all his fanciful notions. Well, the whole
venture with Roberto Mori had been a mistake.

318

Locking the doors of the bank for the noontime closing, Bindo thought about the sad case of the radical priest. It was incredible that the man had really believed in his foolish causes. How could he have embraced the idea of marriage for the clergy and the ordination of women? Marriage for the clergy! Who would accept the body and blood of Christ from a priest who had spent the night in sexual indulgence? Who would receive the Holy Eucharist, consecrated by a woman?

Once again Leonardo Bindo crossed the square to the church of Santissima Annunziata and knelt before the painting of the Annunciation. If, while he prayed, the miraculous Virgin turned her head to look at him, whether in transport or in sorrow, Bindo's eyes were cast down at the knees of his trousers, his fingers plucked at a piece of lint, and he failed to see.

As for Homer Kelly, strolling down Via de' Servi, he gave no more thought to the Banca degli Innocenti and its amiable manager Leonardo Bindo. He was savoring his final hour in the city of Florence. On the way back to his pensione he lingered in the Piazza del Duomo to enjoy a last view of the great bulk of the cathedral.

Today it seemed especially giddy with elaborations of colored marble, frisky with gables and pinnacles and running lines of cusps and arches. The huge punctured holes of the round windows were like shadowy lenses surveying the surrounding hills, the eyes of a personified Florence looking out darkly at the clutter of red rooftops and the narrow streets choked with citizens.

Greedily, with the sense that it was for the last time, Homer stared into the faces of the men and women thronging the sidewalks. The streets were thick with thousands of foreign tourists, but there were plenty of native Florentines shouldering past them, hurrying to appointments, to lunch, to work, to the shops along Via Ginori and Via Cavour. The facial bones of the Tuscan citizens were strong, and as they strode past Homer they met his stare with the same piercing glance that looked out from so many painted walls. They had the same bold physiognomies as the fifteenth-century bankers and guildsmen and merchant princes who stood in such proud clusters to witness an adoration of the shepherds or a beheading of John the Baptist.

Homer ambled along, imagining Dante coming back to the city of his birth, right now, this very year, recognizing on the street the keen visages of the descendants of his sinners. Surely he would discover among them the selfsame sins—love perverted, love excessive, love defective, fraud simple and complex, pride and anger and covetousness, and violence against God.

Did Hell still yawn for the souls of these contemporary Florentines? Did Purgatory rise before them like a many-storied mountain?

The passage of time hardly mattered. In Florence all times were simultaneous. The painted Dominican monks of San Marco knelt before a crucifixion that was always happening, they prayed to the Virgin as though the infant were forever leaping in her womb. The city itself was a majestic representative of that eternity in which justice was forever exacted, Christ forever martyred and yet forever at the right hand of God.

Homer felt a pang of regret at the thought of returning to the United States, to the plain clapboards of New England houses, the modest steeples of Concord churches. On Walden Street and the Milldam he would find the same range of human iniquity and error—there would still be hoarders and spendthrifts and sowers of discord—but the faces would be different, blander, paler, lacking in virile dignity. Nowhere would he find the same universal pride of bearing.

And there would be no stories in stone ornamenting Snow's Pharmacy, no devils supporting light fixtures on the chaste facade of the public library, no miraculous legends painted on the walls of the First Parish Church. The town of Concord was not a city of the imagination.

Homer stopped short in the middle of Via Martelli and turned around to look again at the Duomo. A girl cannoned into him, a van swerved violently, a motorcyclist braked and squawked his horn. Oblivious, Homer backed up onto the sidewalk, still staring at the marble mountain blocking out the sunlight.

As he watched, it swelled and spread, its chapels bulged, it was growing, ballooning, engulfing all Italy, swallowing the entire continent. Before his eyes the Cathedral of Florence turned into a solidified hodgepodge, a jumbled representative of the civilization of the old world, a scrambled conglomeration of all Christian belief. Tumbling into its yawning doors were the prophets and fathers of the church. Thomas Aquinas was striding in, and Martin Luther, shouting. Theologians and saints and artists and musicians were thick on the stairs, thronging into the doorway, Ignatius Loyola and Saint Theresa, Titian and Rembrandt, Palestrina and Johann Sebastian Bach.

What did poor bare Concord, Massachusetts, have to

offer in place of this richness of story and tradition and human suffering and exaltation?

Homer drifted along Via Cerretani, working his way through the waiting crowd at the bus stop, and tried to think what it was that was drawing him home. The image that rose in his head was that of an ordinary summer morning on the Concord River. He could feel the sun hot on his bare knees, he could smell the dank freshness of the swampy shore, and hear the hollow "tunk" of the paddle on the side of the aluminum canoe, and see the water dripping from the blade.

Could one compare the flash and sparkle of those falling drops with the miraculous liquefaction in a vial of the blood of Christ, a holy relic in some Italian church? No, they were only drops of water, visible for an instant, then mingling with the slow-moving river. The trunks of Concord's white pine trees were not carved by generations of craftsmen into gargoyles and the heads of kings—they were only lithe timbers throwing out branches decked with puffs of green.

Nothing in Concord's rural landscape was miraculous except in the profoundest natural way, in the sense that miracles abound in the unsullied sky, in the purling of water over rocks, in the opening and closing of the fingers of a hand.

Comforted, Homer pushed the elevator button in the vestibule of his pensione and waited, twiddling his fingers in the pockets of his coat. When the elevator wobbled to a stop he slid open the door and rode upward, balancing in the two pans of a gigantic mental scale the great rock of the Cathedral of Florence and the drops of water falling from the paddle of a canoe on the Concord River, finding them equal—different manifestations of truths so diverse as never to be grasped in a single system.

The next day Homer and Mary Kelly journeyed to Rome, and within the week they were back in the United States, caught up at once in the life they had abandoned the year before. Local matters closed in on them, Florence receded, their Italian fell away, the levels of Hell grew muddled, and so did the divine heights of Paradise.

But they kept in touch by letter with Julia and Giovanni Zibo, and took an interest in the further history of the American School of Florentine Studies.

One of the original students turned up in Cambridge, Joan Jakes. There she was in Homer's summer session Thoreau class, shooting up her hand as always, eager to ask a cerebral question. It turned out that Joan's whole life was a string of expensive far-flung courses. In the intervening year she had studied Irish castles in Dublin, the zoology of the outback in Australia, and Hopi archeology in Santa Fe. For Joan there was a precious moment in every course when her fellow students discovered she was smart as a tack.

As for Tommaso O'Toole, he was now a settled citizen of Florence, a student of business administration at the university. He had left behind him at the Villa L'Ombrellino his crush on Julia Smith. Julia was the reason Tom had come to the American School of Florentine Studies in the first place. He had seen her at the Bargello that day, listening to a talk about Donatello's Saint George. He had heard her speak to the lecturer, he had watched while she wrote down the name of the new school across the river. At once, abandoning a plan to go to the United States, Tom had signed up too at the American school on the hill of Bellosguardo.

Now he had a girl at the university. She was not as devastatingly pretty as Julia Smith, but she was sympathetic and amusing. Tom visited her family's apartment on Sundays, to be petted by her mother, who gave him artichokes stuffed with mortadella, and *pisellini alla fiorentina*.

The Villa L'Ombrellino was no longer available for any sort of school. The comune had at last found the money to finish it as a trade center for the city of Florence. Tom went to the opening reception and wandered among the displays, remembering with nostalgia the Pleasure Dome of Kubla

Khan, the Pavilion of the Concubines, the Dining Salon of the Grand Duke. The interior of the villa was almost unrecognizable. The spacious rooms that had seen the descent into Hell, the cleansing of Purgatory, and the felicity of Paradise, now sported smart exhibit spaces for Florentine wholesalers.

Tom wasn't shocked. If they were selling word processors there now instead of instructing American kids in *The Divine Comedy*, what difference did it make, really and truly? Florence had always been a city of merchants eager to profit from the latest novelty.

Most of the other students had dropped completely out of sight—Kevin Banks, Throppie Snow, Sukey Skinner, Debbie Weiss, Debbie Foster and Debbie Sawyer. Only Dorothy Orme cherished the memory of her time in Florence.

For the next two years Dorothy stayed close to the nursing home in Worcester where her mother was slowly declining, but when the old woman died at last, Dorothy came into a considerable fortune, and kicked up her heels.

On the day after her mother's funeral she jumped into her car and sped to Boston to talk to the trustees. A few days later she flew to Italy to consult with Zee. Before long there was a new American School of Florentine Studies on the hill of Bellosguardo overlooking the city of Florence.

No longer was it housed in a splendid villa. The new school occupied an ugly modern building. Galileo had never lived in it. No goddesses lined the garden wall. But there were lizards running up and down the reinforced concrete pillars of the loggia, a fig tree dropped its fruit to molder on the lawn, Julia's little daughter toddled in and out of the office, babbling in two languages, and within the classroom a new band of pilgrims wandered with Zee into the dark wood, to be tormented in Hell, and purified in Purgatory, and at last *prepared to leap up to the stars.*

Ay me! how hard to speak of it—that rude
  And rough and stubborn forest! the mere breath
  Of memory stirs the old fear in the blood;

It is so bitter, it goes nigh to death;
  Yet there I gained such good, that, to convey
  The tale, I'll write what else I found therewith. . . .
                                          Inferno I, 4–9.

AFTERWORD

Many people helped with the writing of this book, and I am grateful to all of them, but most especially to Paul Gehl of Chicago's Newberry Library.

J.L.

Biblioteca Riccardiana

FOR THE BEST IN PAPERBACKS, LOOK FOR THE

In every corner of the world, on every subject under the sun, Penguin represents quality and variety—the very best in publishing today.

For complete information about books available from Penguin—including Pelicans, Puffins, Peregrines, and Penguin Classics—and how to order them, write to us at the appropriate address below. Please note that for copyright reasons the selection of books varies from country to country.

In the United Kingdom: For a complete list of books available from Penguin in the U.K., please write to *Dept E.P., Penguin Books Ltd, Harmondsworth, Middlesex, UB7 0DA.*

In the United States: For a complete list of books available from Penguin in the U.S., please write to *Dept BA, Penguin, Box 120, Bergenfield, New Jersey 07621-0120.*

In Canada: For a complete list of books available from Penguin in Canada, please write to *Penguin Books Canada Ltd, 10 Alcorn Avenue, Suite 300, Toronto, Ontario, Canada M4V 3B2.*

In Australia: For a complete list of books available from Penguin in Australia, please write to the *Marketing Department, Penguin Books Ltd, P.O. Box 257, Ringwood, Victoria 3134.*

In New Zealand: For a complete list of books available from Penguin in New Zealand, please write to the *Marketing Department, Penguin Books (NZ) Ltd, Private Bag, Takapuna, Auckland 9.*

In India: For a complete list of books available from Penguin, please write to *Penguin Overseas Ltd, 706 Eros Apartments, 56 Nehru Place, New Delhi, 110019.*

In Holland: For a complete list of books available from Penguin in Holland, please write to *Penguin Books Nederland B.V., Postbus 195, NL-1380AD Weesp, Netherlands.*

In Germany: For a complete list of books available from Penguin, please write to *Penguin Books Ltd, Friedrichstrasse 10-12, D-6000 Frankfurt Main I, Federal Republic of Germany.*

In Spain: For a complete list of books available from Penguin in Spain, please write to *Longman, Penguin España, Calle San Nicolas 15, E-28013 Madrid, Spain.*

In Japan: For a complete list of books available from Penguin in Japan, please write to *Longman Penguin Japan Co Ltd, Yamaguchi Building, 2-12-9 Kanda Jimbocho, Chiyoda-Ku, Tokyo 101, Japan.*